EX LIBRIS
BARBARA HARTMAN

Steve Turville

Conrad Richter

was born in Pennsylvania, the son, grandson, nephew, and great-nephew of clergymen. He was intended for the ministry, but at thirteen he declined a scholarship and left preparatory school for high school, from which he was graduated at fifteen. After graduation he went to work. His family on his mother's side was identified with the early American scene, and from boyhood on he was saturated with tales and the color of Eastern pioneer days. In 1928 he and his small family moved to New Mexico, where his heart and mind were soon captured by the Southwest. From this time on he devoted himself to fiction. *The Sea of Grass* and *The Trees* were awarded the gold medal of the Societies of Libraries of New York University in 1942. *The Town* received the Pulitzer Prize in 1951, and *The Waters of Kronos* won the 1960 National Book Award for fiction. His other novels include *The Fields* (1946), *The Light in the Forest* (1953), and *The Lady* (1957).

Also by Conrad Richter

The Sea of Grass (1937)

Tacey Cromwell (1942)

The Free Man (1943)

The Trees (1940), *which is continued in*

The Fields (1946) *and*

The Town (1950)

Always Young and Fair (1947)

The Light in the Forest (1953)

The Mountain on the Desert (1955)

The Lady (1957)

The Waters of Kronos (1960)

Early Americana (1936), *a volume of short stories*

These are Borzoi Books,

published in New York by Alfred A. Knopf

A SIMPLE HONORABLE MAN

"I have enormous belief in the power

of a simple honorable soul."

JAMES JOYCE *in a letter to Norah*

A Simple Honorable Man

BY Conrad Richter

Alfred A. Knopf · New York

1 9 6 2

L. C. catalog card number: 62-11047

THIS IS A BORZOI BOOK,

PUBLISHED BY ALFRED A. KNOPF, INC.

 Manufactured in the United States of America, and distributed by Random House, Inc. Published simultaneously in Canada by McClelland & Stewart, Ltd.

PUBLISHED APRIL 23, 1962

SECOND PRINTING, APRIL 1962

CONTENTS

BOOK IV *GREEN PASTURES*

BOOK V *THE MOUNTAIN IN THE WEST*

Book · I

MAN OF KRONOS

CHAPTER ONE

The Call

Much of his life John Donner had pondered that which secretly governed man and determined his destiny. Where did it come from and where in him did it reside? It could be found, he had observed, in the grossest of flesh and in the most sensitive and quivering. Seldom could he lay hands on it but it could lay hands on him. Never could he see it naked, revealed and labeled in the broad light of day. Sometimes he had caught a glimpse of it in a man's eyes, a snatch of it in his voice or its shape and pattern in what he did, and then in a burst of unwarranted confidence had called it life, spirit or soul, not knowing what he said, and finding out later that, however he named the unnamable, it remained elusive, formless and past his finding out.

One June evening when John Donner was a boy, he thought he had had a glimpse of the deep and unaccountable working in his father. They were going up Kronos Street together, his father back to the store after supper, his small son trotting to keep up with him. The town seemed full of mute joy, all green and golden in the last rays of the sun. When they reached Boyers' corner, except for themselves, nothing moved. Street, houses and trees stood magically still. Then the spell was rudely broken. Ahead of them the boy saw the tall somber ministerial figure of his mother's father come out of the parsonage door. For a moment Elijah Morgan stood fixing his high hat commandingly on his head, then he began to move toward them like a long dark jackknife solemnly opening and closing.

"Harry," he greeted the father briefly, scarcely acknowledging the presence of the boy, and turned to the church, where he produced a huge iron key from his pocket, unlocked the arched door and disappeared into the cavernous depths.

Now that the grim disapproving figure was gone, the boy waited for the spell of beauty to come slowly back. But nothing happened. He looked up at his father and saw a pale intensity on his face that he had never seen there before, a monkish look of pinched hunger and starved desire. He seemed to be looking on some bright and awful object very far away and invisible to the boy.

"I want to talk to your grandfather a little, Johnny," he said and moved to the church door, but he was like a man compelled, almost to his doom.

The small boy stood troubled and alone on the wide stone

steps. What had happened to his father? What was the matter with him? Who and what had suddenly bereft him of strength and inner power? Behind the counter of his father's store or roaring out bass in the church choir, he was a king of a man afraid of no one. The boy had seen him chase the dangerous six-foot tramp Mike Whalen from their back door, breaking the boy's fishing rod on his back as he went, this because Mike had been given money at the store on the express condition that he would not trouble the boy's mother at the house. Just a few minutes ago Papa had greeted old Mrs. Christ heartily on her porch, passed the time of day with vigor to Mrs. Bonawitz and beamed with unconfined affection on little Sally Brenner running out of her alleyway. And now in a trice all that manhood had been washed out and he had become someone his own son hardly knew.

The boy stared at the open door, then edged toward it. What could be in his grandfather's church today with such heathen, almost demoniacal power over his father? In the dark vestibule it smelled as always of rope matting, of ancient hymnals, damp plaster and whatever else made up the familiar odor of St. John's. Somewhere overhead he heard grave voices and found himself drawn up the stairs to what they called "the church auditorium."

To John Donner as a boy this place had always seemed commonplace enough, like a piece of ancestral property, a kind of baronial or ceremonial hall belonging at least in fee to the family, for wasn't his father head of the Sunday-school room downstairs and his grandfather undisputed ruler of the entire building upstairs and down, as well as of Jacob's and Kinzell's churches besides? But tonight in the twilight the large accustomed church room had a mystic aura about it, different from its ordinary Sunday look taken up with worshippers and the routine of service. From the long western window at the right of the pulpit, a dusty shaft of late golden light still hung in the dark empty vault. The window's stained glass bore the lettering: "Sacred to the memory of Mary S. Morgan." Here by the altar rail, his Aunt Jess had said, the boy's grandmother dead at thirty-nine had lain in her coffin during the funeral services. For a long frightening moment in the dimness the boy thought he saw her figure standing by the altar rail, the deep-set eyes he knew only from a daguerreotype fixed adamantly on him. Then the eyes went out like pools of light and she turned into a high-backed ecclesiastical chair in the shadow of the pulpit.

Now he could see that no one was there but his grandfather, looking extraordinarily tall and authoritative, standing behind the altar rail, while his father, shorter and stockier, almost cowered before it.

"I can't encourage you, Harry, I'm afraid," his grandfather was saying. The family called him Pap-pa with vowel sounds as when a child calls its father Dad-da, perfectly distinguishable from Papa when spoken but to be confused with it when set down in writing. Pap-pa's voice was thin and unwavering as his figure. In telling a humorous story, for which he was famous as for faithfulness to his calling, that plain, homely, almost strident voice was very effective. You didn't know whether you dare laugh, which made you want to all the more. But when expounding doctrine or catechetical instruction, its dry monotony seemed to the boy of the very bone and sinew of the church itself, positive, absolute, without appeal or vacillation. He went on, "Even if you did have the talent for it, Harry, I should be obliged to advise you against it. If I remember rightly, you didn't graduate from high school. Well, a candidate for the ministry in our denomination must be a graduate of both college and seminary. He should be familiar with Hebrew and Greek and a great deal more."

"I hope to still study those things," Papa said in a low voice.

"But you're a family man with three sons. How would they live while you struggled through college and seminary? The church helps promising younger men but I think it would be too much to ask it to feed and clothe an entire family for seven or eight years."

The boy's father didn't say anything. Pap-pa went on. "Most of our candidates for the ministry are dedicated to their calling as young men. Some even as boys. You must be going on forty years of age. Even if you were a brilliant student and covered all your needs in college in a year or two, you'd still have three years in the seminary. You'd be forty-three or -four when you got through, and you'd be just a beginner. You'd need a few years of preaching and practical experience in the service to reach the fullness of your powers. And then you'd be almost fifty years old. You'd be an old man in most people's eyes, competing with younger men who started far ahead of you. I'm afraid they'd get the better churches while you'd have to take what was left. I mean small difficult charges that nobody else wanted or could afford to have. I wouldn't like to see you drag Vallie through that. No, I must disapprove, Harry, and if you ask Timothy and Howard and Peter, I think they'd counsel you the same."

The boy's father stood silent and stricken. Johnny drew back where he wouldn't see him. Tiptoeing down the rope-carpeted stairs, confusion ran through his brain. What was the meaning of what he had just seen and heard? Could it be that his father really wanted to be like Pap-pa and Uncle Peter and Uncle Timothy? But that was unthinkable. Why, he had a store and business here in Unionville. He made a good living, was somebody in the town and region, owned his own house, had friends on every street, and country road and mining patch. And now he wanted to give it up and enter a joyless life and existence peopled with stiff black figures like Pap-pa, Uncle Peter, Great-Uncles Timothy and Howard, a calling streaked with shadows and gloom, with taboos and negations, where dark incomprehensible watchwords like "holiness," "original sin," "the blood of the lamb" and "eternal damnation" chilled the heart of a young boy. Just to think of it drained the green brightness out of the world and all the wild airs blowing.

And yet, he told himself on the stairs, he had never known anything to have such incredible power over his father. He stood like a prisoner shackled and condemned before the throne of some barbaric ruler he wanted to serve, a despot possessed of all magic, whose mere nod of the scepter was enough to throw his enemies into unthinkable torture, not for this year and the next but forever and ever.

Once outside, the boy stood behind the lilac bush on Squire Ammon's lawn so he wouldn't see his father come beaten out of the church and go troubled up the street. But he stared with hard young eyes when his grandfather came, locking the door behind him, a white envelope in his hand. Even in the twilight, Pap-pa's lips were thin and bloodless, a straight line across his long face. The bow of his black tie was tucked under his stiff starched collar on both sides as if to leave no loose ends where the devil or sinful hands might fasten and deter him. But it was his coat that affected his grandson the most, made of some smooth flinty material with something like a ribbon of velvety steel along the lapels, the whole garment of fine hard-finished fibers as of slender wires woven together. It was this hard metallic everlasting quality that suddenly struck the boy. Was this "the whole armor of God" about which from the pulpit he had heard so much?

The boy waited until his grandfather was in the parsonage and the street safe. Then he ran swiftly by Pap-pa's iron fence to the store for the spool of darning cotton that his mother wanted. All the way home it felt indescribably soft and human in his hand.

CHAPTER TWO

Years

Aunt Doty sighed when she heard that Mr. Morgan, as she called the old preacher, had taken to his bed. Why, all his life he had never taken a vacation. He used to say, "The devil doesn't take one either." She had lived across the street from the parsonage since coming to Unionville as Theodosia Garrison, the bride of Major Ammon, and hadn't known Mr. Morgan to miss a service through sickness or bad weather. Many the time she had seen him drive out with the snow deep and still falling so that she could scarcely make out the church. People liked to tell of the time he came to Jacob's through a blizzard when only the sexton was there. On another drifted Sunday at Kinzell's, they said, nobody but himself had showed up. Dr. Sypher told her that when called out in the country at night, he invariably found the old preacher's horse and buggy there ahead of him and the man himself giving communion in the sickroom or down on his knees by the bed. In either case the doctor had to wait.

"Before man, God," Mr. Morgan used to say.

Aunt Doty herself remembered the time she had gone to the funeral of the son of her maid. The place was packed, for the death was a sad and tragic affair. But Mr. Morgan had come into the house of the dead with life and confidence. He was not taken over by tragedy, mourning, the casket or sickening profusion of flowers. He stood there tall and strong, and his voice rang out with authority. She had had the feeling then that here was the master of death.

And now at seventy-two or -three he himself had taken to his bed, a bad sign for so determined and powerful a servant of Christ. She told herself with regret that now she would probably never know why a month or two ago she had seen him go into the church on a Saturday evening and why Harry Donner had followed. Preachers in Maryland where she came from shut themselves up in their parsonage study on Saturday night to write their Sunday sermon. No one had dared disturb them. But then Southern ministers were always comfortably behind time like everybody else in the South, while people up here in Pennsylvania were terrible sticklers to be on time, especially the Pennsylvania Dutch.

In that Mr. Morgan was surely a Pennsylvanian. In other things he might have been a Marylander since he hailed from very near the state line. He blew his nose resoundingly in the pulpit like Dr. Claverty in Hagerstown.

Jessie and Vallie called it Gabriel's horn. There was no processional or gown in St. John's, but Mr. Morgan's entrance into church, they said, was an event all the same. He would move down the aisle, silk hat on arm, the edge of the brim held in his fingers, pause to set the hat at its accustomed place in the deaf pew, mount the pulpit slowly and then stand in silence with his fingers on the open Bible to pray. He had what most Southerners had and many Pennsylvanians lacked, presence. Mrs. Werts, who brought the Ammons their chicken and butter twice a week, told her that when he came into their house it seemed as if the highest person in the world, even God, was calling on them.

"Parra Morgan baptized me," country people used to say, as if it gave them standing in the community.

But it was in telling a story, Aunt Doty thought, that Mr. Morgan showed his Southern blood, drawing it out with deliberate ease, no hurry, never cracking a smile, dry as the hinges on an old stable door. Oh, he minced no words in what he felt was his religious province. "You can write Hell and Damnation with your finger in the dust on most Bibles in this community," he declared once in a sermon, and another time, preaching on prayer, "Some people are as swine. They never look up before they eat." He shirked no duty even to friends. From time to time he preached a fiery evening sermon against gambling and drink and once in the course of it declared, "Within the sound of my voice, certainly within the range of a stone, would I be disposed to throw one, the devil's playing cards are being played and intoxicating liquor drunk at this moment on the holy Sabbath."

His hearers knew he could mean no other than the Major Ammons across the street. Since Mrs. Ammon was Reformed when she went to church, which was perhaps once or twice a year, she didn't hear it in person, but loyal friends duly reported it.

"This is my house and I will do in it as I please," was all Mrs. Ammon said. Besides she and Mr. Morgan were the best of friends and she knew that one of these evenings when he could take time out of his busy schedule, he would come calling on her to make neighborly amends, sit at his accustomed place on the fixed rocker in the library, slipping his hands in and out as he rocked, paralyzing the children with constant fear that his long tapering fingers would be caught and crushed, all the time regaling her with humorous matters of his parish.

He did call, too, as she expected, with courteous dignity as if nothing had happened. The only notice of the sermon reference Mrs. Ammon took was to comment on ministers in general.

"There should be a course at Gettysburg," she told him, "to teach young preachers graciousness and manners before they go out in the world. Most of your Lutherans come out of Pennsylvania Dutch farmhouses where they don't even know to stand up when a lady comes in the room. Not only you Lutherans but my Reformed, too. Since the seminaries don't teach them, I do what I can. My minister is usually sitting in the parlor when I come downstairs. I know he won't budge if I go over to him, so I stop in the doorway and say, 'How do you do, Mr. Kohler,' and stand there with my hand out, and he has to get up and cross the room to shake hands with me."

Mr. Morgan had laughed heartily. After all he could afford to since he had never failed to get up for her, but Mrs. Ammon wondered if his first wife, Mary Scarlett, hadn't taught him. Perhaps he would have laughed anyway, since he enjoyed a good story. Tonight with him taken to his bed, she remembered a few—of the woman at Jacob's who had dreamed her chickens were in the dough tray and had cried out, "Shoo! Shoo!" in the midst of his sermon; of the town preacher of another denomination who had preached at an elderly spinster's funeral: "She was pure and chaste, so far as we know"; and the story he had related to the Major, who in turn had told her, of the preacher across the mountain who when annoyed by boys going in and out of the service, had said in his sermon, "Girls, listen to the Word and stay away from those boys. They have something wrong with their bladders."

Then there was the story of the habitual old drunk at

Crouse's Corners who had been telling his troubles. Mr. Morgan had listened as long as he could before cutting him off firmly.

"Even Christians have their troubles and must bear them," he said.

"Is that so, Parra?" said the drunk. "Then, by Jeez, I must be one of them."

And now with the indomitable old man bedfast they wouldn't likely hear any more like that from the pastor of St. John's. It seemed curious to Mrs. Ammon that such a composed man as Mr. Morgan had always been couldn't lie quiet in his sickbed. A dozen times a day he would try to get up. "I want to go to Jacob's," he would say, or "I want to go to St. Mark's," which was the official name of Kinzell's. Somebody had to sit up with him at night or he'd try to get up by himself and fall to the floor.

"I must get dressed," he would protest. "I must water Mike. Don't you hear him?"

But everyone knew that the neighing horse wasn't thirsty. He would turn over with his nose most every bucket of water brought to him. It was his master that he wanted, the man who had fed, watered, curried and driven him for nearly twenty years. Aunt Doty understood that. Her father had kept horses in Maryland and the Major always had a driving horse or two in the stable.

The first time she had crossed the street to see the sick old preacher he had said when she left, "Doty, will you have

Georgia come over to see poor Mike sometimes? She always had a way with horses." The second time she was shocked by the change in him. His faded gray eyes must have seen it, for he said reprovingly, "The Lord giveth, Doty, and the Lord taketh away. Blessed be the name of the Lord." When she left, the second Mrs. Morgan told her downstairs that he was a great trial, that he couldn't rest and the only one who could do anything with him was Vallie's husband. A dozen times a day he would ask, "When is Harry coming?" Sometimes they sent for him at the store. He only had to touch the sick man's pillows and Mr. Morgan would close his eyes and go to sleep.

Aunt Doty was surprised at that. Mr. Morgan was scholarly, aristocratic, never bent or unbended. She always had had the impression that he had looked down on his son-in-law, didn't think one who had quit school to work with his hands for a time on his father's section gang was good enough for his daughter.

By September a portentous story was making the rounds. They said that during Sunday-morning service at St. John's, a white pigeon had flown through the open window and circled three times above pulpit and congregation before flying out. Never had such a thing happened in the church before, and the people took it as a devout sign of their old pastor's proximity to heaven. Aunt Doty accepted the conclusion but had her reservations about the sign. She told the Major she herself would have to see it to believe it, and if she did see it, she would have no notion it meant anything. Just the same, she wouldn't like any dove, white or black, coming into her house and flying three times over any member of her family.

And now what would Susie do, she wondered, Mr. Morgan's cow, the one that grazed all summer in the cemetery or down the roadsides leading out of town? Only last week she had got out of the cemetery and her head into the Luckenbills' outside oven where Phrany Luckenbill had bread baking.

CHAPTER THREE

The Blessing

The old man lay in his great walnut bed, restless and feverish. Out of the corner of his eye he could see Mrs. Kriner sitting solidly on her chair. Of late there always had to be someone with him. They never let him alone any more, he who had spent most of his life alone on the road, going and coming, just he and his horse. But these women, and the men, too, who came to sit up with him for an hour or two weren't the faithful and obedient horse. No, they were the driver now and he the one to be obedient, to take orders, his powders on the hour, to lie as if he were sticks and stones, not to waste his strength talking, as if what strength he had left mattered or wasn't his own to spend as he liked.

"Lie still, Reverend," they kept telling him. "There's no good fretting. Everything's being done."

What did they know about it, sitting there secure in their health and well-being? They had years ahead of them to perform what they had left undone. He had days, perhaps hours. Once there had been nearly fifty years of labor before him in the Vale of Union. Only last year he still entertained the notion that he had time, would always have time to do the required and unfulfilled matters he couldn't explain to others and wouldn't if he could and which they wouldn't understand if he did. And now all the time given him by the Lord had suddenly flown away. How often these last days had he thought of Romans, seven nineteen, "For the good that I would I do not; but the evil which I would not, that I do." He had read these words many times from the pulpit and no one had wondered. How they would have stared if he instead of St. Paul had confessed them of himself, he who had baptized he didn't know how many thousand souls, preached more than ten thousand sermons, and who, brother-in-law Timothy declared, had traveled in his church labors more miles than all the missionary journeys of St. Paul.

A few of the unperformed things he could still confide and delegate. There was his concern over the unstable foundations at Kinzell's, especially in the rear. Kinzell's was a union church and the Reformed had to give consent and agree to share the costs. Had the Reformed consistory made the first move, all would have been well. His own council would have followed. He could have seen to that. But since his side had started it, the Reformed had been putting the matter off, belittling it, as if the Lutherans were making a fuss over nothing, trying to boss the Reformed. And now the preacher who followed him here would find Elijah Morgan had left a church sagging under the holy altar.

Then the horse sheds at Jacob's were too small. The church had grown and some worshippers' horses had to stand out in the rain or bitter cold and wind. He had urged his council but the council's horses stood in the dry and councilmen were slow to dig down in their pockets for the comfort of other people's horses.

These were matters he should have seen to himself. Nevertheless, others might look to them. On the other hand, matters remained that no one but he could attend to and about which he was loath to speak. Why hadn't he healed in time the hurt he had done to that old dyed-in-the-wool Democrat Tom Rank? Sunday morning after Tom's party had lost to Lincoln, he, a minister of the Gospel, hadn't been able to resist the temptation to choose a teasing hymn and read the first verse aloud, as was his custom, from the lectern.

Come, ye disconsolate, where'er ye languish.
Come to the mercy seat, earnestly kneel.
Here bring your wounded hearts.
Here tell your anguish.
Earth hath no sorrow that heaven cannot heal.

He could still see the dismay on Tom's face in the third pew and the smiles that ran through the congregation.

Tom swore he would never darken the church door again and never had, not even when the President was shot and they should have been quits with the pulpit draped in black and its preacher in mourning. He had always planned to go to "der Tom," confess his sin as any sinner and beg his forgiveness, but never could he quite bring himself to the needful state of humility.

He turned restlessly in his bed. His transgression with Tom was only one of many. He could still see the white face of Tibbie Boltz standing at her parents' gate when he rode away. It had happened on his way to Unionville for the first time, riding Uncle Jerry's young sorrel. He had felt ill ever since leaving his father's home in York County but it was at the Boltz farm along the Blue Mountain that he could physically go no farther. The Boltzes were very kind. They had taken him in and Tibbie had been his nurse and protector. Lying ill and weak in his bed as now, she had seemed to him a ministering angel. Tender words had passed between them. He had never felt toward anyone as he did for her and in the long convalescence they had reached an understanding.

But once up and about he had come to his senses and seen her as she was, an unlettered girl in a white cap and bare feet. What would the Lutherans in Unionville think of such a wife for their new preacher? He had thanked her copiously, far too copiously, when he left, and had never returned. Inquiring later when safely and suitably the husband of Mary Scarlett, he had learned that Tibbie had run off and married some improvident non-member of the Church of the Brethren, and had died early, leaving two children, both girls, one sickly, the other beautiful, the picture of her mother, they said. He had promised himself to go back and hunt up those two girls, to look on the living picture of the mother and to minister to the sickly one as her mother had to him. He had always postponed it. The uncomfortable thought of Mary and the other Scarletts learning of his mountain love affair had made him strangely unhappy. And after Mary had gone, there was Palmyra, still more proper and propertied than Mary.

A disturbing thought kept coming to him since he lay here. In all the years he had led his congregation in the Lord's Prayer and the morning service, repeating, "Forgive us our trespasses" and "We poor sinners confess that we are by nature sinful and unclean and that we have sinned against thee by thought, word and deed," it was the sins of his three flocks that had concerned and troubled him, chiefly the carnality of these men and women of the soil whose forefathers had come to America in the sixteen and seventeen hundreds and whose descendants had been going their earthy and prodigal way ever since.

There was the young and pretty Lyddy Shappell of Kinzell's, who had done away with her newborn babe born out of wedlock, and the astounding young goat of a Kephart, who everybody said had seven unmarried girls in trouble the same year, and Abe Stover's wife, Stella, the mother of five children, only the first of which was said to be Abe's, and yet with whom Abe continued to live together as man and wife. It had reminded him of Gomer, the harlot wife of the prophet Hosea, and if Hosea had put up with Gomer all those years, he reckoned that he as Stella's pastor could put up with her. Just the same it was always a little disturbing to see the five children, the lawful and unlawful, come regularly to Jacob's with their parents, who sat in the congregation as big and much at home as anybody, setting a doubtful example to all the rest as if to say, Look at us and tell if you can what harm defying God and the church has done!

He saw now that the failings and backslidings of his people had taken all his concern, crowded out self-examination. So far as serious sins were concerned, it had not been pressed upon him of late years that he had any. Shortcomings, yes, imperfections, laxities and omissions but nothing to cause bitter repentance or banishment from heaven. And now the realization came over him that this was his greatest sin, his blindness to his own transgressions. Never, that he could recall, had he prayed for forgiveness of his severity and sharp tongue to some of his people. Why, he was looked up to by all, respected and feared throughout Union, Washington, Jackson and a half dozen other townships. When he consented to stay for dinner at a farmhouse, the housewife ran for a chicken and the hand ax. Out came her snowiest tablecloth. In came the children, freshly scrubbed and shod to stand like reverent statues.

"Bete!" he would command with hand on each tousled head, and the frightened child immediately would mumble some incoherent prayer, if only, "Aba, Vater, Amen." The parents overfed his horse with oats—never common corn as to their own horses. They loaded his buggy with vegetables from their garden or cold cellar, fruit from their orchard and wine and vinegar from their house cellar. And yet lying here today looking back, he wondered if these charities might not have been more out of fear than love, fear for his tall commanding figure, for his terrible office and power, fear for him as the high deputy in Union or Washington township of the Gut in Himmel who could blight their crops, strike their household with some mysterious malady or worse.

Closer to home, he remembered painfully when Peter, his own son and a junior at Gettysburg, had wanted to marry. As his father he had sternly reminded him of the year still ahead at college and three in the seminary. Cathy was a wonderful girl. They all loved her. But God and his ministry came first. The father had stood firm. Nothing could sway him. They should by all means wait till Peter was an ordained minister and could support a wife. If Cathy was to be his chosen helpmeet, as they all felt she surely was, she would wait. But Cathy hadn't waited. She had married a young storekeeper, and Peter, when finally an ordained minister who could support a wife, had married this daughter of a Lancaster lawyer, a woman who had been a thorn in their flesh with her slights, never to him of whom she was afraid, but to his daughters, and whose strongest moral conviction was that she didn't believe in breakfast, of which for years she had given Peter none so that he had grown chronically sallow, which she called his "becoming Latin skin." This was the only fault he had ever found in his son, that he should let a woman starve him and snub his sisters while he smiled to her as benignly as ever.

But his own sins and transgressions weren't alone of long ago. Only a few months before he took to his bed he had cruelly rebuffed Harry and the younger man's ambition for the ministry. It was all right to be forthright and firm, but why had he dealt so harshly, showed no mercy, to him whom he loved more than any other save his son and daughters? Was it his love that had really spoken, putting on a hard mask to protect the younger man from burdens and trials the elder had gone through but never dared speak about? For example, the questionings that rose in him sometimes, the sins of doubt and unbelief, bad enough in a man of the world, but unforgivable in a minister of the Gospel. And what about his burden of inadequacy, of utter failure, that came over him at times, especially when he woke up at night or very early in the morning, a feeling so dark and heavy that it could almost not be borne, he who was thought by all to be a new man in Christ and should be filled with the joy of his Saviour? Only after breakfast would he begin to feel better and once on the road with his horse the green or white world become natural and cheerful again, although all the time he knew that tonight or early tomorrow morning the dark shadows and numbness would be waiting, the deep impenetrable mysteries that he in his calling had challenged and whose world he had dared to enter.

Youth, life, strength, these were the antidote. The old preacher moved his skull toward the woman sewing on the horsehair chair.

"How long till Harry comes?" he asked.

"Now don't you worry about Harry, Reverend," she reproved as to a child. "Wait once. I'll fix your pillows for you like he does." She got up and fluffed them vigorously with her strong hands. "Now that's just like Harry. He couldn't do it any better. You can go to sleep now, Reverend."

But it wasn't at all like Harry. Something was lacking. Lou Kriner might be an experienced practical nurse but she hadn't in her hands what Harry did, nor did light and life accompany her into the room.

"When he comes, I want to see him," he said.

He had made up his mind. This time he would do what he should have done long ago, abandon his father-in-law severity, show the younger man some of the affection and respect he had long felt for him. That Saturday evening a few years ago when Harry had found him in the church looking for notes he had left on the pulpit, he should have told him the story of what had happened on a similar occasion. It was his first year in the ministry. He had been having trouble with his sermons and had discussed their sterility to old Pastor Kreiser of the Summer Hill church, who had proposed a remedy. He was told to leave his sermon notes in the pulpit Scriptures overnight so the Lord might fertilize them. Skeptically the younger man had tried it for a few weeks and thought he could notice the difference. But the young rapscallions of Flat Hill had got on to it. One Saturday night they had broken into Kinzell's, taken out his notes and put a piece of blank paper in their place. Sunday when he went to the pulpit to give his sermon, the paper was blank and so was his mind. He knew now the reason for the unusually large congregation. The word had gone forth and "die leite" had come to hear what the young preacher would do.

Looking down, he could see delight and anticipation in many faces. For a moment his head swam, then the spirit of the Lord had descended and steadied him. He announced that his text would depart from the Bible reading. He would take it from the first chapter of Genesis, the first verse, "In the beginning God created heaven and earth." He held up the blank paper.

"You see," he had said, "there is nothing on this side." He turned it over. "And nothing on that side either. And so far as we are informed there was nothing in the world on the eve of creation. But out of that nothing God created the heavens and earth and all manner of life upon it. And out of nothing with the help of God I will preach my sermon to you today." When he got through, he thought it one of his best.

Harry would have appreciated that story, detected in it evidence of fraternal confidences and encouragement for his clerical ambitions. It was still not too late to tell it. Right after the story would be the propitious moment for the difficult words of reversal, for transforming the old relentless disapproval into permission and accord. He lay anxiously waiting for the chance to redeem himself. It seemed like a very long time and he knew who it was when he heard the front door open. No one had to tell Harry to come up. He took the stairs two at a time and his hearty beaming face appeared in the doorway.

"How are you tonight, Pap-pa?"

"Mrs. Kriner, you can go down now," Pap-pa said briefly. "I want to talk to Harry a little."

Mrs. Kriner obeyed with reluctance.

"Now don't let him talk too much, Harry," she warned.

"I will decide on that, Mrs. Kriner," the old preacher said sharply.

"Can I fix you up a little, Pap-pa?" his son-in-law asked.

"Not right now, Harry," the sick man said. "Just sit down." But when the younger had taken Lou Kriner's chair, the old man found it hard to speak. Now exactly what was the comfort and approval he had wanted to say and just how had he planned to say it? Why was it that instead of joy and encouragement only grim admonition rose to his lips? Had he spoken sternly so often and for so long that the meek and mild, the sunny and bright, were not in his heart any more? Now that the moment had come, all he could begrudge the younger man was a warning not to expect too much from the ministry. It was true, he hastened to say, that the older Scriptures held promise for the man of God. The psalmist had said, "No good thing will he withhold from them that walk uprightly." And when Solomon had refrained from asking for riches, or for a long life for himself and short lives for his enemies, the Lord in return had heaped on him great riches, full years and everlasting honor. But Harry must remember that was the Old Testament. The New Testament was different, promised no reward in this life to its servants, only what Christ, his disciples and the saints had received, prison, scourging, stoning and the cross.

When he finished he lay striving to get around to the sweeter things he had outlined in his mind to say. Why in God's name wouldn't the words of favor and support come, the gentle and affectionate, the accordance and rejoicing? He gave up at length, frustrated and exhausted.

"After hearing this are you still determined to answer what you feel is the call, Harry?" he asked.

"What you say about lack of material reward makes no difference to me, Pap-pa," he said. "My mind is fixed. I can think of little else."

The aged preacher closed his eyes. Inside he felt a faint shivering as if from some mystical chill. When he opened his eyes he found the younger man's gaze fastened on him with concern. The old man wet his dry lips.

"Kneel down by the bed, son," he murmured. Thank God the humble and compassionate had come into his voice at last. "I pray the blessing of the Father, the Son and the Holy Ghost upon you." He breathed for a few moments heavily. "I commend you to him especially who is our Lord and Master." He struggled to sit up and, failing, lifted his hand. His voice grew suddenly loud and clear. "Grace be unto you and peace from Jesus Christ our Lord. Now unto him that is able to keep you from falling, and to present you faultless before the presence of his glory with exceeding joy, to the only wise God, our Saviour, be glory and majesty, dominion and power, both now and ever."

Then his hand fell but his eyes kept fixed wonderingly on the pale intensity of the faraway gaze and the twisted, almost cruel emotion on the strong tradesman's face of the younger man.

Book · II

SEMINARIAN

CHAPTER FOUR

Port Oxford

With his father still at home, the boy, Johnny, hoped that the dark, theocratic cloud might yet pass from over their heads and lives. But once his father had actually left for West Shore College and Seminary, he knew the die had been cast, the vows taken. There was no turning back.

"Now that your father's gone in the ministry, Johnny," Aunt Jess told him, "you'll have to stand up for Jesus."

Even she, the boy thought, the lively irrepressible Aunt Jess, was in league with the implacable powers, a cog in the iron ring of Christian gloom that had been forged about them, with all the constraints, obligations, solemnities, rites and ceremonies native to those made captive by the cross. The exact identity and appearance of those to whom his father had become slave were still unintelligible to the boy, obscured by ancient mists and mysteries, but that they were powerful and even ruthless rulers to be reckoned with remained clear from certain edicts uttered long ago and preserved in black Biblical letters, not the more compassionate sentences like "Come unto me all ye that labor and are heavy laden," but the more frightening ones like "There shall be weeping and gnashing of teeth," and those strange, incomprehensible orders "Take, eat, this is my body" and "Drink ye all of it; for this is my blood," all words to trouble the tender mind of the young.

Now when he ran from the sunlight into his mother's house, shadows met him. The rooms with bare walls, crated furniture and boxes and barrels partly packed gave him the feeling of an empty house. Indeed the house had already taken on something of the barrenness of a church which had benefit of neither kitchen, cupboards, china, dinner table, beds, pots and pans nor other warm vestiges of life and living. When he went uptown, his father's store no longer welcomed him as an extension of home. It had become the property of another. His father's voice and hand had vanished.

"When are you going to move?" people kept asking as if the Donners no longer belonged to Unionville, enjoyed no more its rights and privileges.

"When we're good and ready," Gene, who never lacked an answer, told them.

"Hal's coming for us when he gets a house," Johnny's mother kept promising.

"But how can you live this way?" ladies asked.

"We better get used to it," Mamma said. She meant used to the packing and moving that was most ministers' lot.

Winter came early this year. By Thanksgiving boys were skating on the canal although falling snow soon spoiled that. They swept and shoveled for a while. Johnny went about his new frozen world with certain lines of the poet running undesired through his head, "Thicker, thicker, thicker grew the ice on lake and river." It was, he knew, their new desolate life that was being foretold.

Then suddenly his father descended on them, almost a stranger, in a great impatience to get back to classes, with hardly enough time to talk, spending day and night hammering shut boxes and barrels, getting all on Lib Fidler's wagon and down to the coal siding where the furnishings of home, now hardly recognizable, were swallowed up in a frigid, drafty freight car with flour stains on the ceiling and oats on the floor. Then his father was gone again on the three-ten, leaving them to stay at Aunt Jess's till a telegram should summon them with the word that the freight car had arrived in Port Oxford.

It was late in the day and year when they followed. There had been a holiday thaw with rains and the train barely crawled over the mile-long bridge across the dark river running with dangerous cakes of white that battled the piers. The flood was crossed and they were presently in what the conductor informed them was Port Oxford.

Street lamps glimmered and a beaming Papa stood waving jubilantly in the fog.

He hustled their baggage off the cars to a hand truck. A limber old fellow Papa called Squawky began to trundle it down a dark unfamiliar street. Johnny had never remembered seeing his father so young and cheerful.

"Now see if you know our house, Gene?" he challenged but for once in his life Gene was silent, eyeing every strange door and window.

"Well, here we are!" Papa declared, stopping at a tumble-down place behind an unpainted paling fence. Johnny's heart sank. His father opened the gate and started for the door. Then he gave one of his hearty laughs, closed the gate and went on. He was in wonderful fettle. The boys, all three, stared at him.

A block or two farther on he halted again. There was a cemetery across the street and a log house at the edge of it.

"Well, how do you like that place over there, Tim?" he asked. "No stairs to climb. No cellar to carry coal out of. It shouldn't be too bad. How about it, Squawky?"

"No, sir, not too bad. Handy for the undertaker and plenty of grave-digging tools. Shall I take the suitcases over, sir?" Squawky waited dutifully.

But Papa only laughed again and went on, past the cemetery to the very end of the street, where he stopped at the lower half of a small white house on the corner. It had short boxlike benches on either side of the tiny roofless front porch.

"Well, how would this strike you?" he propounded casually as if about to turn the corner and go on.

"It's not our house," Gene said. "There's light and people inside."

"Wouldn't you want somebody in your house getting supper for you?" Papa asked and turned to Mamma. "It's Mrs. Herr, my boarding-house lady." He threw open the front door and there lay the familiar ingrain carpet on the floor, the old reddish square of Brussels carpet at the door. Beyond were the golden upholstered chairs and sofa in the front room and in the next Mamma's mahogany sideboard with the claw feet, dwarfing the little house. Everything was there, even the faithful crokinole board leaning against the wall at its accustomed angle.

"Why, we're home!" Tim quavered.

They found others there besides "the boarding-house lady," a Mr. Schubert who looked like Schubert the composer, but heavier and with a mustache, a solid-looking man with glasses whom Papa introduced as a classmate studying for the ministry. The other was a slender personage in well-cut clothes, high red spots in his cheeks and a cultured voice and manner, whom he introduced as Professor Barbado.

"Schupe is a professor too," Papa said. "He teaches Freshman Greek on the side."

"Your husband invited us to supper to welcome you to Port Oxford, Mrs. Donner," Mr. Schubert said ponderously.

"It's a great pleasure, Mrs. Donner," Professor Barbado bowed. "We've heard a lot about you. Poor bachelors like Schupe and me who have to live on the campus are grateful for the civilizing influence of a house to come to. We hope you like it here and that your spouse invites us again."

Mamma looked pleased and very pretty. At supper she sat with her head up in a way she had only on special occasions. Her gray eyes stayed bright even after the talk had turned to dry, heavy things like Post-Nicaeans and the Arabian philosophers. Mr. Schubert was very earnest and learned, using words Johnny had never heard before, like "teleology" and "theodicy." Professor Barbado used new words, too, but was lighter, making snide comments and puns on grave subjects, poking fun at the Greek philosophers to bait Schupe, all the while trying to steer the conversation to English literature, which he taught. Presently Mamma helped him to get going on Shakespeare. He flashed her a surprised look and started a scholarly speculation on the identity of the mysterious "Mr. W.H." When Mamma told him that her Aunt Cassie could repeat whole acts of the plays by heart, he displayed his own memory by reciting his favorite sonnets.

"What's the name of that one?" Papa asked.

"It's the fifty-fifth," Barby said.

"I think he must have got the idea from the Gospels," Papa commented. " 'Not marble, nor the gilded monuments of princes, shall outlive this powerful rhyme.' Isn't that pretty much like what Christ said centuries before, 'Heaven and earth shall pass away but my words shall not pass away'?"

The discussion grew lively and exciting. It appeared to Johnny that Professor Barbado was a non-believer like Billy Pomeroy in Unionville, who quoted Robert Ingersoll at every opportunity, but he noticed that his father was fond of Barby just the same, and Schupe, too. Some of the talk became unintelligible, even tedious, to the boy but he had never seen his father more awake and alive. There was something here that reminded him of a book he had read, *The Three Musketeers*, with three quarreling but loyal companions in a splendid and adventurous undertaking. When the boy awoke in his new bedroom during the night, fragments of the talk and fellowship came back to him like snatches of riches and a warm life. Where, he wondered, was Christian gloom now?

Next day was the last of the year. Mamma had much to do in the new house but Papa insisted on dragging them out the back way to see the college and its grounds, which he called the campus. He showed them all five buildings including the new brick gym and its smell of steam, where, he said, when the holidays were over, young men in gym suits would be swinging on bars and tumbling on mats. In the conservatory despite the holidays a piano pounded out one piece while a violin sawed out another, neither bothered or thrown off tune by the other.

This central building, Papa said with elation, was Old Main. That had been his room up there where the window was cracked. Mr. Schubert roomed next door with a senior from Nebraska. The fourth building was Augsburg Concordia Hall and here was the chapel, empty today. During services Westy, the college greyhound mascot, lay with his jaw on the president's foot. Watch for Westy. He was around somewhere wearing a blue-and-orange blanket lettered with WB. A few seminarians also were around.

"Fine fellows," Papa said, naming them. "I'll introduce you one of these days."

He was all wound up. He tried to take them to his old room in Old Main but found it locked, had given up his key and couldn't get in.

"Pshaw!" he said. "I wanted to show you where they put an eel between my sheets one night. I never knew it till I put my foot down." He laughed, still pleased to be treated as a younger man. "We'll go home by College Avenue. I'll show you the president's house and where Professor Unwin lives. He's leader of the glee club."

Late that night Johnny felt his shoulder shaken. It was his mother. She wakened his two brothers, too, all sleeping in the two white iron beds in the back room.

"I want you to see something," she told them.

"I don't want to," Gene struggled to get back to his warm nest.

"But you'll never have a chance to see it again as long

as you live!" his mother insisted. Her face had something significant in it as it had the other night at supper with the two professors. "I've never seen it myself, nor anybody else my age."

"What is it?" Johnny wanted to know.

"You'll find out," she said mysteriously, bundling them up in blankets and taking them to the side window.

"It's dark. I can't see anything," Tim complained.

"Just wait," Mamma said. "It won't be long."

She kept looking at the alarm clock. Suddenly the sound of a cannon broke the stillness, rattling the windowpane, then the clatter of shots rang out and church bells over town started ringing.

"It's the new century," Mamma said. "The old one's just gone and the new one's come in."

The three small boys peered out of the dark window, fully awake now, listening to the racket. The moon broke through the clouds and shone for a moment on a ragged snowy world, only to go under again.

"I saw it!" Gene crowed. "I saw the new century. What's a century, Mamma?"

"It's a cycle of time," she told them. "A new one never used before. Like a fresh sheet of paper taken out to write on. When you first saw it there, it hadn't a mark but now Father Time has already started to set down things on it."

CHAPTER FIVE

Halcyon Days

Never, Mamma told Jess in a letter, had she ever dreamed that the pleasantest years of her life still lay ahead of her in a place called Port Oxford.

"Do you remember, Sister," she wrote, "how we listened when Peter came home and told us about Gettysburg? We thought how wonderful to be a boy and go to college. Now we have that life around us every day. Hal says the air here blows fresh from Mt. Olympus and the Pierian Springs."

It blew warm and cold around their small eddy on Wood Street half a mile from the campus. Even mealtime was shot through with symbols of a new existence, the antique shape of Greek and Hebrew letters studied by Papa with fried potatoes and mush for breakfast; textbooks on logic and philosophy underlined and scribbled in margins and flyleaves with ham and eggs for midday dinner; and Latin quotations and scholarly discussions with one of Papa's college friends along with mush and milk for supper.

Seldom had Mamma heard so many new words. They

came, she knew, bright and shining from college halls and classrooms to be hoarded by the men and boys who heard them and carried away for spending in living and dormitory rooms wherever the opportunity presented itself. Some of the words Mamma thought worth little, some pretentious, some lacking in life as from a dead language. "Jejune," "strabismus," "antithesis" and "calisthenics" were some of these. Others captured her, like "flutingly." How it brought up the voice of Lutie Markle now dead in Unionville. Some haunted her, like "quadrant," especially the phrase "Northern quadrant." Just what it meant she didn't exactly know but she felt a cool sweep of Canadian air. On the other hand, "incommunicable" chilled her. It was good after that to come to a cozy civilized word like "coterie."

One evening Professor Barbado kept using the word "halcyon."

"I know I get a pleasant feeling from it," Mamma said. "But exactly what does it mean?"

"It means something very peaceful and nice," Papa answered.

"It means a bird," Barby said. "The ancients thought the halcyon bird cast a spell on the winds and waves to lay its eggs on the quiet waters."

"It was a very nice and peaceful bird," Papa insisted. "A golden bird with a beautiful voice."

"I think the halcyon was a kingfisher," Barby said dryly.

"The kingfishers I know are blue and have a very raucous voice."

"Doesn't the bird live any more?" Mamma asked.

"I'm not sure that it ever did," Barby said. "It was an ancient myth."

"Not all ancient myths are necessarily unfounded," Papa declared stoutly. "The quieting of the winds and waves was true in Biblical times and can be true today. We still have nice quiet stretches of weather. Those happy golden days are halcyon days to me."

Mamma smiled to Barby as if to say, that's Papa, believing good about everybody and everything. She had to admit he had been right about Professor Schubert. She hadn't known at first how to take him, a solid serious man with a mustache who said surprising, enigmatic things. He seemed far from a student minister of the Gospel. She thought now her early prejudice may have come from his tobacco chewing. The *Luminary* had printed a little squib, "Lost, remaining half of a plug of rope tobacco. Can be identified by large Grecian tooth marks. Reward if returned to Prof. Schubert." Sometimes at the house he would go to the door to expectorate, once explaining how in Greek the word was suited to the act, a word that sounded like "spit-tu-o." Until she got to know him better she couldn't understand why Miss Hoke, the dramatics and voice teacher, could be "sweet on him," making overt attempts to interest and conquer him, all of which the campus knew and which

Schupe stolidly refused to notice. Now Papa had liked Schubert from the beginning, declaring him "a whiz at Greek and an all-around good fellow."

Hal and his older fellow seminarians talked more than once of doing something to bring the two together. One May evening when Barby was at the house, Hal spoke of it again. He had sung Miss Hoke's praises ever since taking public speaking from her.

"The term's almost over," he announced. "Two more years and Schupe'll be an ordained Christian clergyman thirty-nine years old without a wife."

"It's almost sinful," Barby agreed. "In fact, it's conducive to riot. The spinsters of his first charge will fight over his poor two-hundred-and-fifty-pound body."

"Miss Hoke's too nice a person to be a disappointed old maid," Papa declared. "She'd make an ideal minister's wife."

"And a shapely one," Barby said. "Maybe Schupe would take some notice of her if we could get those actressy hats off, and her corset. Of course, I mean something else on," he hurried to say to Mamma. "For instance, a bathing suit with ruffles at the knees. And bare arms. I hear she's a wonderful swimmer. What do you think, Mrs. Donner?"

"I think you're getting on dangerous ground," Mamma smiled. "You sound more like undergraduates than a professor of English and a candidate for the ministry."

"Hal has to uphold seminary standards," Barby said.

"I'm sure President Lang would agree. You know, he's been missing chickens. The other evening he heard a noise in the henhouse and when he went out and counted, three were gone. He talked it over with Mrs. Lang, then went straight to Augsburg Concordia Hall and made the rounds till he heard a festive air and commotion from one of the rooms, also a suspicious odor in the hall. He knocked. 'Who's there?' somebody called. 'It's Dr. Lang. Open the door.' But nobody opened it. 'Go away,' they told him. 'Nobody can come in here. We got the smallpox.' Dr. Lang went home and sighed to Mrs. Lang. 'I'm afraid,' he said, 'our chickens have entered the ministry.' "

Mamma laughed. Papa looked at her eagerly.

"Why don't you give a picnic on the island, Mamma? You could invite Schupe and Miss Hoke, and we might do something."

"If I did that, just what would you do?"

The two exchanged glances.

"Oh, something cunning and despicable," Barby declared. "Schupe can't swim and I've thought if we could lure him into deep water and have Miss Hoke save him from drowning, they might live happily ever after."

"Just like a man," Mamma said. "I'm surprised at you, Professor. You might drown them both. And even if she rescued him, it would be the worst thing you could do. He'd never look at her again. He'd cross the street when he saw her coming."

"I don't see why," Papa protested. "I don't think I would."

"You wouldn't like to see her around every day either, Hal—not the woman who saved you from drowning. She'd make you feel small—not manly or grateful. My Cousin Rose knew a young man in Maine who rescued a whole family from a capsized boat out at sea. They clung to the boat and he brought them back one by one. All this time the poor husband was sitting on the porch of their cottage. He saw everything but was helpless. He couldn't swim and had no other boat. Afterwards people tried to get a medal for the young man. To save money they thought they'd take the affidavits to the husband to be notarized. He was a lawyer in Portland. They thought he'd do them for nothing. But he charged fifty cents for each name. And this young man had saved his whole family."

The two gazed at her with respect but unsubdued.

"We'll have to find something then just as good that meets your approval," Barby said.

"I refuse to have anything to do with your schemes," Mamma said firmly. "But I'll give the picnic if you like and invite them both."

It was warm late-May weather when the day for the river outing came around. Papa enthused over the sun, sky, the clearness of the air and the refreshing breezes on the river. He had rented two boats, one of which he and Johnny rowed, Barby the other, the assistant professor of

English coatless in a blue shirt, his sleeves rolled up over his starched cuffs with gold cuff links. Mr. Schubert looked cautious, a bit heavy and silent, almost glum, but Miss Hoke was striking in a low-neck dress and a huge shapely summer straw. She made a picture sitting in the bow of the boat, her skin fresh and clear, the ribbon on her hat flying. Both Papa and Barby seemed unusually elated, calling lively remarks to each other and exchanging gleeful glances across the water.

They found a clear sandy place under red birches and had a wonderful time. Miss Hoke and the boys and Papa, looking very white, swam. Later they induced Schubert to take Miss Hoke for a ride in one of the boats. Papa and Barby went out in the other. They came back presently, but the other boat grew farther and farther downstream.

"I think I see somebody fluttering a handkerchief," Mamma said.

"Probably Schupe drying it off after wiping his sweated brow," Barby told her.

It was getting dark, and Papa and Barby had grown anxious as the rest when the other boat returned under a rising moon. Miss Hoke sat in the front like a classic figure on a bowsprit. Mr. Schubert poled heavily from the rear.

"What happened?" Mamma wanted to know.

"Those two men!" Miss Hoke said dramatically, looking very accusing. "Your husband, I mean, and Professor Barbado. They took the oars from us and let us drift downstream. I don't know what we would have done if it hadn't been for Professor Schubert."

"Why, what could that helpless Greek do?" Barby asked.

"Helpless! He waded out to an island when we drifted close and pulled up the boat on the sand while he cut a birch pole with his pocket knife. Then he brought me back safe, all the way upstream with his pole. It was magnificent."

Professor Schubert's shoes were still off and his trousers rolled high on his white pudgy legs. Papa gazed on him with admiration.

"He looks like Poseidon coming up out of the waves," he said.

Slow anger grew in the heavy face.

"You traitors. You two miserable barbarians." He followed with an unintelligible but unmistakable tongue lashing.

"Donner, I think he's cussing us out in classical Greek," Barby said. "Schupe, remember you're a candidate for the ministry. I dare you to translate what you just said into vulgar English."

"Don't mind them, dear," Miss Hoke said, at which Papa and Barby fairly whooped.

"What went on down there in your boat, Schupe?" Papa demanded.

"And your desert island? What went on there?" Barby wanted to know.

"Now that's enough, boys," Mamma said. "You'll destroy any pleasure they had in their adventure. If you two are so full of satanic energy, why don't you build a fire to roast our marshmallows? Then we can go home and put these tired and sleepy youngsters to bed."

The river had never looked so difficult to leave as on the ride back, a sheet of rolled silver, the shores distant in the moonlight, Mount Herndon to the south so milky and far away that the reach of water between seemed like a great inland sea. Hardly a ripple moved in air or water. All was the soft perfume of the river except when a bit of breeze brought faint traces of land. The only sounds were the dip of oars and the murmur of a distant riffle.

"Are these the wide waters where the halycon nests, Hal?" Mamma murmured.

But Papa was too set up to descend from his high state of jubilation. He started to sing "Juanita," and across the water from the other boat Miss Hoke joined in. Soon they were all at it, their voices raised in that spontaneous phenomenon of their species which, although Mamma did not know it then, was soon almost to vanish from her land, the untrained and unaccompanied paean of man and woman raised against the vast unhearing and uncaring sea of nature that surrounded them, a strange and touching sound like that of a bird singing alone in the dark night.

Not that it sounded strange to Papa. He was elated for weeks afterward. One day during the summer vacation he came home pleased as punch with his mustache shaved off. Mamma almost cried.

"Why did you do that, Hal?"

"I looked too ancient," Papa said. "Last year Hebrew and Greek kept me busy. I hadn't time for the glee club. Now that I'm a middler I'm trying out for it."

"Professor Unwin has a mustache," she pointed out.

"Yes, but a very stringy one. Mine was too bushy and black. Besides, he's the leader. I'd look too old with a mustache singing with the undergraduates. None of them have any."

When Gene and Timmy came home they hardly knew their father.

"Your upper lip bulges out so," Timmy cried.

"Your face looks bald as the side of a barn," Gene said.

"Nonsense," Papa declared, going to look at himself in the kitchen glass. "I look very well and ten years younger. The barber thought so, too."

He had got hold of a book entitled *College Songs* and now most every evening devoted a few minutes to the unfamiliar tunes. He owned a tuning fork of bluish steel color. This he would bite and hold to his ear, immediately to run up and down the scale till he found the key. During this time he'd sit leaning forward on his chair, either in the kitchen or front room, the book in one hand, keeping time with his tuning fork in the other.

"Do re mi sol," he would sing, "do re fa, do re fa, do re

si do, do re si do," waving the fork and at the same time lifting and lowering the toe of one shoe, doing just a bar at a time, going over it again, nodding to himself when he felt sure he was right, then on to the next bar.

"Isn't that pretty? That's 'Uralio,' the Yale College song," he said.

Neither Mamma nor the boys could make head or tail of it as yet. It was just a meaningless string of do-re-mi's. But Papa went back to it with energy, finally tackling the thing as a whole, not attempting the words, yet full of expression, drawing out a do here or a re there, turning his head to one side with feeling and rounding out his mouth as if to imply, "Isn't that beautiful?"

At last he was ready for the final stage. He got hold of one of the boys. His hand with the tuning fork went around a small shoulder while with the other he held the book for both to read.

"Now!" he said and led into the printed lyrics, his tuning fork keeping time, jostling the boy with every beat, urging him to join in eating the fruits of what was a small miracle, the creation of tune and time out of nothing, like a magician pulling a live rabbit from a hat.

Flushed with success, he took them all to Mrs. Unwin's recital in the chapel. The Unwins had that new marvel, the talking machine, the first to be heard publicly in Port Oxford. The audience sat silent and respectful seeing nothing but a horn out of which came sounds of an unseen world preceded by a spoken announcement ending with the words "Edison record." Mamma felt it a little weird and flat with no singer to watch, no living person on the platform at all except Mrs. Unwin, who rose from time to time to take off the old record and put on a new one like a human midwife attending a robot prodigy.

Afterward Papa insisted on taking Mamma up and introducing her to the midwife, who graciously invited Mamma to call. Papa enthused on the way home. She must go at the first opportunity.

"It's really her duty to come and see me," Mamma protested mildly. "I'm the newcomer. I already came to her recital. I should feel uncomfortable going to see her so soon again."

"Nothing of the sort!" Papa declared with great vigor. "You can't turn her down after she went to the trouble of inviting you specially."

"I don't think it was very special, Hal," Mamma said. "It was just something nice and courteous and conventional to say."

"It might even affect my getting on the glee club," Papa pointed out. "Your giving her the cold shoulder could offend the professor."

Mamma sighed.

"Professors aren't offended by the absence of a poor student and his wife. But if you insist, I'll call on her sometime."

"You really ought to do it next week," Papa said.

Mamma looked beaten. She felt that Papa did some things too quickly. When a letter came he invariably sat down and answered it the same night or the next.

"In social things there's a principle of time involved," she had said. "People don't like to have their call or letter answered too soon. It rushes things, is too eager. It also takes away the satisfaction the other person has in paying his debt. If you answer too soon, you only give your friend another social debt to pay."

But nothing would halt Papa's impatient energy. Meekly Mamma gave in and agreed to go.

"Do you want me along?" Papa asked helpfully.

"No, thank you, Hal," Mamma said with firmness. "I'll take Timmy and Gene. They'll give me the support I need."

She wrote Jess later what had happened, how glad she had been for the two boys flanking her as she went up to the front door of the professor's house on College Avenue and rang the bell. Mrs. Unwin hadn't remembered her and she had to introduce herself. All through the call two of Hal's sayings kept coming back to her, "I had to talk uphill" and "It fell flat." Mrs. Unwin showed them a box of candy. It seemed that her daughter Carolyn was engaged to the son of a candy manufacturer in Harrisburg and Mrs. Unwin brought out the largest candy box the visitors had ever seen. The contents were tied in dainty miniature white sacks, many of which she opened to show them how delicious it looked.

"We never found out really how good it was," Mamma wrote Jess, "because she didn't offer us any. And me with two young boys with their mouths watering."

When they left, none of them spoke until they reached the railroad although Gene and Timmy had kicked savagely at trees they passed. Once safely across the tracks Mamma spoke warmly.

"I was proud of you boys not hinting for anything."

"She can keep her old candy," Gene said.

"Mamma," Timmy asked plaintively, "what was that kind she had that's sometimes white and sometimes pink and you can see something dark and chewy inside?"

"I don't think I ever heard the name," Mamma said.

When they got home, Papa had arrived before them. They knew it by his hat downstairs although he didn't show himself from his upstairs study until they called him for supper. He looked tired and didn't ask where they had been.

"We're late," Mamma volunteered. "We called on your friends the Unwins. Then we stopped for a few minutes at Mrs. Ferrebee's. She wanted to make fudge for the boys."

Papa didn't say anything. He must know Mrs. Ferrebee's tiny house across from the cemetery. He asked nothing about how it had gone at the Unwins', which was most unusual, gave a heavy sigh when he laid his forehead on his propped-up hand to pray. Mamma waited to press him until he had fortified himself with a second cup of coffee.

"I had bad news about the glee club," he said glumly. "They don't want me. Unwin himself told me." He had always called him Dr. Unwin before.

The family sat stunned.

"Not you and your voice!" Mamma said incredulously. "But why?"

"I don't know. I guess I'm too old."

"Dr. Unwin must be still older than you," Mamma protested. "Look at Carolyn, how much older she is than Johnny."

"That stingy Carolyn!" Gene broke out.

"Gene!" His father glared at him.

"Papa!" Tim's voice came out like a small angel's. "When you had the store what did you call that candy that was sometimes white and sometimes pink and tasted so good?"

"I don't know which kind you mean."

"It had something dark and chewy inside. You could see it showing through."

"Oh," Papa said. "I think we used to get them from Brenheiser's. They had a fancy name, Ultradura or something like that."

"What did that mean, Papa?"

"It was just a made-up name like Nonpareil. I think it meant only that it was extra hard and you had to chew on it a long time."

CHAPTER SIX

Papa's Ruddy Drops

This was the summer that Mamma worried about Papa. Something had happened to him since his rejection from the glee club. He had had disappointments before but not to the voice that had been his pride and joy. Why, everyone in Unionville had looked up to that voice. Its range was unequaled. It could take with ease any part in a male quartet, from second bass to first tenor. Seldom had his home town put on an operetta without securing him for one of the principal singing roles. He had led St. John's choir for years. And now here at Port Oxford his voice had been spurned in front of the whole college.

"Be careful with your father. He isn't himself," she told the boys.

She thought it might tame them down a little in the house, stop their eternal wrangling. But it was too much to expect them to believe their father unwell. All their young lives they had never seen him sick in bed. They had known him hoarse as a crow with a bad cold, and they had heard him cough as he did everything else, with violent energy, as if to tear out the lining of his lungs. But they had never seen him off his feet.

"You mustn't think he is not sick simply because he's up and around," she told them. "He wouldn't go to bed even when he had typhoid. Dr. Sypher called it 'walking typhoid,' but your father looked like a dead man walking around."

"I don't think Papa feels sick like we do when he gets sick," Gene said.

Mamma gave up then. It was no use telling them about his blood pressure, that Dr. Sypher had warned her he might go suddenly of a stroke like his mother. The one thing the doctor had said that he mustn't do was get excited. Dr. Sypher might as well have told her not to let Papa breathe. He had also said that he daren't worry. Now he had been worried all summer. Had he been more like himself, his "dutch" up quickly and done, she believed he would have overed this thing sooner. Now for three months he had gone about as meek as Moses, his only complaint an old song intoned reproachfully.

They say that you are false
But I still believe you're true.
You're my bonny blue-eyed Scotch
Lassie Jean.

Whether the false Lassie Jean was God or Professor Unwin, Mamma didn't know. She dreaded the end of vacation, when he was bound to have another shock. All summer she had kept Johnny's final report card from him. Sooner or later he must find it out, but she hoped he might be in better spirits then. The latter didn't come to pass, and on the second day of school in the fall he found out about Johnny.

"What's this?" he sputtered to Mamma. "Johnny in the same class as last year! What does that miserable creature mean?"

Johnny shrank. He thought that he was the miserable creature. But Mamma sat calmly. The time had come for the truth.

"He just wasn't passed, Hal," she said.

"Wasn't passed?" Papa repeated. "You mean you knew it last spring? Why wasn't I informed so I could have had it out with that red-headed fellow?"

Mamma felt troubled.

"I don't think you should have done anything, Hal. This is between Mr. Bowdich and Johnny. You know, I was a teacher myself and I always felt that parents shouldn't interfere."

"You mean you accept this monstrous libel?" Papa demanded. "You agree that your oldest boy is a dummy and an ignoramus?"

"No," Mamma said unhappily. "I talked to Johnny. I think the trouble may be Mr. Bowdich's temper. He had a feud all last year with some of the bigger boys, especially a Macgonigal boy from the country. Johnny says when he gets mad he gets really violent. He tore out the footrest from one of the scholars' desks and broke it over young Macgonigal's back. He's never touched Johnny and many of the others, but they all see what happens to young Macgonigal, and a few of them don't care about school any more. They don't care if they study or pass."

"I should think they'd study all the harder to get out of his miserable dominion," Papa said. "Be that as it may, I have no intention of letting my son be the victim of fits and tantrums. I intend to have a little talk with this fiery fellow at once."

"Please don't do that, Hal," Mamma asked. "You must remember he's an older man than you and has such a big family. He's taught for over twenty years and I'm sure he thinks what he does is right. Besides, he's much bigger than you, really a very formidable person. I would rather if you didn't see him tonight—at least not until you think it over."

"But that's exactly what I've been doing the last five minutes," Papa declared. His voice grew louder. "I have no intention of putting off my duty and lying awake all night going over in my mind what I'm going to say to that hothead tomorrow."

He left the house in the quarter hour, heading up Penn Street in the direction of the school. Mamma looked around her uncertainly. She felt that as a wife and mother she should sink into a chair in distress. At the same time she thought she felt a curious relief, a kind of growing brightness in the room.

"For three months I've been terribly worried about your father," she told Johnny. "But now don't you think he seemed a little more like himself?"

She busied herself to prepare a nourishing supper. Papa would probably need it. When suppertime passed and he hadn't come, anxiety rose. Perhaps she shouldn't have let him go. She could imagine only too well what could happen when two heated and immovable forces met. It grew dusk and still no Papa. And now she could no longer conceal her uneasiness and concern.

Timmy ran in to say that the lost was found and in sight. He had passed the cemetery and was coming fast. Mamma bustled at the stove, turning her head away so she might not see a beaten Papa at the door. Then his step, she heard, was firm and his voice as well.

"I'm sorry I'm late, Vallie, but it couldn't be helped."

She was dying to know what had happened and so, she could tell from their faces, were the boys, but they all had to be content to wait. Papa sniffed the kitchen air hungrily, observing with apparent surprise that instead of the usual mush and milk for supper she was frying eggs, a full half dozen, which meant an extra one for him. His glance at her seemed puzzled as if impatient for her to question him. In the end he couldn't hold back any longer.

"Well, Johnny, it's all right," he said forcefully.

"Mr. Bowdich passed him?" Mamma said, not knowing how to feel about it.

Papa's face darkened.

"No. That insufferable old red mule! He wouldn't give an inch. He said if I was president of the school board, he would treat me exactly the same. I told him I *was* president of the school board in Unionville for six years, and if he had indulged in such unbecoming conduct with a pupil like Macgonigal, I would have seen that he was summarily dismissed and lucky not to get worse."

"Papa!" Mamma protested, and after a little, "Then Johnny has to go back for another year?"

"Not at all." He waved her aside. "I informed Bowdich I wouldn't let him or any teacher like him waste a school year in the life of my son. I left him sit and went out to see Professor Crane. That's what took me so long. He wasn't at home and I had to wait. He asked me lots of questions about Johnny. I told him he was twelve years old, that his mother was the daughter, sister and niece of clergymen with honorary degrees and that I would personally guarantee the boy's intelligence. He said he thinks it will be all right, and Johnny can enter out there tomorrow."

Mamma, Johnny and the other boys stared, overwhelmed by Papa and his prodigious feat. They all knew Professor Crane was principal of the Academy, formally known as the West Shore College Preparatory School.

"But Johnny's only eleven. He won't be twelve till October."

Papa waved that aside.

"I promised Professor Crane that I'd see the boy made the grade if I had to study along with him. He told me the age didn't matter too much. Just so Johnny didn't flunk out. He said he was twelve years old when he matriculated at the Academy. He was a day scholar, too."

Mamma looked at Johnny. The Academy was on the campus. It was like going to college. Johnny himself could hardly gaze on his father. The latter seemed too powerful tonight, his plan to pay for a boy's schooling too grand and magnificent. Who else would have entertained such a daring thought and brought it to such a victorious conclusion? Mamma had been right. Papa wasn't sick any more. He looked like when they had first come to Port Oxford. Never had he raised a finger when he himself had been rejected from the glee club. But let somebody try to reject or hold back one of his young sons, and he was a raging lion abroad in the night seeking whom he might devour.

From that time on, as Mamma predicted, Papa was Papa again. He let his mustache grow. It came out black and rank, ranker and blacker it seemed than in Unionville, and as strange-looking now as his bare upper lip had been when first he had shaved it. Mamma and the boys had to get used to him all over again. When Johnny saw him on the campus now, he stood out among the undergraduates and seminarians as a man among boys.

Along with the mustache, Papa went back to smoking. Mamma had said nothing about the mustache, but she wondered aloud delicately if he had given the latter suitable thought.

"None of my clergymen relatives with honorary degrees you spoke about went back to smoking," she mentioned.

"They never did smoke in the first place," Papa declared. "So it would be impossible for them to go back to it. Now I always did. So it's perfectly natural for me."

"You'll soon be in the ministry, Hal," she reminded him.

"So will Schupe," he said. "And he still chews. Perhaps you'd consider Schupe's vice less noticeable or objectionable for a preacher. If you'd prefer—"

"No, Hal. Not that," Mamma said hastily.

It was settled with Papa promising not to smoke on the street, campus or at home in front of anyone. Some who came to call or for supper and crokinole used to sniff and look a bit puzzled when they stepped into the house, but it smelled good to Johnny, especially up in the study, much better than at Unionville, where Papa had smoked cigars from the store. Now for economy's sake he smoked a pipe. Only when Grandad Donner visited them did he indulge in cigars supplied from his parent's pocket. "Twofers," Grandad called them, and then the house smelled rank, even vile, but Grandad was there to get the blame.

Papa's new energy reached out and took in elocution. It would help his future sermon delivery, he told Mamma, and the little house on Wood Street, which had been bereft of Papa's singing of late, began to be filled with the memorizing and practice of his "pieces." For the rest of their lives Mamma and the boys could recite lines, and Gene whole verses, from Port Oxford days.

Papa liked especially "The Road to Heaven."

He stood but a moment looking
How it happened, I cannot tell.
He seemed to lose his balance
Gave a short shrill cry and fell.
Fell over the bridge's coping,
And I heard his poor head strike,
With a thud on the bridgework under,
And splash in the Thames went Mike.

There was another piece Papa used to bring out with meaningful voice and reproach. Mamma had the feeling it was directed toward her, a kind of warning and prediction of the future. It was spoken in a curious Down East accent which Miss Hoke had taught him.

Nothin' to say, my daughter,
Nothin' at all to say.
Gyrls that's in love, I've noticed,
Gener'ly have their way.
Yer mother had afore you
When her folks objected to me—
Yet here I am, and here you air,
And yer mother—where is she?

Johnny had told her that Papa recited most every day walking to college by the railroad tracks. Once he gained the eminence of the railroad bank, Johnny said, Papa would break out either in elocution or deep-breathing. He taught

Johnny as Miss Hoke had taught him, demonstrating vigorously as he walked, calling out, "Inhale, one, two, three, four. Exhale, one, two, three, four!" each count to a railroad tie, all the while slapping his abdomen to give vent to his resulting vitality and well-being as well as to direct that it was down there and not up in the chest where the breath was supposed to go.

You would never know now that Papa had been humbled, shamed and made to eat humble pie. He declared that Johnny's late teacher had done him a good turn failing to pass him and insisted the boy skip first-year Latin and Greek classes to attend along with other students and former students the funeral of Mr. Bowdich, who in February shocked the town by his sudden collapse in school while opening the morning session with prayer. Then in March Papa was elected president of the seminarians, joined the debating team and was named to an intramural contest. Mamma was pleased.

"Have they settled on a question?" she wondered.

"Indeed, yes, and a very good one," Papa said. "Resolved that alcohol is the curse of mankind."

"I hope," Mamma ventured, "that they haven't put you on the wrong side."

"There is no right and wrong side," Papa assured her. "This is an exercise in reason and persuasion. I happen to be on the negative. But I might as well be on the positive. It's immaterial to me."

Mamma confessed to the boys that she wished Papa was on the side against alcohol. Not that Mamma was fanatic. One of her favorite songs was "Little Brown Jug, How I Love Thee." She still spoke with pride of the wine that had been served her at General Acgrigg's dinner when she was a young girl, and all her life she had taken a tablespoon of whiskey for acute indigestion attacks, this on doctor's orders until he could get there. Just the same, she didn't feel it fitting for a man about to become a minister of the Gospel to argue publicly against temperance and sobriety.

"I hope," she told Papa, "you won't give anybody the idea you advocate strong liquor and intoxication."

"I hope so," Papa said briskly. "But I can't be held responsible for what my hearers happen to think about me. I daren't be a traitor to my side. My duty is to do justice to the negative proposition, not to give aid or comfort to the enemy."

For a week or two Mamma and the boys heard new and vigorous phrases drifting down from the tiny upstairs hall study, "The affirmative holds," "I must disagree with my honorable opponents," "Let us reason together without bias or prejudice" and "It follows then without the possibility of doubt." These fragmentary utterances used to disturb Mamma, especially the words "I confidently dare to believe" and "Whatever our religious beliefs, let us face the facts I make bold to present." What were these disturbing facts that Papa made bold to present and what creed favorable to intoxication and debauchery did he dare to confess that he confidently believed? She felt almost relieved when Gene developed a croupy cough and she had an excuse to stay at home on the big evening.

The boys were asleep when their father returned but next morning at breakfast they knew something out of the ordinary had occurred by Papa's face and air. He sat at breakfast like a victorious mustached chieftain, with Mamma, his slave, waiting on him hand and foot.

"Papa won last night," she told them.

"It wasn't I alone," Papa said modestly. "Bill Murdock was on the negative with me and together we did a pretty good job on them."

They saw him off happily to seminary classes but the wreaths of glory had somewhat fallen from him when he returned at noon. Mamma got after him.

"Oh, it seems that whenever I open my mouth, I put my foot in it," he said. And when Mamma persisted: "Well, I believe there were some on the seminary faculty who didn't like one or two things I said last night."

"Why, what did you say that they didn't like?" Mamma wondered.

"Oh, nothing that wasn't entirely true," Papa declared quickly. "I just reminded the judges what Paul had told Timotheus, 'Take a little wine for your stomach's sake,' and that Christ himself must have approved of alcohol when he changed the water into wine at the wedding feast in Cana and gave his disciples wine to drink at the Last Supper."

"I don't see how the seminary could object to the Bible," Mamma said.

"Oh, they didn't say they objected to the Bible. What they objected to was that I, the president of the seminarians, quoted such things to support the side of alcohol."

"And that was all you said?"

"Well, not exactly," Papa said slowly. "I gathered they also didn't like my rebuttal of their contention that exposure to alcohol meant becoming its victim. I informed them that the smell of beer and schnapps was familiar to me as my mother's milk, that my father used to take me along to the saloon as a child and lift me up to sit on the bar while he drank and visited with his friends. I said all the narrow-minded people of town predicted my father was bringing me up to be a drunkard. I pointed out that instead of such an eventuality I had taught the men's Bible class for many years, was superintendent of the Sunday school nearly as long and was now fulfilling my lifelong ambition to go out and preach the gospel of Jesus Christ."

Mamma looked grave.

"They didn't like these things?"

"That's what I can't get through my head," Papa declared. "It was the unvarnished truth. I told Dr. Mecklenburg so. He admitted it was necessary for me to present a case for the negative since I had been named to that side, but he said in view of my status in the seminary and church, he didn't think I had to go as far as I did or show what he called such zeal for my subject. I got the idea he would have been happier if I had—I don't say suppressed but—glossed over certain facts and arguments so we would lose. The Christian tradition, he told me, has always been to lose, from the martyrdom of the saints down. I told him I thought it had been their lives they had lost, not the cause of truth. He made a face when I said that."

"Well, anyway you won the debate," Mamma said. "They can't take that away from you."

"No, but they can make it so it doesn't mean anything," Papa told her gloomily. "Dr. Mecklenburg came right out and said he was afraid he couldn't recommend me to supply a city charge this summer. He said honesty was a virtue but not indiscretion. He said big-city congregations called for judgment, tact to know what to say and what to leave out. He as much as hinted I didn't have any. He said he thought I'd do better in a country charge. He told me he was recommending me to supply a place called Bairdsville in the Muncy Hills. There're five churches, I believe, three sermons to deliver on Sunday, one on Wednesday and one on Saturday night. He said I'd have to buy a horse for the summer or rent one. I believe there's seven miles between the nearest and farthest churches."

Mamma refused to be cast down.

"It sounds good, Hal. Just think! Out in the country for the summer. The cool hills instead of the hot city. Why, I think, Dr. Mecklenburg's done real well by you and all of us, Hal."

CHAPTER SEVEN

North Mountain

Already in early May it became evident to young Johnny Donner that a change had come over his father. The boy had noticed it first the day the latter had brought home a book and showed it to them at supper. It was very small as books go, slim enough to slip into a side pocket, flat and quite thin, a slight thing to affect a strong man like Papa. But its color was a peculiarly deadening black with nothing to relieve it save a faint golden cross with its crossbar slanted upward. There was also a cloudy mark or two on the black cloth as from a perspired thumb, and this together with the slanted crossbar made it appear as if the cross were some supernatural object floating among the clouds, without visible means of support, which gave it an unearthly effect like God's handwriting on the wall.

That afternoon the boy heard new and solemn sounds coming from the little hall study upstairs, a grave voice practicing sentences he had never heard his father recite before.

"Man that is born of woman hath but a short time to live, and is full of trouble. He cometh up like a flower and is cut down. He fleeth as it were a shadow and continueth not . . . Forasmuch as it hath pleased Almighty God in his wise providence to take out of this world the soul of our deceased brother, sister or child, we therefore commit his or her body to the ground, earth to earth, ashes to ashes, dust to dust . . ."

Troubled and yet drawn, the boy found himself mounting the stairs to the hall study door. It was as he had guessed. His father had the little black book open in his hands. Presently he turned to another page headed THE ORDER FOR HOLY BAPTISM! The boy felt relief. This would surely be more pleasant and cheerful, for the words were to be said over tiny creatures fresh from the Lord's hand himself and consequently pure and sinless. But his father's voice came out dutiful and grim.

"This child is by nature corrupt and depraved through sin and is subject to everlasting death and condemnation. Wherefore I beseech you that ye would earnestly intercede for this child . . ."

The boy turned and fled downstairs out into clean air free from death and condemnation, purified with the scent of new grasses and growing things. Here he could shut out the incomprehensible words from his ear but not the sound of his father's voice or the sight of him sitting there with sternness and judgment on a poor child. It reminded him of his grandfather stiff and unbending behind the altar rail of his church at Unionville while his father stood crushed in front of him. Never before today had the boy heard his father call anyone corrupt and depraved, let alone a small child. Why, he always made a fuss over children. Only a few days ago he had been filled with the undergraduate's joy of living. How could a little black book do this to a man? A feeling of rebellion rose in the boy, a feeling he was to remember years later when first he read Lafcadio Hearn's cry addressed to the same revolutionary causes, "Woe! Woe! Thou didst destroy it—the beautiful world."

Aunt Jess noticed it, too, when she came to visit.

"What's happened to Hal?" she asked her sister. "He's like a black crow. He could almost be St. John gazing over the sea at the Isle of Patmos."

"I think it's Bairdsville," Mamma said.

"He's like the priest I read about in the paper. The one put on trial by the Vatican."

"We have no priests in the Lutheran church, Sister," Mamma reminded.

"We may not," Aunt Jess replied airily. "But Hal could very well be one."

"It's to be his first 'supply,'" Mamma explained. "He's been licensed for a year by the synod to preach, baptize, marry and conduct funeral services. I think it frightens him a little."

"Hal will never be stumped," Aunt Jess declared loyally. "Not even if he has to preach a funeral sermon over some old drunk. But I'd like to hear him and his first Sunday sermon, too."

"Why don't you stay and go along up to Bairdsville, Sister?" Mamma said.

They deserted the house at Port Oxford on a May day clear as a desert morning. Papa's new black clerical coat and vest made him a kind of austere stranger. They went on the cars. At the depot in Muncy most of them waited till Papa came back from the livery stable driving a pair of bay horses hitched to an ancient black carriage with green upholstered seats and a patent-leather mudguard that curved down grandly to make a step for Mamma and Aunt Jess to climb in.

After six miles of Aunt Jess's easy chatter, Papa halted the horses on the top of a long hill. A country town lay scattered in the green valley below. Johnny thought his father had stopped to tell them about it but Papa had his eyes elsewhere.

"That's North Mountain!" he said, pointing one reinheld hand to a long blue mass against the horizon. "It's not like our mountains at home, I understand, up one side and down the other. It looks like a ridge from here but when you get up, they say, it's flat on the top and runs back for miles. It's very high and right where we're looking, I've heard, there's a paradise of lakes and summer resorts and big hotels for rich people. They say you can see the lights at night from the Seven Stars church. I want to take you up sometime."

Did he mean, take them up to the Seven Stars church or on North Mountain? Johnny wondered. At his father's words the shaggy range against the sky had turned into a purple Chinese wall upholding some ancient cloudlike kingdom rich with palaces, casinos and places of pleasure including the good food that Papa had always loved.

"What's this down here, Hal?" Aunt Jess brought them back to reality.

Papa sighed.

"This is Bairdsville," he said. Then he clucked to the horses and started down the long decline.

Bairdsville turned out to be a single dusty street, the parsonage a faded brown house with darker brown shutters. An untrimmed vine overran the sagging roof of a side porch that held a wooden pump and the house's back door. In after years all Johnny was to remember of that house were the porch, the shutters and the oilstove, a long rickety and tinny range with three burners of bright blue circular flame sending its peculiar Bairdsville scent through the house. Forty years later the smell of a diesel engine exhaust would take him straight back to the brown house in the Muncy Hills although he could no longer recall anything else in it, neither wallpaper nor furnishings, not even the room he lay in when Papa preached his first sermon.

For the first few nights in the house Papa had sweated

and groaned over it. When Aunt Jess asked how it was "getting along" he answered gloomily. He looked "down in the mouth." The boy found himself dreading the ordeal of hearing it. When Sunday morning dawned it was almost like waking to his own and his father's execution. At breakfast he felt actually ill. By church time Mamma said he looked so badly that she let him go back to bed, which he did with hasty grace.

It seemed extraordinarily peaceful in the house after the rest had gone. His illness had suddenly and mysteriously vanished into thin air. Well-being rose in him so that it was hard to lie abed. After hearing the first hymn from across the street and knowing he was safe now from conscription, he got up and dressed. After the second hymn silence ensued and the listening boy felt a sense of rising suspense. Had his father got started all right and how was it going? Careful to keep himself out of range of an inadvertently opened church door, he crossed the street. Presently he stood under a tall side window, ears straining. He was relieved to hear that Papa was speaking but the words escaped him. There was only a low blur.

Suddenly his father's voice rang out, a preacher's shout he was to become more or less inured to. But today the words fairly blasted him at the window.

" 'Depart from me, ye cursed, into everlasting fire prepared for the devil and his angels.' "

Startled, the boy fled back to the house. Hastily he undressed and crawled into bed, coming down only when called for midday dinner, finding it a kind of celebrant and victorious event. Evidently Papa had done all right. He stood at the head of the table carving the chicken, while Aunt Jess relayed what certain ladies in the congregation had told her. Papa looked the vigorous conqueror, too busy to pay attention, shorn of all apprehension now. It was true that he had two more sermons to preach today but they were to be at country churches and would be warmed-up replicas of "this morning's discourse," a custom the boy was to become familiar with during the summer, often hearing the same sermon two and three times in one day, the monotony made bearable by observing its variations and judging whether the changed parts had been improved or spoiled.

"Hal," Mamma said at dinner, "Johnny didn't hear your sermon this morning. Why don't you take him along to Brown's church this afternoon? The ride and fresh air should do him good."

The only solace of the boy on his journey of penance was that he rode behind Pet. She had been rented by the month from the livery stable at Muncy, and they all exulted and took pride in her as their own. Papa liked her, too, but despite her beautiful lines, smooth coat and gentle manners, she was only a mare and not to be compared to people who had souls.

At the sight of a passer-by on the road or someone in a yard or barnyard, Papa would come to life in the buggy.

"How are you? Nice weather we're having," he'd call eagerly.

"Who was that?" Johnny would ask.

"They're the people who live there, I guess," Papa would say, "I don't know their name."

"Do they go to one of your churches?"

"Probably not," Papa admitted. "But they're our neighbors."

The failure of many to acknowledge the greeting didn't affect Papa. He refused to notice that most of them gazed with some surprise and suspicion at this stranger in a preacher coat and vest who called to them so ingratiatingly as if to proselyte them from their established faith. Papa greeted the next one he passed as warmly as the last.

"I don't believe I heard your name," he kept saying to hearers after his services at Brown's, pumping hands, trying to fix the spoken name in his mind when they gave it, beaming to children, shaking even the tiny meaningless hands of babies, and saying some hearty greeting. It baffled the boy. What could his father see in these people? He must know that after the summer he would probably never see them again. Yet he treated them as God's elect in whose company he expected to pass eternity. Brown's church was a rough, faded, yellow-steepled building not much bigger than a country schoolhouse, with a small cemetery on one side and a woods on the other. Only a score or two of people had come to hear the new supply preacher, but Papa addressed them as a multitude, praying manifold blessings upon them, pleading with God for their sick and afflicted, shouting "Depart from me, ye cursed, into everlasting fire prepared for the devil and his angels," when again he came to it, fully as loud and terrifying as at Bairdsville that morning.

All afternoon and evening the boy watched and listened in a state of perplexity. The postmistress who kept the small store across from the Summer Hill church had invited them to supper, a meal of bread, butter, apple butter, creamless coffee and an opened can of salmon from her shelves. The table looked shockingly bare to Johnny, surely a slight to a preacher of the Gospel, doubly so on Sunday. He expected Papa, who loved a good table as well as any man, to treat her with the summary coolness she deserved. Instead he smiled on the table as if at a feast and delivered one of his longest and most prodigal of prayers, praising God that "the lines had fallen in pleasant places," and asking generous blessings on "the bounties prepared by kind hands."

Johnny couldn't understand it. At home that dinner Papa had been calm and impassive, too secure to take notice of far more than this. Here among his "sheep," he was different, his fervent spirit turned on everyone alike, the well and the poorly dressed, the homely and the pretty. He saw nothing amiss in the heavy long-haired farm horses, the muddy buggies and spring wagons, the small rudely furnished churches. There was a naive credulity about his smile, the boy thought, an almost foolish eagerness, like that of Billy Bubb, the lamplighter in Port Oxford, a small roundish man with clothes soaked in oil, so that people said if he ever dropped a lighted match on himself they would see the conflagration in Sunbury. Billy went around with a rickety wagon and bony rack of a horse. His face would crease with pleasure at children who liked to follow him from post to post. His job seemed to delight him, his lamps and polished globes, the wicks he trimmed and the cigar butts he picked from the gutter.

It was on the way home from the Summer Hill service that evening that Papa woke him.

"You see those stars up there, Johnny?"

"Where?" the boy stammered.

His father had halted Pet on the top of a hard hill. Straight ahead in the sky hung a cluster of stars twinkling with all the mystery of distant heavenly bodies.

"I'm not sure they're stars, Johnny," Papa said. "I believe they're the lights from the hotels on North Mountain."

The boy stared. It seemed almost impossible that lights so high could still be on the earth. Even after his eyes were able to separate the bulk of North Mountain from the sky, he still felt the bright constellation belonged to a distant and higher world than this, a world of pleasure and ease, of lofty and rarefied pursuits. In his mind's eye he conjured up the big hotels and cottages, the lighted woods paths, the reflecting glimmer in the lakes, and the girls and ladies in the sheerest of shimmering dresses.

"You said you'd take us up this summer," he reminded.

"I fully intend to," Papa promised grandly. "I'd like to see it myself, and I want Mamma to see it. I want her to have dinner at one of the big hotels."

All summer the promise remained in Johnny's mind, a lighted lantern slung ahead in the dusk. But June went by and July. August heat settled down in Bairdsville. Mamma haunted the side porch fanning herself, trying to get her breath. Dust from the road hung in the air. Scarcely a bird could be heard but frogs called throughout the still close nights. Papa said that on North Mountain it would be cool with blankets called for at night, the air fresh and bracing. Rich folks from Philadelphia and Baltimore and all their gay young people would be there.

At first the boy fully expected they would go.

"Next week," his father kept promising.

But something always turned up to postpone it, summer festivals at the churches, calls on the sick or communion to administer, a funeral or a wedding. It was the time he spent in the buggy on the road between the five churches that held him back, his father said. If he had all that wasted time in one stretch, they could go to California. August heat waned and then rose again over the Labor Day Sunday. Mamma told them tales of the hottest weather she ever knew, on the Maryland border in mid-September. It was mid-September presently and they were still in Bairdsville so Papa might earn an extra month's salary to help carry them through his last winter at the seminary. Dr. Mecklenburg said they would let him make up his classes when he returned.

Suddenly the day came. Lute Reed had told Papa he'd like to see North Mountain himself. He had been there only once, as a child. He'd furnish one horse and the carriage if he could bring Fanny Lore along, the girl he was to marry. They had been going together for seven years, Papa said, adding that he'd never get the wedding, that the engagement might run another seven years. The ancient carriage had three leathern seats. Papa sat in front to drive, with Johnny on one side and visiting Cousin Polly on the other. Mamma was on the middle cushions with Timmy and Gene, while Lute and Fan stayed in the back so they could spoon without being seen. Lute had picked the seat himself, and since the carriage belonged to him, there was no help for it.

Misty dawn broke along the road long after they left. For hours the carriage wheels turned and the horses' hooves muffled in the thick dust, but North Mountain seemed to get little nearer. It was early noon at the foot of the mountain before they ate the cold dinner Mamma had packed in tin kettles and a huge basket.

"For supper, Mamma, you'll be at one of the hotels," Papa promised.

Now came invasion of the mountain itself, scaling the great Chinese wall. The road climbed on and on, always in the leafy shade of the big trees, always getting higher and never the sound of running water very far off. The boys and Lute walked, lightening the load. Sometimes Papa walked and let Johnny drive. They had to stop often to wind the horses.

"The air here's like wine," Papa enthused. "Can you taste it?" They all said they could. Mamma found it easy to breathe. Papa said they were nearly a half mile "up in the firmament." The top wasn't far off now. Any minute they would come out among the big hotels, the casinos and gaily painted cottages.

But when they stopped to rest the horses again, all remained quiet as the woods below. The most silent place was their first sign of life through the trees, a very large house to be called a "cottage," with other "cottages" farther down the road, most of them painted a mossy green or dove gray, all with deep porches and many windows, the roofs sharp, often a half dozen smaller roofs over upstairs porches and windows. But where were the people? Porches and yards were empty. As they came abreast they saw that the windows of some of the houses had been boarded up.

"Why, I don't believe anybody's here," Lute said.

Papa said nothing. He drove slowly down the beautiful wooded street with empty houses on either side till they could see the gleam of a considerable lake through the trees and on the bank a tremendous yellow barn of a building with porches running around upstairs and down, and a hundred windows. FOREST INN, the large white sign read.

"Here's where I wanted to take you for supper," Papa said.

There was no sign of life except a squirrel. A rusty chain hung between the stone pillars that marked the drive.

"I think we're too late," Mamma said. "I think they're closed for the season."

Papa couldn't believe it. Why, the most beautiful time in the woods and mountains was still to come, he said, the season of Indian summer, of painted leaves and running game. He gave the lines to Johnny, got out and read the notice fastened to one of the stone pillars. His lower lip stood out like a child's, as if God had let him down.

The boy felt unhappy for all including himself, but for Papa the most. He had never shown such bitter disappointment, not even at his glee club rejection. There was something here the boy couldn't name, something hidden, something more than the chance bringing to nought today's dreams and expectations. What was it then? Were preacher folk never to know the rich, highly flavored life of the well-to-do and well-born? Fate, God, call it what you will, was speaking to them from the rusty chain between the pillars. The voice was quiet, firm, gentle and, at least to Papa and himself, very, very sad.

Book · III

THE DARK FIELD

CHAPTER EIGHT

Mahanoy

Preacher Harry Donner stood under the round blue altar window looking over his congregation as it sang the last hymn of the morning service.

The month was June with the church pleasantly warm and the scent of flowers on the pulpit. The sun streamed through the stained-glass windows putting a sparkle of red, purple and green over the scattered faces and garments in the pews. This should have been his moment of assuagement, for the morning sermon lay behind him and refreshment for the carnal man not far off. The choir had done very well with that "As the Hart Panteth after the Water Brook" thing. He had never heard it before this last week. They were lucky to have the Calebs as members. Mrs. Caleb's calm soprano and the deep bass of the organ were the best things about the charge. It was a good enough church, of solid stone, with a bell that lifted the ringer off his feet as he clung to the rope to keep the wheel from turning over.

The pastor liked both bell and building. He had been duly ordained, with high synodical hands laid on his head to bless him and his work in this place.

And yet he did not feel blessed. He had looked forward to the charge but now that he had it, something was lacking. He didn't have to look at his hymnbook. He knew the words by heart.

Peace, peace, wonderful peace
Coming down from the Father above.

But he didn't feel peace. His sermon today had gone uphill. Nearly all his sermons here had to be pushed. Even then he fancied an empty ring in the half-empty church. He was hardly a stranger. His native Unionville lay in these same mountains, less than ten miles away. The hard-coal region that surrounded him had been familiar since childhood. Mahanoy wasn't a mining patch but a considerable town, an anthracite trade center with streets, churches, a dozen stores and a bank. Businessmen lived here and the retired well-to-do. He could see some of them below him now, church pillars and councilmen: Mr. Greenawalt, starched both here and in his shoe store; Mr. Wolfe, who watched him in the pulpit as sharply as the accounts at the Rhodora Colliery; Charley Waltman, who worked for the Reading Coal and Iron; and Mr. Rennsler in his formidable white beard, flanked by four unmarried daughters.

Even the benediction failed to satisfy Harry Donner today. As a rule, holding his hands out over his flock in the blessing was when he felt closest to the Ineffable Source, closer than at the altar. In other churches the altar had at times awed him with the holy and inscrutable. Here in his own church, God's table seemed strangely just a table. If there was any essence of mystery or sanctity about it, he felt too mortal and sinful to detect it.

But when he gave the simplest benediction, he felt the Presence.

"The grace of our Lord Jesus Christ be with you."

He noticed it less when he used the routine form, perhaps because all his life he had heard these words.

"The Lord bless thee and keep thee. The Lord make His face shine upon you and be gracious unto thee. The Lord lift up His countenance upon thee, and give thee peace."

His favorite was the benediction from Jude that Pap-pa had blessed him with. When he spoke that to his congregation, it never failed to move him. This was when the Unutterable brushed closest to him. For a few moments he felt convinced of his discipleship, that he was indeed an instrument of the Almighty. He could sense power coming through him and out to the congregation. Why couldn't he know it more often? How could he hope to convey the exaltation of his Lord unless at least for the time being he were made holy and acceptable, partaking of the indescribable grace?

While Mrs. Mosely softly plied the organ, holding the supplicant chords until she saw him safely at the door, he hurried down the aisle between bowed heads, feeling like a small boy sneaking out of church or a housewife hurrying home to put her Sunday roast in the oven. The sudden joyous peal of the organ told him that the people were released and coming, the young and fast steppers first, then the main stream of the congregation. As a layman he used to feel joy in this final ceremony, the organ making triumphant sounds while a lively chatter rose from cleansed and edified worshippers in recession along aisle and stairs.

Perhaps he expected too much of those whose hands he shook as they passed by.

"It was very warm in church," Mrs. Siegreid said to him almost accusingly and Mrs. Orwig boasted she had had a letter from Reverend Sanner, a former pastor, now at Atlantic City. Most of the congregation simply shook hands, said how-de-do and went on, but he tried to have something to say to each. He told Miss Mary Thomas that her flowers on the altar were fragrant and beautiful. She said she would get them after the evening service. Mr. Jones complained he couldn't hear him, only that part about Absalom, My Son, My Son, and he heard that because he knew it by heart. Mrs. Yost, who came right after, told him she didn't hear some of his sermon either, but she wasn't deaf like Willy Jones. They oughtn't to let them bring crying babies into church, she said sharply. Mr. Rennsler spoke the longest, holding up the line with the authority of his patriarchal beard. He thought they should call a special council meeting. He would have a great deal to say over their apportionment, which was too high. He happened to know the Tar City church apportionment was less. Also, they better order next winter's coal. The spring and summer discount of twenty-five cents a ton would be off before they knew it. Miss Nellie hoped they would hold the meeting at their house. Her father shouldn't walk home from church alone at night. The pastor didn't object. It would mean refreshments and very good ones. Mrs. Caleb said she was going to Philadelphia next weekend and wouldn't be in the choir. Old Mr. Wilkins, who, Preacher Donner heard, had fought with the Methodists before he came to the Lutherans, complained excitedly that he had lost a five-dollar goldpiece. He thought he must have put it in the collection. It was a mistake, he said, and he would give George Wolfe a nickel for it. He had intended only to put in a new penny.

So it went. Afterward the preacher couldn't remember a good word for his sermon. He had given his best. He had looked on one and all with love, but he guessed it must have been only human love. Not enough of the divine had been able to get through his mortal flesh. After all, his flock expected him to love them. Wasn't he their pastor, paid for out of their own pockets, his services to them part of the contract? Perhaps, the preacher mused, it was their house rather than God's. He wondered about that.

When the last had gone, he sighed and told Jimmy Neal he needn't wait. He would lock up. Even as he said it, he didn't like the sound of the words. The Catholic church on the hill right behind them—they could throw rocks down on the Lutheran church roof if they wanted and some of the Irish boys did—never locked its door. Sometimes he wondered if his own Protestant churches mightn't be too austere and bare, too vigilantly literal about the first commandment. The images in Father Keleher's church helped to draw the people up the long wooden steps to light a candle and say a prayer at all hours of the day and night. Surely the Lord God of mercy was not jealous of his saints. If so, the Protestants had better look out when they put the likeness of apostles in their stained-glass windows.

After Jimmy had gone, St. Peter's seemed another place, quiet and deserted. The familiar church scents of carpet, hymnbooks and of the departed congregation rose silently and took over. He closed the front door and climbed the stairs. The long church room and its furnishings looked almost lifeless, the organ incapable of sound, the pulpit shorn of power. The altar seemed wooden, inert. He went up the aisle, passed through the altar rail and knelt. Under his tightly folded hands the Lord's table remained passive, the sanctuary about him mute.

No words came to his lips. He only wanted to kneel here in this quiet place and open his unquiet heart to the hoped-for Presence. Professor Munger at the seminary had once quoted a Hebrew saying that every unspoken aspiration rising from earth is heard and understood in heaven. Preacher Donner told himself in that case the Lord would have to know from his wordless yearning what he himself didn't care to put into words, that after he had been called, schooled and given a church to preach in, it would be ingratitude to cast up to him that his joy wasn't all he expected. After all, trial was the Christian's lot and the pastor's duty to pray for others before himself. If he had fancied that once he had a church, his days would be peace and bliss, the fault was his own and not that of him who had called him. Without sin or tribulation in the world, what would be the need for holy orders?

There were, of course, times when he yielded to selfish petition. One of his subterfuges was to pray in song.

Even me. Even me.
May some blessings fall on me.

Since it was only a hymn, he could do it with good conscience. To all appearance he might be doing no more than praising God, but anyone hearing the plaintive way he drew out the words might guess what lay in his heart.

He felt faintly refreshed when he rose. He got his hat from a Sunday-school bench and retraced his steps to the front door, locked it and struck out in the hot sunshine for home. The sky looked brassy over Catholic Hill, the street abandoned. Everyone must be eating his Sunday dinner.

Middle Creek flowed clear when he crossed the arched bridge, sad testimony, if he hadn't known it, that the collieries had shut down for the summer.

As he opened the front door he smelled Vallie's Sunday steak, something she could get on the table quickly after church. He also glimpsed a caller in the small parlor. The Donners called it "the front room." It was a man sitting stiffly on one of the yellow upholstered chairs. When Harry Donner got closer he recognized him as a miner from Primrose whom he hadn't seen for five or six years.

"Why, Tom!" he exclaimed, pumping his hand. "I'm glad to see you. How are you and Carrie?"

"We're fine, Reverend," Tom said, pleased, managing the new religious title all right. He sobered. "Sally Barrett asked if I'd come down. Mike's pretty bad. You know, his mother died on ship and Mike's never been baptized or confirmed. He never would go to church. Sally thought maybe you could come up and sprinkle him. She'd hate to have him die like a dog or the heathen, she said."

Harry Donner stood there remembering Sally Barrett, the mother of five, at whose house he had eaten more than one dinner when out with the store team. Even then Mike Barrett couldn't lie down at night, had to sleep sitting up in a chair. His trouble was miner's asthma, silicosis the doctors called it. He kept on working just the same but the last Harry Donner heard, Mike was in bad shape. The slightest thing exhausted him, he who had been one of the strongest and wildest men on Broad Mountain. The patch was filled with stories about him. But glory set no table, and after the last strike that outlawed the company store, Harry Donner heard that Sally had started a small store in her front room.

"Why, sure, Tom," Preacher Donner said. "But what does Mike think of it?"

"I don't know. He didn't say. But he knows it would please Sally and the girls. He hardly squeaked through last night."

"I'll come right away, Tom," the preacher promised.

"You have Sunday school this afternoon and services tonight, Hal," Mamma reminded.

"Johnny can run over and ask Mr. Rennsler to teach the Bible class," he said. "I'll catch the six-o'clock train at Lost Creek and be back in time tonight."

"But how will you get up, Hal?"

"On Shank's mare," he said. "You walked down, didn't you, Tom? Well, you stay now and have dinner with us and we'll go up the mountain together."

They left the house in an hour. Mamma saw that he had the little black Ministerial Acts in his pocket and the portable service under his arm. Their way lay a long mile through town, across two creeks and the railroad, past the Old Lutheran Church and up the west end of the rising street with frame houses clinging to the steep side hill. When the two men passed the last gate they were already well up on a flank of Broad Mountain.

Ever since he had come home and found Tom Sheridan there, the preacher had noticed a change in the air. Although the sun felt hotter than when he left the church, a fresh breeze seemed to blow through town, and when they reached the green shade of the woods, the preacher felt more like himself than for a long time. This was the mountain he knew so well from Unionville days, laden in summer with the scent of bush, and vine, of hardwood and pine. They passed aromatic sweet fern he used to fasten in the store horses' bridles to keep off the flies. By the time they reached the broad summit and saw ahead against the sky piles of coal dirt like the pyramids of Egypt, the preacher felt his lethargy completely gone. The air was better here, the sky bluer and everywhere at the edge of the gashed earth the green fingers of the forest worked, trying to erase the scars and to hide with rich verdure the grimy buildings. Young sassafras crowded up from the edge of the dark roads and luxurious banks of fern came out of the coal-black earth as from gardens.

They could see now the roofs of New Summit off toward the north ridge and Old Summit to the south. Lost Run, the largest patch of all, lay in the mountain flats hidden by the forest. They started off the mountain to a broad bench heaped with prodigious culm banks, passed the Primrose boiler house and its brick stacks, the dark eye of the slope, and the flat maze of narrow- and broad-gauge steel tracks where idle wooden mine cars and steel gondolas simmered in the sun, into a cool sulphurous layer of air from the yellow water vomited by the pumps and on toward the patch itself.

"Well, here are three nice little boys out for a walk!" Harry Donner greeted cheerfully, stopping to bend over and shake their hands one by one.

"We're not little boys. We're girls," they told him.

"Oh, is that right!" he said, as if greatly surprised, beaming at them and going on.

He felt the old well-being as he came up the dusty road between the one-and-a-half-story houses, unpainted except for the red window sashes, with the selfsame stoops in front of most of them, many with green creepers over the back porch; some with whitewashed palings to keep out the cows and goats. The houses looked alike but he knew or used to know them apart and all who lived within.

A group of men stood under the tree outside the Barrett house as he approached. Some of them had owed Kipps, Donner and Company money when he left. Beside him and Tom they looked a little shabby and uncomfortable in their weekday clothes. They needn't, Harry Donner thought. After all, there was no church nearer than six miles to tell them it was Sunday, and in the patch the first day of the week was little different than any other, especially in the summer, when the mines were idle.

He spoke to each heartily to rid him of his unease. He had always felt an affection for patch folks. So long as he was in the store business, he had to hide it sometimes. Miners were plungers, ready to buy far more than they could ever hope to pay for. Tradesmen had to call payday or the day after to collect what pittance they could, and in the summer with no pay at all coming in and overdrawn at the Company store, miners had to be kept in reasonable limits. But today he had no reservations, nothing to hold back from them. They could come and take from him the bread and water of life freely.

"Harry Donner!" Pete Conningham said when his turn came to shake hands. "They said you might be coming but I didn't believe them."

"He's a Reverend now, Pete!" Tom corrected.

"I know it," Pete said. "Reverend, will you stop and see Katie before you go back? She's not good either and many's the time she's spoke your name."

"He's not a father," Tom reminded. "He's a Protestant."

"Reverend, I don't care what you are," Pete said, clapping his shoulder affectionately. "That reminds me of a story. Two micks seen a High Church of England priest coming along. 'Hi, Father,' said one. 'He's no father,' said the other. 'He's got four kids.' Now wait a minute. I have another while we're on the subject. My cousin came over on the Immigration and wrote home from Shenandoah to my Uncle Pete, the one I'm named after. 'Uncle Pete, it's a wonderful country over here. I'm tearing down a Protestant church and getting paid for it.' Now don't take offense, Reverend. Come in and see Katie before you go. You don't need to mention you're Catholic or Protestant. I won't and she won't either."

"I'll do that, Pete," Preacher Donner said. "How's Mike?"

The men shook their heads.

"Not so good, Reverend," Jim Doran said. "The women are fanning him for breath now. Annie was up with him most of the night."

He could hear Mike breathing when he got to the door. It almost struck him in the face, a loud whistling and wheezing that shouldn't come from a human being. And could that be Mike Barrett himself, propped up in bed in the little parlor behind the storeroom, a wreck of a man wasted away to his bones, frail and transparent as glass, his hair turned to a kind of tarnished silver? It was a shock to remember him as he used to be, filled with life and the devil. When he came home from work evenings, they said, he would dance a jig by himself on the back porch, and him black as the ace of spades, his eyes white and sparkling with the Old Nick. He'd whistle his own tune to dance to, a hornpipe or the "Irish Washerwoman." And him down in the mines all day. They worked twelve hours then. He claimed he danced for his supper. Tom said he thought he danced that he was safe out of the blackness for the day and home to his shanty, woman and young ones. But Sally insisted Mike danced for pure pleasure. She said he'd sooner dance than eat, that his overalls could be patched but his shoes had to shine.

Harry Donner reckoned that Mike's wife ought to know him best. Most of the men who drilled the rock tunnels tied bandanas over their mouths to keep out the rock and coal dust, but Mike said he wasn't ashamed of his face. He could eat rock and live off it. He mocked those who claimed that the coal regions were damned, the mines accursed, that sooner or later a man would get hauled up in a bucket. The mines would never get him. Besides, where else could an Irish lad with blood in his veins from County Mayo earn a dollar and twenty-five cents a day?

Sally saw Harry Donner from the kitchen and came hurrying in to shake his hand. The look of thanks in her eyes was reward enough for missing Sunday school and walking six miles up the mountain. She had been raised in the country near Unionville. Now she showed him her youngest girl and led him over to the bed.

"Harry Donner, me lad!" Mike Barrett greeted him faintly. "How'd they ever get a black coat on you, man?" Talking as little as that made him choke and cough till he brought up some thick black stuff which he spat in the can Sally held for him.

Pete Conningham pushed in and took the can from her.

"So you know this man, Mike, in his high-church collar? Reverend, Mike claims he's County Mayo but he never saw it. His father did but his mother was Church of England. So Mike's neither mackerel nor red herring and you can give him all the holy water you want. Did you ever hear the story, Reverend, of the man from County Mayo who looked like the king? The king of England, I mean. The king heard about him over in London and sent for him and looked him over. 'Yes,' he said, 'it's like looking in a mirror. Was your mother ever in England?' The County Mayo man never batted an eye. 'Never,' he said, 'but my father was.' Now don't take offense at a shady story, Reverend."

Harry Donner tried to draw out his old friend. But Pete did most of the talking, fanning him with Annie Doran's fan. It took a little time to realize Pete was trying to save Mike from talking and coughing.

"It's a pity Mike never saw Black Sod Bay above Galway, Reverend, or Broadhaven Bay either one. They're the beauty spots of the world. It's where the Spanish Armada come ashore and the shipwrecked men stuck around because of the colleens. If you look at Mike you can see the long Spanish face. That's what makes him such a stubborn headstrong lad and nobody can lead him around."

"Except Sally," Tim Cochran put in, a foolish thing to say with Sally wanting him baptized. Pete Conningham talked on a while trying to let Mike forget it.

At the end there was nothing to do but come around to it. Harry Donner laid his hand on the sick man's shoulder.

"I'd like to baptize you while I'm here, Mike," he said.

"You mean Sally'd like it!" Mike jeered.

"Well, of course she would. But I'm your friend and I'd like it, too. Will you let me do it for you?"

Mike sat there fighting the idea and fighting himself for fighting it.

"If Sally wants it, go ahead," he brought out at last.

Harry Donner took the Ministerial Acts from his pocket. The small black book in his hands lent him a sense of holy orders, made him feel suddenly more than himself, taller, of surer authority. The men withdrew to the store-room door and around the bed it became quiet except for the breathing. Harry Donner opened the book and his voice came out strong with life in this sickroom.

"Dearly beloved: forasmuch as our Saviour, Jesus Christ, hath said, Except a man be born of water and the spirit he cannot enter the kingdom of God . . ."

It went well enough until the time came to interrogate the candidate.

"Dost thou renounce the devil and all his works and all his ways?"

The only answer was an endless fit of coughing with Mike's eyes mocking him as if to say, "How do you expect me to renounce the devil when he has me by the windpipe?"

Sally waited a long minute, then spoke in a low voice.

"Can I answer for him, Reverend?"

Harry Donner considered. After all, Mike and Sally were one according to God's own word. He supposed it not unreasonable. He continued the questions with Sally answering till the coughing stopped and Mike answered for himself. The preacher took the miner's wasted right hand in his and held it up.

"In the name of the Lord Jesus whom thou hast confessed, I hereby declare thee a member of his church and authorize thee to receive the Lord's supper and to participate in all the spiritual privileges of the church."

He turned so as to face Sally, Annie Doran and the men bunched at the door.

"And now I admonish you to acknowledge and receive this man as your brother and heir with you in the Lord and ever to pray for him and that God may perfect the work which He hath begun by His Holy Spirit. The blessings of Almighty God, the Father, the Son and Holy Ghost be with thee always. Amen."

"Amen," Sally said fervently.

When they saw it was over the men at the door pushed back into the room, Pete Conningham in the lead talking.

"Do you know, Mike, you're a bloody Lutheran now? How will an Irishman get along when he wakes up in purgatory and finds himself with the Dutch?"

Sally pushed warmly between them.

"If he could get along with the Dutch for thirty years, Pete Conningham, he won't find it any harder over there." She turned to the preacher. "Can he take communion now, Reverend?"

"If he wants it," Harry Donner said. "We won't push him. He doesn't need to take it if he doesn't want to."

The eyes of the bloodless miner were like pieces of coal. He seemed curiously calmed by the service and unaware of the terrible sucking and whistling sounds from his own chest. He motioned the others to leave.

"I know you, Mike Barrett," Pete Conningham told him. "You want all the wine for yourself." But he left with the others while Annie Doran and Sally went to the kitchen. The preacher took his silver set from its cloth bag, then tapped on the kitchen door for the bread and wine.

The words and heart of the Eucharist ceremony had never seemed so rich and moving or yet so mysterious and inscrutable as when he repeated them today to this dying miner propped up in his unpainted Company house on Broad Mountain.

"Our Lord Jesus in the night in which he was betrayed took bread; and when he had given thanks, He brake it and gave it to His disciples saying, Take, eat; this is my Body which is given for you; do this in remembrance of Me."

He poured out some of Sally's wine and put the cup momentarily to his own lips.

"After the same manner also, He took the cup when He had supped, and when He had given thanks, He gave it to them, saying, Drink ye all of it. This cup is the New Testament in my Blood which is shed for you and for many, for the remission of sins; this do as oft as ye drink it in remembrance of Me."

At the end Harry Donner closed the little black book. "That prayer was printed in here, Mike. Now I'd like to pray one of my own for you, if you want me to." He knelt by the bed and knotted his hands on the covers. He did not need to think what to say. Words of entreaty and intercession, as seldom came to him in his Mahanoy church, flooded the room. It seemed that he could almost hear his father when as a boy he had listened to him one night long ago pleading in the darkness with the Unseen, his voice rising and falling in slow, imploring, unforgettable German.

When he left, Sally tried to press a bill on him. He pushed it back.

"You need it yourself, Sally."

"But I want you to come again, Reverend." He thought he knew what she meant.

"Any time," he told her.

"I'll never forget what you've done for us. It's the first time a minister's been in our house since your wife's father used to come and see us."

"Well, it needn't be the last, Sally," he said. "Call me when you need me."

The truth was, he told himself, that she had done more for him than he for her. It was her summons that had led him here, had let him bring God's word and sacrament to an old friend in his last bitter hours. More than that, she had opened his eyes to this field of destitution and need lying unseen almost under his nose. At Mahanoy he felt his people were well off in spiritual possessions. They took them all for granted, a church home, religious services four and five times a week, pastoral calls in their houses, religious instruction for the young. Here in the patches they had nothing of that, neither sheep fold nor shepherd, no Sunday school or altar, no man of God moving among them to remind them of their heavenly Father who knocked unseen on the doors of their rude houses or of the Holy Spirit ready to descend with the men in the dangerous breasts and headings of the mines.

When he stepped outside the men were still there, flanked now by some women and children. He sensed a respect he had never felt when out with the store team. Warmly he shook hands with them all. Several asked if he would stop in at their houses to see them.

"He's coming with me first to see Katie," Pete Conningham bragged. "Then I'm walking him over to the Lost Run station to catch his train. He's got to preach in Mahanoy tonight."

CHAPTER NINE

Rock and Rye

As a boy Johnny had seldom thought much about his mother. She was too incontrovertible a fact, too familiar a substance and being, more real than his own flesh and blood. His likes and loyalties he might question but his mother's never. There was always this tender rock in gingham to resort to, always the fine steady gray eyes and sweet smell about her to depend on and reassure. Cordial to most, she was never intimate save to her three sons. With all, there remained a clement earthy quality about her like a spring in the field or the soul at the moment of death or revelation. In all his life the only times he knew it to be broken were at the agonized cry she gave at the telephone when Polly's boy, Tod, was dead of diphtheria at eight and her shaken prayer aloud the night the parsonage was struck by lightning.

Not that she lived without mysteries. They were only part of the familiar reality. One was her alien personality in silk at church, sitting in the pew repeating religious forms that meant little to Johnny but which always brought from her lips the soft sibilants of reverence and belief. Another was the deep sadness that came over her at times. When aware that it had been observed, she quickly threw it off. She would never explain or discuss it. There were also the incredible colors she told them she saw when she closed her eyes, colors unlike anything on earth. If only she knew how to paint them, she would make their fortune.

His father was different, up and down, strong and positive, a phenomenon the boy continually resisted, a turbulent stream whose current bore him along no matter how he struggled against it, never to be kept to the seclusion of fields and forests but always intent on towns and people.

The boy felt uncommonly aware of this the day Maggie Moore called. Evans, her name was now, she said, but her man had died of a siege of intermittent fever. Papa made a great fuss over her. You might have thought this strange woman his long lost younger sister. When he asked after her mother and her family, it was as if after his own.

"This is Maggie, your old nurse girl, Johnny," he beamed at the boy. "You were only a baby and Maggie was, let's see, just fourteen or fifteen years old."

"Thirteen," Maggie said. "We were talking about it last week when we heard you'd been up to Mike Barrett's in Primrose. Mom thought maybe I could 'live out' with you again. She said I know a little more now than I did then."

Papa welcomed the idea with enthusiasm. This was the Lord's doing, succor sent to Mamma by Heaven. But Mamma explained kindly and firmly to the girl. They had no store now to fall back on. They were just a poor preacher's family, and a maid or even another mouth to feed was beyond their slender affording. Papa looked frustrated and Maggie took out her disappointment on Johnny, stroking the embarrassed boy's arm, reciting how as a babe he used to wet himself at all hours of the night and scream to get her up and attend him. The more she went on, the grosser the injustice seemed to this thwarted woman to deny her the small work she craved. But Mamma held her quiet ground. The boys were no longer babies and she could manage.

"Could I take him up to Lost Run then for a few days, ma'am?" Maggie begged. "I'd like to show him to Mom and the rest. They've heard tell of him and never seen him."

Johnny struggled to escape. He knew Mamma would come to his rescue, and she did, but this time Papa would not back down. There were lost Lutherans at Lost Run he had long been wanting to hunt up. Maggie must stay for dinner. Then he would go along up on the mountain with her and Johnny on the afternoon miners' train, stay at her mother's house overnight and bring Johnny home tomorrow evening.

The miners' train was dirty and bare to the boy's eyes. Three hard narrow benches ran the length of the car. Papa seated himself on one as on a throne. While the train climbed the mountain he expanded to Johnny on Lost Run and the woman at whose house they were going to be guests. He knew no more saintly person in the patch, he told the boy, a Lutheran whose Irish husband had been killed underground leaving her to raise a big family. She had help from nobody but had found time to help others, generously baking for a funeral or wedding. She still did, Maggie said, either that or nursing the sick or hanging paper for somebody. Papa nodded. Should a baby be due in the patch, he told Johnny, they got Mrs. Moore instead of the Mahanoy doctor and when the doctor came to the patch to cut out tonsils or amputate an arm or leg, she was the one who stood by him and lent a hand with the bloody work.

Johnny didn't know as he liked the prospect of staying at the house of someone so ready to cut off legs and tonsils. The unmistakable reek of anthracite in the car faintly nauseated him. At Lost Run when the miners came swarming on the train before it stopped, he seemed in some foreign world peopled by black-faced natives who brought fresh and stronger reminders of the deep Cimmerian veins.

His father plainly reveled in it, piercing the black disguises to call most of the miners by name and then to stride with greetings from all sides to an unpainted Company house which he entered like a lion.

"And who is this?" the big stout woman he called Mrs. Moore asked when she saw Johnny.

"This is my oldest," Papa declared. "The one that Maggie

had to change so much." He laughed heartily while the boy flinched.

"Well, Reverend," the large woman said placidly, "he looks like he's big enough to go to the outhouse himself now. I hope he'll take after you and his grandpop and make another preacher in the family."

With indefinable gloom the boy heard the last train leave for Mahanoy that evening. The night that followed was a fantastic one in this strange house on Broad Mountain. At home he slept at ease in the back bedroom with Timmy and Gene. Up here he lay among the whole unfamiliar Moore clan, both women and men, all sleeping in the unpartitioned half-story attic they called "upstairs." Walls had been left unfinished as was the ceiling. Board shelves nailed between the rafters held food and toilet articles. Slab bacon, shirts, petticoats, underwear and a half-used ham hung from nails. The tin of a later roof showed through the broken shingles.

It was the most remarkable place to sleep the boy had ever known, but his father took it as if going to bed in public was his accustomed wont, undressing in the darkness with the others around him, kneeling down by the larger of the beds with legs—some were only ticks on the floor—taking a long time with his prayer, a silent one except for the audible sighs and occasional impassioned whispers interjected, it seemed to the boy, to give it more of a semblance of holy petition and devotion in this unseemly place. Then he laid himself down beside Johnny and recalled in a voice for the benefit of all the last time he had slept in the patch and what a sight like Pentecost it had been early next morning with the street filled with miner's lamps, the tongues of flame bobbing and flaring in the darkness, the men singing on their way to Primrose and North Summit collieries and to No. 2 at Lost Run. Some had come from far down the mountain, tramping to save miners' fare pennies, and the boy wondered how anyone in the cold and darkness of an early winter morning could be so preposterously cheerful on his way to work and danger in the mines.

In the morning when he awoke all the beds were empty save his. He dressed and went downstairs to find them at breakfast. Mrs. Moore stood huge and commanding by the stove. Something smelled good.

"Now, Johnny," his father said, "I'm glad you're along to see some of the womanly Christianity I told you about. The people next door haven't been the best of neighbors to the Moores. They think sometimes they've missed milk from their cow and cabbage from their garden—"

"We don't think so, Reverend," Maggie interrupted. "We know them devils done it."

"Now that's enough of that kind of talk," her mother called.

"Forgive and forget, Maggie," Papa said. "What I was about to explain to Johnny was that death came to this questionable neighbor family during the night, and yet

Maggie's mother is ready to help what she can and bake a custard to take over."

Johnny felt let down. He thought the good smell meant something for their own breakfast.

"Mom can take it over, Reverend," Maggie said significantly, "but she can't make them let her in."

"Oh, yes, I can," her mother put in piously. "I tell you I didn't try to keep anybody out the time your father lay a corpse in this house. I was glad enough for anybody to come around and give me a hand, let alone a custard."

"I think, Mrs. Moore," Papa said, "I ought to go along and offer a prayer. Johnny, you may come, too."

The boy would have given much to escape but there was no eluding his father. They were both a step behind Mrs. Moore as she marched up to the back-porch steps next door. An Irish woman with wild-looking hair narrowly opened the door.

"Good morning, Mrs. Shott," Mrs. Moore said in her most polite tones. "It's a sad day for you, we hear, and I thought I'd come over and tell you how we felt for you."

There was no answer from Mrs. Shott, whose eyes were fixed on the custard. Neither did she open the door any wider. Maggie's mother went on.

"It happens that a preacher of the Gospel has been staying at our house. You've heard of the Reverend here from Mahanoy. He's the same Harry Donner who used to come up from his store in Unionville, and his wife's the daughter of the Reverend Morgan who baptized so many on Broad Mountain. The Reverend thought he should stop in for a few minutes and pray for the dead if you wanted him to."

The door opened an inch or two wider.

"I don't know," the woman mumbled. "She was Catholic."

"That's all right, Mrs. Shott," Johnny's father assured her. "I'm not here to try to make a Lutheran out of any of you. I just thought I might offer a prayer and ask if there was anything I could do. After all, we and the Catholics are both Christians. We pray to the same God and hope to go to the same heaven."

"I don't know about that," Mrs. Shott said again, but she opened the door an inch or two still wider.

"Also"—Mrs. Moore played her trump card—"I thought I'd bake you a custard. I hope you like custards."

Mrs. Shott, who hadn't taken her eyes off the custard, looked sharply at her neighbor now for malice.

"Oh, I can eat anything, Sophy Moore," she said, letting the door give away at last so Maggie's mother, the custard, Harry Donner, Maggie and Johnny could pass into the kitchen, where a red-faced man sat by the table.

"Good morning, Mr. Shott," Maggie's mother said. "You know the Reverend, I guess. He was just telling Mrs. Shott he'd be glad to go in and say a prayer for the poor soul."

"Hold on!" Mr. Shott said. "He can't go in there, Mrs.

Moore. Not where the old woman was lying and dying. The dirt and stink would knock you over like a feather."

Maggie's mother stood there huge and mountainous, looking anything but like a feather.

"Well, maybe me and Mrs. Shott better go in first and scrub up a little for the Reverend."

"Ah, did you hear that, Kitty? It's a nice neighborly thing to do, Mrs. Moore. But I couldn't let you be imposed upon. Not without the protection of holy water." He put a hand under the table and lifted up a gallon jug partly filled with wicked-looking amber liquid at the bottom of which lay the jagged crystals of rock candy together with a small rusty hinge and still rustier nails.

Mrs. Moore turned her lip with distaste.

"I've been laying out the dead for twenty years, Ben Shott, them that died in bed and them that had to be brought up in pieces, and I've never had to drink rusty nails yet. Now if you'll give me a rag, a basin and tea kettle, Mrs. Shott, you and me can go in and do our duty."

Armed with the objects in question, she led the way firmly into the back room off the kitchen which some called "the summer kitchen." The Shotts had used it as a bedroom. She was back in a few minutes to send Maggie for a scrub brush and bucket of hot water from home. Her face was kind of mottled red and green.

"I told you," Ben Shott said. "We're all weak and sinful

and in need of purification. What do you say, Reverend?"

"There are occasions that a little alcohol may be prescribed," Johnny's father said.

"Well, only a sip then, Mr. Shott," Mrs. Moore weakened, "I don't touch it as a rule."

The hinge and rusty nails clicked and slid as he poured her three quarters of a tumbler, which she lifted and tasted, taking another taste or two till Maggie came with the bucket, when her mother disappeared into the room only to come out from time to time and fortify herself a little more, finally to take the glass in with her as Mrs. Shott had done before her.

Johnny's father had taken a chair and entered into conversation with the man of the house when voices began coming under the door. One was plainly that of Mrs. Shott but the other sounded as from a strange woman.

"My lights and livers!" it called. "How in the name of God, Mrs. Shott, did you let it get so rotten filthy in here?"

"I had nothing to do with it, Sophy Moore," Mrs. Shott said. "You tend to your business and I'll tend to mine."

"Do you mean to say it's the fault of this poor dead woman lying bedfast in a bed she couldn't get out of when all the while you were here healthy and able with sound legs and arms in the same house?"

"I was busy feeding and taking care of her, Sophy Moore, and feeding and taking care of my man and seeing he got to work every morning to bring a dollar or two in the house so we could keep on feeding and taking care of this dirty old woman."

"You have the cruelty to call her a dirty old woman, your poor aunty lying here with her mouth shut and at peace after all the mean things she said in her lifetime?"

"Maybe she did, but that has nothing to do with me."

"Nothing to you? You'd deny you take after her, Myra Shott!"

"I'd deny it if you said it, Sophy Moore, and anything else you said."

"Come over here, Mrs. Shott," Mrs. Moore coaxed. "Take a good look at that mouth and say whether or not it's your own flesh and blood that could never tell the fair, decent and unpolluted truth!"

"Are you insinuating now and accusing me of prevarication and foul language, Sophy Moore?"

"I'm not insinuating and accusing you of anything, Myra Shott. I just want you to cast your eyes like you might at a sow in the pigpen and tell me if that wasn't the way your mouth turned down the time Mr. Shott was hauled off to jail for beating to death with a sprag one of the mules on the eighth level of North Summit."

"That's a dirty and dastardly lie, Sophy Moore. They never could prove that Ben even touched the mule."

"I didn't say there was anybody there to prove it on him in court. I only say if you come over here and look at the corpse from where I'm standing—"

"I don't need to come over there, Sophy Moore. I've been looking at this corpse in my house for twenty years. Everybody knows I don't take after the Tobins but the MacSweens."

"So you take after the MacSweens?" the other voice said with dangerous sweetness. "Maybe you could tell me about Paddy MacSween who kept a woman at the other end of Broad Mountain?"

"I can not!" Mrs. Shott shouted along with a sound like the spatter of water hitting the ceiling.

"Then can you tell me of Leo MacSween who they wanted to hang as one of the Mollies the time they shot poor old Mr. Raddabaugh at Primrose and stuck their fingers in his blood and wrote threats and warnings on the walls against anybody and everybody who didn't fall in with what they wanted?"

"That's enough, Sophy Moore!" Mrs. Shott warned. "I didn't ask you over to blacken and besmirch my uncle, God rest his soul!"

"No!" Mrs. Moore said loudly and unsympathetically. "And you didn't ask if you could milk the cow either."

"Cow! What cow is that you're talking about?" Mrs. Shott answered with great loftiness.

"It's our cow I'm talking about, Mrs. Shott. Up in the mountain you milked her when you thought nobody could see you. We didn't see you either. But we seen the custards you made. You even had the gall to set them to cool on the window sill on our side so we could stew in our own milk custards."

"It was never your milk in them custards, Sophy Moore."

"Then whose was it, I'd like to ask?"

"It was nobody's milk, Sophy Moore. Them was water custards."

"Water now, was it?" Mrs. Moore's voice was so high and sarcastic it sounded like a child's. "I'd like the receipt for water custards you can make rich as butter and yellow as a orange."

"Well, don't worry. I'll give it to you sometime. But don't expect a sloppy Dutch cook smart enough to make them."

"Ai, yai, yai!" Mrs. Moore moaned. "Now I'm a sloppy Dutch cook and the one that tells me keeps no garden in summer and smokes no ham and bacon in winter but has to eat bread and molasses when the mines shut down."

"Sure we eat bread and molasses and we like it," Mrs. Shott shouted. "We talk the king's English, too, and not the pig language."

"What kind of English is that?" Mrs. Moore cried. "Why didn't you talk it in Ireland then instead of having to wear shamrocks on monkey-hunting days so the English didn't shoot you by mistake?"

So it went minute after minute while things banged against the floor and walls and water slopped so that it finally flowed in rivulets under the door. Now how could his father, Johnny wondered, sit there all this time so natural and unaffected, talking to Mr. Shott about people of the patch, bringing out a dozen names or more the boy had never heard of before? And how could his father, once it was all over and the door opened and a bleary, disheveled Mrs. Moore looked out startled to see the preacher as if she had forgotten all about him—how could his father go to the door of the room in sight of the awful object on the bed, and how could he stand there and pray in such a strong, fearless voice as if untouched by all the taint and smell of death and dissolution? How especially could he speak to God so kindly of these terrible people and ask tender loving blessings upon them, both the quick and the dead, so that when he had finished, the boy found to his astonishment water cropping from the eyes of Mr. and Mrs. Shott and Maggie's mother?

The latter spoke little or nothing until they went back to the house.

"The Lord strike me dead, Reverend," she said, "if you ever catch me like this again. When you come to preach my funeral sermon, I hope you won't have to say nothing about it."

CHAPTER TEN

A House for Isaac and Rachel

Halfway up the path to the mine superintendent's house, the preacher halted. He wanted to catch his breath. He would stand here a little while and look down on Lost Run. In Mahanoy he knew some murmured against him. They said he was neglecting his church. Mr. Rennsler had brought it up at council meeting.

"I preach two sermons for you on Sunday," Harry Donner had replied. "I hold catechetical classes and Wednesday-evening prayer meeting. I try to call on every parishioner twice a year. The sick and afflicted more often."

"But lots of times you're not here," Mr. Rennsler said. "When we send for you, we find you're up in one of the patches on Broad Mountain that pay nothing toward your salary."

"They have no money," Harry Donner explained. "And no church. What do I say when they come to me for help? Do I tell them I'm too busy for God's work—that I won't minister among them unless I get paid? I'm his shepherd and they're his sheep, too."

Looking down now on one of these same Broad Mountain patches, he felt glad for what he had said. The late-afternoon sun shone on Company house roofs. The winds at this elevation had fallen. Leaves scarcely stirred on the trees and the birds in the surrounding forest were silent. For an hour or so now time would seem to stand still up here as if in the presence of the Almighty. The slow, steady light, the clear mountain air and calm, he felt, marked that nearness. The culm banks glittered with a thousand tiny facets and even the ugly black breaker looked almost beautiful. Distant cries rose from barefoot children at play. The lazy sound of cowbells drifted from mountain pastures.

Down near the slope he could see a dark object moving. He recognized the black wagon and white horses. It was the ambulance, of all things on wheels what mining folks hated most to see. As the word ran through the patch now, he knew, women and children would be standing at doors and gates, still as death, waiting to find at whose house, perhaps their own, the wagon would stop. More than one injured miner, Harry Donner heard, had climbed out short of home and made the rest of the way on foot. Better for his family to see him crawling into the house than the shock of the black wagon at their door. But the white horses now had left the patch and were on the road to South Summit.

Preacher Donner closed his eyes to say a prayer for the

unknown man in the black wagon. When he opened them again, a cloud had come over the face of the sun, and shadows lay on patch and colliery as if God had summarily departed, taking with him the inexplicable source of peace and repose. The children's cries, which had ceased for a time, grew harsher while a string of oaths rose from Isaac Gottschall's back door. None could swear with such frightening violence as the Pennsylvania Dutch, the preacher reflected, perhaps to make up for the mild often nonsensical meaning of some of the fierce-sounding German words.

It was a hard place, he thought, to live and work and try to raise a family, close by the black slope that led to so much sorrow and disaster. Most patch people here he had known before he took holy orders. He could see Lizzie Yoh's house now, near the prop and lagging piles. Her first husband had been squeezed to death between a mine car and gangway timber, her second badly burned in a fire damp explosion so that he was afraid of fire ever after and would let no matches in the house. Close by were the Housers, two of whose boys had been lost in the mines, one up Gilberton way. Behind them on the next street Pete Shaw still lived though his back had been broken by a fall of rock eight or ten years ago.

Not that misery, sadness and gloom were the temper of the patch. Far from it. There was the Irish wife of Al Madenford, who made the highest wages in the patch contracting inside, and spent it on whiskey, cock fights and shooting matches at a couple hundred dollars a side. She seldom had a dollar to spend herself but she could still tell her thanks to the unknown railroad conductor who, when she was a slip of a girl coming from Canada on the Immigration, had touched her on the shoulder and told her to look out the other side of the train, and if she hadn't, she'd have missed seeing Niagara Falls. Another cheerful one was Pete Malarky, who always could make you smile like the time he was drawn for jury duty and came home saying, "What do you think they've thought up in Pottsville now, boys? Screening the air. I seen it myself, in the hotel window." Next door Henner Kline would tell you about his mine mule, Topsy, who liked tobacco and followed him around like a dog. Nobody else could get any work out of her. Farther down the street, Solly Moyer, the fire boss, let no miner kill a mine rat if he could help it. He claimed they were an intelligent and sociable race, that the same rat waited for him at the same place underground every morning to run along and help inspect the inky breasts and headings to make sure they were safe for the men to follow. And Yuny Kestler usually had something new and acrimonious to say about Bat McGurl. Both were watchmen at the crossing, one by day, one by night. Two years before they had quarreled. That night Bat took home the watchbox stovepipe he had put up himself and Yuny had to go out and get his own. And now just for spite each went to the trouble of taking down his own stovepipe at the end of his trick and carrying it home to bring back and set it up next day while the stove smoked and sulphured.

Harry Donner liked to chat with one or the other at the crossing, and if he could help it, he never missed seeing the Conleys to visit with their boy, fair as a girl with a whole gamut of grunts and exclamations for language, all the time giving smiles of secret joy and amusement that would break a weaker man's heart. He was fond, too, of the Eckerts and their eight girls, all musical, who took turns singing to lighten the work of those doing the dishes, especially washing the hated dinner cans and bottles with chains that dirtied young girls' hands.

Harry Donner liked patch people. The worst miner he knew seldom failed to let something in his dinner can to bring home "for the kids to fight over" if only a lard sandwich with black finger marks. And the best miner seldom bought his coal. The women and children loaded it on a hand wagon or wheelbarrow and then hid it in the bushes so the men could fetch it to the house after dark.

"Taking coal from the Company isn't stealing," they argued with the preacher. "The Company has more coal than it can sell. That's why the collieries have to shut down in the summertime. The coal we take keeps them running a little longer."

Oh, patch people were a little like children, poor lost children, the preacher thought. It's what kept them happy through dark days, hard times and bare tables. Their greatest deprivation, he felt, was something else. Standing here on the path to the superintendent's house, he reflected on its nature, a house that was no Company house but a dwelling for the Lord. It needn't be large and of stone like at Mahanoy. Small and frame would be holy enough. The idea had possessed him since his first visit with Mike Barrett at Primrose. Lost Run was the better site with North and South Summit and Primrose and other patches in walking distance. He had even collected money for his dream, a quarter here and a half dollar there, mostly from the patches themselves. Catholics helped. Wiley Drumm, the engineer, gave him a dollar several times but most came from those who had very little. The money, a hundred and thirty-five dollars, lay in a special account in the Mahanoy Miners Bank. He had the spot for the church picked out, could see it now down there where those young pines grew, a tabernacle painted white among the coal banks and unpainted Company houses, a symbol of purity in all this black wilderness of sin against earth and man.

But it wasn't the Lord's house, rather another that troubled him today, the house of Isaac Gottschall, the man he had just heard cursing. His first arm lost in the breaker when a boy, he had gone inside, become a miner, and few were the men with two arms, it was said, who could dig and load more coal in a day than Isaac Gottschall with one. Then in March his second arm was crushed under a fall of rock and last week final notice had come to get out of his

Company house so a productive miner and his family could move in.

"There's nothing I can do, Reverend," Tom Hughes, inside boss, had told him. "The order's from higher up. If he'd lost a leg this time, it wouldn't be so bad. He could get a peg and keep on working. But what can an armless man do around a mine? And he can't stay in a Company house without working."

Harry Donner looked up now at the superintendent's house. It had been built on a flat bench of the mountain to the specifications, they said, of a mine operator's house in Wales, three stories of solid stone, with long stone-sill windows on two floors and dormers on the third. A veranda ran across the front of the house with a bay window upstairs and down on the southeast corner. Lawn and a flower garden lay around it, a stone stable stood to the rear and a fenced-in vegetable garden was adjoining. The Company furnished everything together with a man to take care of it, but the superintendent's wife had to pay her own hired girl. Since becoming an invalid, she had kept two. Few in the patch had seen the inside of the house but the story ran that a relative of one of the hired girls had asked if she could go through. She told Mrs. Grace afterward that it was true.

"What's true?" Mrs. Grace had asked.

"Why, the sleeping rooms," the woman said. "I heard that they didn't smell, but I wouldn't believe it."

The preacher didn't know the hired girl who came to

the door. He greeted her heartily as any girl of the patch. She failed to ask him in, but left him to cool his heels while she went to give his name. He knew by her face when she returned that the name had meant little. She said he could come to "the library," and he followed her into a great wide hall, then to a room lined with bookcases that reached to the high ceiling. A well-dressed man his own age leaned competently on a walnut desk as in an office. His black mustache was bruskly clipped. He looked solid and capable. At the sight of him sitting there upright and decent, the preacher had difficulty believing stories going the rounds about his affairs with women.

"What can I do for you?" he wanted to know.

"I'd like to talk to you a few minutes," Harry Donner said, stammering a little. Why was it, he asked himself, that he felt inept and inadequate in a big house like this, strangely deprived of the power of the Spirit that was always with him in a miner's house? Could it be true, as Vallie's father had once hinted, that the son of a section foreman on the railroad was out of place among men his father would have called "tony" and "high muckety mucks," that he belonged among the common people, the humble and the poor?

The superintendent of the Lost Run mine, he grew aware, was watching him narrowly.

"Aren't you the preacher who's been collecting for a Dutch church in Lost Run?"

"I guess I am," Harry Donner said.

"Well, if you've come to me for permission, I'll have to disappoint you," the superintendent declared. "Your Pennsylvania Dutch have been giving us a great deal of trouble. They're too independent, even insolent if I may say it. They've been especially troublesome and uncooperative during strikes. I don't think the Company would look with favor on a Dutch church on Company ground."

"I didn't mean to talk to you about a church today," the preacher said, sobered. "I came to see you about the Gottschalls."

Almost at once something alive and powerful entered the superintendent's face as though to say, So that's it, well, we'll see about it.

"If it's a Company matter, the place to take it up is the Company office." He waited. "May I ask what you have to do with it?"

"The Gottschalls are Lutherans," Harry Donner said, "and I'm their pastor, or the only one they've got. Mrs. Gottschall asked me to come up in January when her husband was first hurt. In fact, she had asked me a month or two before when he said he heard what they call the death tick. You know, the men think it's Vince Madden's watch. They never found the watch when Vince's body was dug out. They believe it's still in the mine and whoever hears it will be next."

"I'm quite familiar with the story," the superintendent

said coolly. "It's pure superstition. The sound, if it's heard at all, is caused by borers in the timber. Or possibly by the roof settling down on the props. In that case it might precede a fall of rock but the sound has nothing to do with the man who hears it."

"He would have to be dangerously close, I think," Harry Donner pointed out. "But whether it's superstition or not, the miners believe it and Rachel Gottschall was frightened when she knew about it. She wanted me to persuade Isaac not to go back inside. She wanted him to get another job, give up mining, anything but work underground. I talked to him and he asked me what else he could do? Where could a man with one arm and no schooling get a job? All he knew was digging and loading coal. And how would his wife and children live if he gave up his job? I couldn't do anything with him. I told his wife I'd pray for him. It seemed to make her feel better."

An ironical cast came over the superintendent's face.

"I understand the miners say your praying for him kept him from getting killed?"

The preacher resisted the temptation to belittle his own prayer or minimize the possible protection of the Almighty.

"These things are in the hands of a greater and more mysterious power than you and I, Mr. Grace," he said with dignity. "She sent for me again when Isaac wouldn't let the doctor take off his arm. I stayed with him all day. 'What would I do for a living if they took off my arm?' he said. 'It's the only arm I got left. How would Rachel and the young ones eat?' I told him I didn't know the answer but God did and if they didn't take off his arm, the doctors said, he would die. I said, 'You know the gas bubbles you see coming up out of the water in the mines? Well, those bubbles coming out of your arm are gas, too, from the gangrene. Don't you want to live for Rachel and your children?' 'No,' he said, 'they'd be better off if I'm dead.' It took me a long time to get the notion out of his head. Before he gave in, he asked if I'd stand by them. I said I would. Now they've managed to get along without wages so far. She and the young ones tramp all over Broad Mountain picking huckleberries to sell. They sell the milk from their cow. I tried to keep my promise. When the cow was bitten by a rattlesnake, I got the veterinary from Hegins Valley and stayed till the cow was better. I had a wedding in Mahanoy at the time but there I was in Lost Run holding the cow's tail so it wouldn't swish in the veterinary's face. Now I'm trying to keep a roof over their heads. It's the only roof they have. They've got no other place to go."

The superintendent's face hadn't changed.

"I can only follow Company rules and practice," he said. "We're not unphilanthropic with our men. We take care of them as long as feasible. We've never yet laid a man off for age so long as he could work. We even create jobs like watchmen at crossings so faithful old men can keep working at something. Gottschall was right when he said there's nothing in the mines that a man without arms can do. Besides, he's a Dutchman and a stubborn fellow. They tell me he's mighty short-tempered since his accident. If you ever heard him cursing, Reverend, I don't think you'd feel so much like helping him."

"I heard him today," Harry Donner said. "I don't like his taking God's name in vain any more than you. But the Bible says there's more rejoicing in heaven over one sinner that repents than over a hundred righteous men. A man who curses like that needs help more than one who doesn't."

"That sounds like strange theology to me." The superintendent shook his head. "But even if I agreed with you, I could do nothing about it. It's a Company ruling. The Company can't afford to let its houses to men who don't work for the Company."

The man's face and words were final enough but the preacher didn't quit. He told the superintendent he couldn't see himself returning to an armless man with such a verdict. He reminded him of his duty to man, of his own physical wholeness, good fortune and mercy at the hands of God. He persisted and badgered the man till he rose from his desk chair.

"No!" he shouted. "I don't want to be rude to a clergyman but if you keep on I'll have to ask you to leave the premises."

Harry Donner gave up then. He had prayed for the

success of the meeting. Throughout the interview while his tongue spoke as it could, his mind had begged for guidance, for words to say and for the feeling of love for this man that might beget its kind. But, he judged, the Lord must have further hardship and destiny for the Gottschalls. Then he looked up and saw the superintendent's wife in the doorway. She was an emaciated woman with the fever spots that bespoke her fate.

"Will!" she pleaded and Harry Donner didn't see how the man could refuse her with her children around her, the youngest a boy of three or four.

"This man Gottschall is a troublemaker like all his kind," he told her. "If I break the rules for him, others'll want the same. Our houses would soon be occupied by the lazy and jobless. Besides, how would a cripple like Gottschall be able to pay rent and how, if he doesn't work for the Company, can we deduct it? A man who isn't a Company man simply can't stay in one of our houses. Unless, of course, he happens to buy it."

"How can a man without work, Will, possibly buy a house?" she asked.

"I agree with you. He can't," her husband declared.

The preacher stood there uncomfortably.

"How much would a house cost?"

"I don't know definitely. I think we sold one a year or two ago at North Summit. If I remember rightly, the buyer paid three hundred cash."

The woman in the doorway must have seen the preacher's face.

"You can't ask a man without arms such a sum, Will."

He turned angrily.

"We're not trying to get cash out of him. Personally, I should be very dubious about such a transaction. The Company is reluctant to sell any part of its property. I only answered his question. The house in North Summit was Class B, if I remember rightly. Class C houses like the Gottschalls' are listed at two hundred dollars."

"It's sold!" a voice said suddenly and the preacher felt startled, for the voice had been undeniably his own, yet he was aware of no such decision.

"Very well," the superintendent said, sitting down and turning back to his desk as if this were a small matter unworthy of much attention. "If you think there's a chance these people can raise the money, I'll hold the ouster until the end of the week."

Now that the deed was done, Harry Donner felt shaken and uncertain. He thanked him and turned to the wife to thank her and greet the children.

"May I say a prayer before I go?" he asked, and stood silent a moment, conscious of the curious young eyes turned on him. It was their presence, he thought, that made his voice sound suddenly clear and strong as in other households. "We come before thee today," he began, "to ask a blessing on this house and its people. Be thou with the man of the house, in whose charge thou hast given the lives and welfare of many human lives, who like the centurion of old sayeth to this one go and he goeth and to another come and he cometh. Remember also the wife at his side. Strengthen and comfort her and let her return to the bloom of health so she may be a pillar of joy and refreshment to her husband. Bless also these children. Feed them so they may walk in the nurture and admonition of thy Word. We ask thy blessing, too, on what has taken place here today. May it redound to thy glory. We ask that thou continue to be with the family that only a short time ago had no place to lay its head. Comfort and sustain them. Prepare the living to live and the dying to die and in the end save us. In Jesus' name, Amen."

When he raised his head he found the wife looking at him with an indescribably piteous expression.

"May I ask your name?" she begged, and when he had told her, "I hope you will come again."

He said he surely would, shook hands with each, asked the names of the children and left. Down in the patch he stopped at the Gottschalls' briefly, telling them not to worry, that he thought they could stay in the house. He would know more fully when he came Saturday. He had two more calls to make in Lost Run and it was late when he reached home. The boys were in bed but Mamma had waited up for him.

"Is anything wrong, Hal?" she asked.

"I don't know," he said unhappily. "I may have committed transgression against God. I've been worrying about it all the way down the mountain."

"You, Hal!" she said incredulously.

He told her what had happened, that the money collected for God's house he had pledged for a house for humans like himself. His wife looked relieved.

"Let's think you just borrowed it from the Lord," she said. "I believe if you went to Unionville and explained it to a few men like Mr. Boyer, they'd help you put the money back in the account. They helped you out when you needed it at Port Oxford."

"The trouble is," he confessed, "I need two hundred dollars and the money in the Lost Run church account is only a hundred and thirty-five."

He lay awake a long time that night pondering his dilemma. Mamma's Scarlett cupboard had been cut down to get into the house here, so it wasn't worth much. But her Scarlett sideboard would bring fifteen or twenty dollars. An antique dealer had offered as much. After all, it was intended for a larger house and crowded their small sitting room. Moreover, it was mighty heavy and had been a nuisance to crate and move. Of course, he guessed it meant something to Mamma, especially its claw feet and tremendous mirror. But she would still have left the Scarlett cut-glass decanter, the Scarlett andirons and the cannonball that Pap-pa had picked up on the battlefield at Gettysburg.

CHAPTER ELEVEN

The Confession

The black-coated figure tramped the mountain road between Primrose and Lost Run. It was cold. His shoes were muddy. He should have put on his rubbers. His legs felt played out. But it wasn't the weariness in the flesh that troubled him so much as the spirit. This was the first time he remembered dreading a visit to Lost Run. He would rather today have avoided sight of the ugly black breaker, the unpainted houses and the people.

It had been three years since he started making the patches on Broad Mountain his missionary field, and he was no nearer a church in Lost Run than before. The chippers still had their Sunday barrel of beer and their ribald songs in the little grove where he thought a white church should stand. The Company continued to deny him the land. He had a growing conviction that he had failed both God and man. Even the most faithful of his people, the Moores and the Eckerts, looked at him with pity, he thought. They knew his God had not backed him against the coal company as he had Daniel against Nebuchadnezzar. Once Harry Donner expected that the Lord's hand, which the Psalms declared was not shortened, would work in its mysterious way through the mine superintendent's Lutheran wife. But when she died last year he had not been asked to conduct or even assist at the funeral. They had the Episcopalian minister from Pottsville. Harry Donner kept going to see the children. After all, they were half Lutheran, and the mother's religion commonly determined that of her children. He had planned to call on them in the big stone house today, although he noticed they were always strange with him when their father was at home.

Here on the road he couldn't think at the moment of any real good that had come out of his ministry. His congregation at Mahanoy continued to grumble at the time he spent in the patches. Last June his oldest son had shamed him by saying he couldn't speak at high school commencement. The school board had refused to let him graduate and the father had lost his temper with them before they gave the boy a diploma. And last Sunday his youngest son had given his mother a bad time in her pew during the sermon. He had ordered Tim up on one of the pulpit chairs behind him and when his congregation tittered, he looked around and found the lad making faces at the people.

Why was it that a minister had to have the worst children in town? It hurt to be let down by those you tried to do the most for. There was Isaac Gottschall, who seemed to welcome him of late only as somebody to light his pipe. He had a little store now in the front room of his house, like Sally Barrett used to have before she remarried after Mike's death. Rachel said they could get along now, owning their own house, with Isaac making a few dollars a week selling tobacco, candy, knickknacks and groceries including bread that came six days a week on the miners' train. He could open the door with his foot, make change with his stump, set down his pipe on the counter's edge by bending and picking it up in his teeth the same way. But he swore more than ever and complained bitterly that he had to have his wife or one of his boys go along to the outhouse with him to button and unbutton him.

What sobered the preacher most tonight was the "taking down" Wiley Drumm, head mining engineer for the Markles, had given him. They had been walking together from Primrose to catch the late train down the mountain from Lost Run. There were just the two of them. Wiley was a consistently heavy drinker but Dan Markle said that as long as he could read a blueprint and run a line, he could keep his job at Primrose. It was right about here with a glimpse of the lights of Lost Run through the tops of the trees that he had got on the subject.

"You're too damn good for this godforsaken country, Reverend. You ought to go to the city where there's money and something going on."

"I can't be very good, Wiley," Harry Donner said. "I've never had a call to the city. You know in my line you've got to wait till somebody asks you to preach a trial sermon."

"You can wait till the cows come home, Reverend. The church is no different from any other business. If you want it, you got to go after it. That brings me to something. Now mind, you brought this up yourself. You're the one, not I, who said you'd never had a call to the big city and never went after anything. But now that you've said it, I've got to agree. You've got a fault there, Reverend, a bad one, if you'll excuse me for saying such a thing to you."

"I have many faults, Wiley," the preacher said.

"No, not many, Reverend. That's the trouble. But it's enough. It's your mortal sin. It's what holds you back with God and man. Do you know Francis Thompson's poem: 'I fled him down the nights and down the days; I fled him down the arches of the years'? Well, you don't flee him. He doesn't need to follow you. He doesn't need to beg you to go his way. He doesn't need to cross your palm with gold and silver. He can let you starve and do without. He knows you'll stay with him just the same no matter what. Do you follow me, Reverend?"

"No, not yet," Harry Donner said doubtfully.

"Well, can you get it better if I put it another way? I like you, Reverend, but you're too damn good for your own good. Now I don't mean goody-good. You're not that. I don't mean pious and mealy-mouthed. I don't know exactly what I do mean except that you don't look after yourself like the rest of us. When commonsense was handed around, you were left out. If a man asks you for a dollar, you're liable to give him two. If he asks you to listen to his tale of woe, you pray and go to bat for him to boot. You were the same way when you kept store in Unionville. That's how you lost out, giving credit to all these lousy miners who never paid you. I bet you haven't got a dollar on those back debts since you're here though they see you walking around with your elbows sticking out and your sole leather worn through."

"They have a hard time getting along themselves, Wiley," the preacher pointed out.

The engineer laughed.

"Oh, I know you, Reverend. I could feel the fault in you the first time I met you, and if I'd missed it then, I'd have known it the minute you opened your mouth. You never changed a hair when you got close enough to smell my breath and found I had a drop or two. You didn't lecture me. You didn't try to save me. You didn't try to chalk up my soul as a mark on your account in heaven. If I wanted to go to hell, that was my business, but you'd say a prayer so I'd slide down a little slower and hell fire would be a little cooler. When I bragged, you didn't try to show me you were as smart and important as me. That's the trouble with this damn goodness. It doesn't get any better or learn anything. It's satisfied with itself and other people as they are. It's satisfied living in a black hole like this just so it can look after other people in this black hole it thinks it has to look after. That's you, Reverend, and that's the main trouble with you. Do you know something else, Reverend?"

"I guess I know very little, Wiley," Harry Donner said sadly.

"Well, just let me tell you this. Goodness never gets you anywhere, not even with the Lord. Or with yourself. It doesn't drive you. It doesn't keep you awake at night scheming how to get back at somebody who did you dirt or how to beat him out of an honest dollar. A good person gives too much time to people who can't help him. The smart one plays up to the right people. Take Andy Christenson down here in Lost Run. Most everybody likes him and he likes everybody. He'll do most anything for you but what will it ever get him? He'll be station agent in this hole the rest of his life. On the other hand, take Mel Dicer. Nobody liked him much when he was at Mahanoy. He wouldn't go out of his way for you unless for a reason. But he knew the right things to do for the right people. Now he's superintendent of the Reading division. They call him a leader. He never gives you his time unless Mel Dicer wants something. He sees you with that in mind. He watches you like a cat. Everything he says and does is to soften you up and get you around to his way of thinking. But what do you do? You give every Tom, Dick and Harry your time just because you like him. You baptize him, confirm him, marry and bury him and all his kin. You visit with him and get down on your knees for him and, if you can get away with it, sing for him. You just like to sing. You don't need to be coaxed. You went to bat for that armless Gottschall and got him a house and what did it get you? Poor devils like him and the miners you kept eating during the strike can't do a lick for you. But Will Grace could have, and you crossed him up by implying he was doing a dirty thing putting a man without arms out of his house. Sometimes I think what griped him most was making him sell you a house for one of his own men. Now I hear he has no use for you, won't give you a couple square feet of his stinking black ground to build a ten-by-four church and graveyard. He hates your guts. I'd say it's a kind of honor to be hated by him, Reverend. If I'd had as good a wife as he had, I'd sooner be lying dead drunk in the gutter than run around with all the women he did while she was alive. And he's still doing it now that she's dead. Lately I hear he's been laying out with that hellcat of a Minersville woman."

"I'm sorry to hear it," Harry Donner said with feeling.

"I'm sorry, too," Wiley Drumm said. "Not for Will Grace but for you. Remember, I'm not God, Reverend, I don't want you different. I like you pretty much as you are. I hope I haven't made you feel bad. I always talk too much this time of day."

Harry Donner didn't say so but he wished the engineer hadn't mentioned that last thing about Will Grace. There were plenty of unpleasant things he could tell, too, if he wanted, accounts of sin, disease and death in the patches around him. Now why did the flesh itch to hear and repeat all the bad things of the flesh? Only the spirit seemed to welcome things of the spirit. What was that which Jude had said? "He is of purer eyes than to behold evil."

He felt bad enough for the mine superintendent and sorrier for his children. He had wanted to see them today but not with Wiley Drumm's picture of their father soiling his mind. It was hard enough to visualize and believe in Will Grace as a son of God, to love him as a friend and brother. Well, he would visit ailing George Akers first. Then perhaps he could still call at the big stone house on the hill and be gone or at least his mission half done before the superintendent came home from the office.

The call took longer at the Akerses than he had thought. It was always hard to get away from these nice people. On leaving, the poor Conley boy saw him four or five houses away and called in his high eager, wordless, almost birdlike voice. The afternoon was more than half spent, but Harry Donner couldn't resist going in to see him for a while. The boy made such a fuss when he called. Sometimes he thought he almost understood his gibberish and sometimes that the boy understood him, but what each understood, he guessed, were the smiles, the tone of their voices and the fellowship between them.

He had heard at the Akerses that Meg Madden was "in

bad shape" and now as he passed, Mrs. Bogle next door ran out to say that she was dying.

"She heard you were in the patch and wants to see you."

"Isn't Old France at home?"

"She was better at noon and he went to work."

Harry Donner passed in the gate with Mrs. Bogle behind him. He had known Meg Madden from his store days, a big Irish woman old enough to be the mother of most everyone in the patch, once a veritable mountain of life, gossip and sly humor but of late an incredible little old woman so ancient they called her lad Old France to tell him from his married son of the same name.

There was almost nothing recognizable in the face on the bolster when he came into the front room downstairs. It was a sagging muscleless face, the white hair an anachronism, as if belonging to some other day and time.

"The Virgin fetched you to the patch today, Father," she greeted him, clutching his hand with a frightening grip.

"It's all right, Granny. You can never be out of God's presence." He tried to calm her while she held to him like a drowning soul to a root. He offered a quiet prayer but her grip refused to loosen until toward the end when her fingers gradually weakened and her eyes lost some of the wild look.

"Shall I ask Andy Christenson to phone for Dr. Fegley for you?" he asked.

She shook her head and he went on.

"Is there anybody or anything you want?"

"My confession," she begged. "You could hear it and give me absolution?"

He looked troubled.

"I'm not your father-confessor, Mrs. Madden," he pointed out. "You know but have probably forgotten that I'm Protestant. But I can stop and see Father Keleher for you when I get back to Mahanoy."

"He'd never get here in time," she said. "Besides, I know you a lot longer than him. You wouldn't deny the last request of a dying old woman?"

"But, Granny," he persisted. "What would an old woman of nearly ninety have to confess?"

Her eyes stared blackly, enigmatically at him and he had the first faint premonition of what was to come. He paged through his Ministerial Acts with helpless fingers. There was, he remembered vaguely, a form for private confession. He had never been called on to use it before. He felt her watching him anxiously. He would have to go through this with fitness and decency.

"In the name of the Father, the Son and the Holy Ghost," he began in a strong, resolute voice.

"Get her out first, Father," the dying woman hissed.

He turned and saw Mrs. Bogle standing piously behind him, intent on everything that went on. She left with reluctance and he closed the door before returning to his small black book.

"Make haste, O God, to deliver me!" he continued. "Have mercy upon me according to thy loving kindness. According unto the multitude of thy tender mercies, blot out my transgression. Behold I was shapen in iniquity and in sin did my mother conceive me. Thou desirest truth in the inward parts. And in the hidden parts thou shalt make me to know wisdom. Purge me with hyssop and I shall be clean. Wash me and I shall be whiter than snow. Hide thy face from my sins and blot out all my iniquities—"

He grew aware that she was making violent hissing noises.

"Not yet, Father," she protested hoarsely. "I must talk first."

Examining the fine print at the head of the order, he found that she was right and the confession came earlier.

"You may say it in your own words, Granny," he said kindly. "Or you can use the general order of confession that I can read to you."

"I want to say it myself, Father. That's the way I was used to. But you better sit down like the other fathers do."

Afterward he thought he knew why his Catholic brothers sat down to hear confession. But whence came their fortitude to take it and whence the sudden vitality that rose in the dying woman now that she was engaged in baring her soul? Her admissions came in a growing stream, mostly carnality in thought, word and deed but principally in thought that filled him with shock and incredulity. He didn't know that such conceptions existed in the world. At length she fell back spent and exhausted but not before his eyes and ears had defensively dulled against the spectacle of this toothless old woman before him pouring out thoughts and things some of which he had never heard of before and which he hoped he never would again.

In his confusion it took time to find his place in his little book. He wondered if his own church authorities had had the experience and knowledge to deal with such extraordinary matters. Then he found and declared in a loud ringing voice what he was not sure at the moment he wholly and completely believed.

"Almighty God, our Heavenly Father, hath had mercy upon thee, and for the sake of the suffering and death of his dear Son, Jesus Christ, our Lord, forgiveth thee of all thy sins. Upon the confession which thou hast made and in obedience to our Lord's command, I declare unto thee the entire forgiveness of all thy sins, in the name of the Father, the Son and the Holy Ghost."

He added a short prayer the words of which he could not remember clearly afterward, gave her what comforting words he could muster, bade her good-by and called Mrs. Bogle. He had to make another call, he said, and must get back to Mahanoy before dark.

The air outside had seldom felt so fresh and clean as when he emerged today but he made no immediate attempt to visit the house of the superintendent. He had small relish to see the children with this additional foulness upon him. His respect grew for priests he knew who must listen year in and year out to such defilement. They could give cleansing absolution to those confessing but who would give cleansing absolution to them, the hearers and vicarious partakers? Here at Lost Run he had no Palestinian desert such as the Lord sought in trouble but there was wilderness enough and a mountain to go up in to pray. Perhaps they would do, he thought, and his feet found a path.

In the woods boys called to him to watch out for air holes. He felt thankful they had been here. He had been going almost blindly along the mountain when this black break in the earth opened almost under his feet. The boys said there was still a bigger hole farther on. Neither one had bottom, they said. With the preacher as an audience, they proceeded to show off, carrying up rocks to throw in. He could hear them crashing down in the pit from pillar to post, giving up deep sinister rumblings as they went farther into the earth, the sounds growing fainter until at last they ceased altogether. Even then he imagined the doomed rocks still falling through impenetrable blackness too distant under his feet to be heard.

The preacher stood there uncertain. There was something about the spectacle, after coming from Meg Madden's, that mysteriously troubled him, and yet as it continued he thought he felt relief as if each of the falling rocks carried with it some of his ugly burden into obscurity.

When the boys tired of their fun, he turned back to the patch and climbed the path to the big stone house. Their father wasn't at home, the children told him. He had been away all last night. They seemed doubly glad for a caller this evening. As a rule when he called, the house seemed to have a faint reek of carbide from the lighting plant. To-night the odor was very strong, but he got used to it by the time the maid came in to light the parlor chandelier. Still the superintendent hadn't returned.

Wiley Drumm's words came back to him, "He's been laying out with that hellcat of a Minersville woman." He threw himself into a livelier exchange with his young hosts, teasing and bantering, getting them to laugh, encouraging them to talk about themselves, especially the boy, who was shyer and more reserved than his sisters. Men, he had noticed, were generally able to do more with girls than with boys. He didn't know why except that girls were quicker to respond, catch on and enliven, were more appreciative of a man and attention. He and Vallie had had all boys at home. He sometimes wished it had been otherwise. He suspected that the children turned back by the disciples from the Lord must have been girls. Not that he himself had trouble with boys except his own. Most boys seemed in his own words to "take a shine" to him. Before the evening was over he had the superintendent's young son singing a song that his sisters said he knew, after which the preacher taught him another. The boy took to it quickly, perhaps because his own name was Jack.

I'm a jolly old quack, quack, quack,
Who carries his pack on his back.
I've rhubarb and quills,
Plasters and pills,
And they call me Medicine Jack.

They were still singing and laughing when sudden steps sounded on the veranda and the front door opened. All was silent for a moment. Then with a strong oath the superintendent rushed in, threw the parlor windows wide, turned out the lights abruptly and left them in darkness. Presently they could hear him banging around in the cellar.

Harry Donner felt discomfited. He waited a little before standing up, said he guessed he had to go. He made a brief parting prayer in the darkness, uncertain whether any of the children were left in the room to hear him. Afterward he said good-by and found his way to the door, grateful for the peace and starlight outside. All the long road down the mountain that night he pondered the happening, the strange behavior and the unhealable breach between him and the superintendent who went to such lengths to oppose and eject him.

Monday he came back to Lost Run to find the incident the

talk of the patch. They told him the superintendent had come home from Minersville to find the house filled with escaping gas and had shut off the plant in the cellar by flashlight.

"Didn't you notice the carbide?" they asked the preacher.

"I couldn't help but notice the smell," Harry Donner admitted. "But I didn't know that I should do anything about it."

"He told the maid," Mrs. Tom Hughes said, "that he couldn't figure out how the house never blew up with the lights turned on full in the parlor and the gas thick enough to cut with a knife. He said there you all sat laughing and talking as though nothing was the matter. He said the only thing that saved his young ones was the presence of a good person in the house."

"Which person did he mean?" Harry Donner asked, puzzled. "I'm sure his maid is a good woman and I know all his children are."

Book · IV

GREEN PASTURES

CHAPTER TWELVE

The Church and the Pig

It was a sunny afternoon in spring, and the preacher was driving home from one of the three churches of his new charge. He told himself again that he had never seen more beautiful country than Wetherill Valley, that the Lord must have laid it out in person, this magnificent triangle of meadows and rolling farm land shut in by mountain walls on two sides and by the broad river on the other. For six years he had been in the raw Mahanoy region, among mountains gashed and plundered for coal. Summer and winter he had tramped the black roads of Broad Mountain. Now he labored in what he liked to refer to in his sermons as "God's green vineyard." Sometimes he felt licentious and a little sinful to be carried over the roads here by his own horse and buggy.

The Lord had surely been good to him, allowing him to build and dedicate his church at Lost Run before he left. It was not a big church but it had given him joy to see its gold cross lifted over the patch, then to come upon it tidy and clean among the black dirt banks and unpainted Company houses, and finally to open the front door and glimpse the bright golden oak pews inviting the weary and heavy-laden to rest, while over altar and pulpit hung the stained-glass window of the Good Shepherd holding the lost sheep in his arms. He hoped his part in it had not made him vain but there was something in him that always leaped at the sight of the white church standing where there had been none before, its doors open to all, a kind of symbol of the heart of God and also of one of his humble servants ready to be called on day or night, in sin or in trouble, in sickness or death. Vallie had wanted him to name it St. Mark's-of-the-Mines. He had thought that a little pretentious. After all, it was not a Catholic or Episcopal church but plain, very plain, Lutheran.

Had this small church and its people been able to support his family, he might never have left. But the synod had kept it in the older, richer Mahanoy charge, and the council of the latter had objected. They pointed out that it was they who paid the minister's salary yet most of his time was taken up with the welfare of the missionary church. They hadn't authorized him to build it in the first place, and the time spent on it and money collected might have been better used to enlarge and improve their own stone church building. After a year or two of reproach and widening rift in the Mahanoy congregation, the preacher had come to the conclusion that a new pastor who had nothing to do with building the Lost Run church might find less feeling against him and do more for the charge as a whole. When the call came to Wetherill Valley, he had regretfully accepted and left.

Not without misgivings, he admitted to himself. How did you ever really know the call of the Lord from that of your own restless heart? He told Mamma he hoped he hadn't jumped from the frying pan into the fire, for he had found a rift in one of the Wetherill Valley congregations wider than that which he had just left. The Piatts wanted a new, imposing, brick church on their hill. The others felt the old gray clapboard church good enough for Christians. It had gone hard to persuade them to get together and compromise. With the help of the Lord the job had been done and all seemed milk and honey between them now.

As he drove along the ridge road the preacher could see the prosperous places of the Piatt supporters on his left toward Nippenose Mountain; first the white buildings of George Piatt, who with the help of his wife and daughter ran the valley telephone exchange in the back of his Sugar Hill store; the large red barn of Ray Piatt, who had a prosperous milk route in town; and the yellow barn of Quincy Piatt, who owned the first and only automobile in the valley. "Quincy's machine," they called it, and when the mud or snow permitted, he brought his family in it to church. The only Piatt place you couldn't see from here was Oliver's, who had a brick house and stone barn on the Long

Run road. His was said to be the best farm in the valley. He also had much timber land, was squire for this end of the valley and sent his only girl to study music in Boston.

"The Piatts," Jenny Rodey told the preacher, "have big ideas. They think themselves more than common people. They got to live up to their brother Morris, who has the iron works in Hancock."

On the other side of the ridge road as he drove, Harry Donner could see the farms and roofs of the Rodey supporters: the faded green house of tough old Cap Waltman, who smoked a pipe in his barn and hay mow; the log house of Gus Sheffer, who prayed in a deep quivering, unintelligible voice that almost put the preacher's boys in stitches; the farm of his brother Cal Sheffer, whom Gene called Old-Finally-and-Eventually because he always said "and now finally and eventually" in his prayers; and the swamp farm of Dave Ney, who last winter had invited the preacher's family to a squirrel and wild turkey dinner, and whom Harry Donner called "like Nimrod, a mighty hunter before the Lord." Also down there out of sight in the swamp lived Mrs. Kelso, famous as the cook who belittled her inimitable pies, bread or roast, complaining "It didn't get good today" or "It's not fit for a hog to eat." Still ahead was the blacksmith shop of Sammy Glass, who liked to call from his shop to his wife in the kitchen, "Kate! Cook beans. Cook a whole potful. God, I like beans!"

And now the preacher's horse was climbing the easy grade to the Manada Hill church and the white house and unpainted barn of Phillip and Jenny Rodey, who lived close by. Vallie said she wouldn't want better neighbors. Harry Donner felt the same. Without Phillip to stand by him for fairness and reason in council meetings, he believed the rebellious ones would have bolted the Manada Hill church long ago. He told her more than once he would have to watch out that he didn't show favor to Phillip over the Piatts.

And now he could see the parsonage and across the road the new unfinished church itself, a series of low brick walls and high brick bell tower, all enveloped by skeleton work of two-by-fours and larger timbers to be faced later by brick. The old clapboard church adjoining had stood here for a hundred years, he had been told, and a log church before that.

He unhitched Pompy and had come into the house when five short rings sounded from the yellow telephone box.

"Hal-loa!" he answered in rich greeting and testimony that God was in his heaven and all right with the world.

"Reverend!" It was Jenny's stricken voice. "I just seen you come in. Could you come over?"

"Why, I guess so, Jenny," he said with strong reassurance which after a moment or two, remembering her tone, he did not entirely feel. He looked thoughtfully at Mamma as he hung up. "She seemed upset over something." A few minutes later his black ministerial figure was crossing the road and church grove.

He was gone a long time. When he came back, Mamma met him at the door. Her face sobered at sight of his.

"Phillip's been arrested," he said. "He's had to give bail for a hearing."

"What in the world for?" Mamma demanded.

"For stealing a pig," Harry Donner said, and when Mamma laughed, "It's no laughing matter, I'm afraid."

"But Phillip stealing a pig!" she protested. "Everybody knows Phillip. He's about the most honest and fair man in the valley."

The preacher looked grave.

"Jenny and Phillip think it isn't the pig. It's the church."

"What could the church have to do with it?"

"Well, they claim Estes Croy would never dare to have him arrested on his own. They say somebody must be behind him. They say when Estes needs money he borrows it from Oliver Piatt and then cuts timber for Oliver to pay for it. They think it's Oliver getting back at Phillip for voting down the Piatt plans for a big church."

"But that's too outlandish. To go to court over a pig just because of the church."

"If the church had nothing to do with the pig before, I'm afraid it's going to now," Papa said gravely. "Phillip is bitter. You know he and his group control council. They say they only agreed to go along on the new church for my sake. They still think the old church is good enough. They can stop the building any time they like, next Monday at council meeting if they want. Phillip said as much. Then we'll have a stalled church and the fighting all over again."

"But Phillip always seemed so reasonable."

"You can't expect a person to be reasonable, Vallie, once he's been arrested for stealing a pig."

"Oliver must know Estes never could win."

"I don't know about that," Papa said unhappily. "This thing happened, I think, before we came, but it seems we're mixed up in it. Jenny says Estes' pigs used to push down the rail fence between their land and come over and eat up Phillip's crops. Phillip would have to drive them back and fix the fence. This went on for a long time. At last Phillip told Estes he'd keep one of the pigs for damages if Estes didn't put them some place else. Estes didn't do much about it and the next time they came through, Phillip kept one. Jenny said it was only a shote. You know how Phillip is, soft and quiet spoken till you tread on him too far, then nothing will change him. He says Estes wouldn't mend the fence, so he put the pig in his own pigpen."

"Where is it now?"

"Phillip says he kept and fed it till spring. Estes still wouldn't pay any damages so Phillip turned it loose in Estes' winter wheat. He said he hoped the pig would do to the wheat what it had done to his own corn. Estes claims he never got his pig back, that Phillip and Jenny butchered it last winter."

"He can't prove such a thing, can he?"

"Maybe not. But a lot of people heard about it and came to see the pig in Phillip's pigpen. Jenny says at the hearing Estes will have lots of witnesses. She says Oliver will throw the case into court. If that happens, she says it's proof that Oliver is footing the bill because Estes wouldn't have the money or stomach to do it. The Piatts, she says, can then sit back and enjoy it and not have to mix in except what Oliver does legally as squire. Jenny says it's not only to get back at Phillip but at me."

"You? Why would he want to get back at you?"

"Well, we're close neighbors here to Phillip and Jenny. In council, Phillip's always my man. He supports me, tries to put my ideas across. Jenny asked if I'd be a character witness for Phillip. I said of course I would. She warned me if it got to court and I testified for Phillip, Estes' lawyer might try to make it look like we got some of the stolen meat. You know, they did give us a ham and slab of bacon last winter."

"This is ridiculous," Mamma said indignantly. "Such a fuss over a pig could never get to court."

But as time went on in the triangle of Logan and Nippenose mountains, Mamma had to admit she had been wrong. For the good part of a year the matter of Phillip Rodey accused of stealing a pig was kept before the people of Hancock County and Wetherill Valley in particular, first in news and talk of the hearing, then the throwing of the case into court, the setting of a date for the trial, the announcement of several postponements, the summoning of witnesses, rumors of what one or the other would say, and finally the hour of decision with the Wetherill Valley hucksters closing their market stalls in Hancock as early as possible to spend the rest of the day in the crowded court. All through the clever testimony for the plaintiff, and the helpless character witnesses for the defendant, and through the shocking verdict that Phillip Rodey was found guilty of willfully possessing and disposing in some unknown manner of a shote, the property of his neighbor; and through the court sentence that Phillip pay a fine of forty dollars and close to a hundred in court costs while Estes was let go with instructions along with Phillip to keep the fences pigproof between them—all through this nightmare of defeat and refusal of Phillip Rodey to attend church services thereafter, the preacher had to swallow his feelings and follow the peaceful pursuit of his calling, visiting and praying for the sick and well, preaching the meek and humble doctrine of the Lamb to all who came to hear his sermons, including the Piatts, who never before, he thought, had sat so smug and righteous in their pews in front of him, while Phillip's place was conspicuously empty, Jenny coming alone and white-faced with her two small boys.

But if Phillip failed to attend church, he never failed to

attend council meeting. Despite the preacher's pleas and protests, Phillip's motions were made and carried to halt what he called the mounting burden of debt on the congregation and to spend no more on the new building until plans could be revised within the ability of the congregation to pay, which could mean only one thing.

"I find it hard to pray for the Piatts, especially the one who brought this about in the first place," Papa confessed to Mamma. "Although God knows that Phillip's stubbornness is a thorn in my side, too."

Everyone who passed now could see that construction on the half-finished church had stopped. Not a workman was left, and the Rodey men promised that's the way it would stay. The stalemate went on, with Oliver, they said, cutting timber with his own hands to work out his frustration, and Phillip digging a well under the same compulsion. That's what he was doing when he slipped from the windlass and fell to the bottom of the hole, breaking a leg, which swelled so badly by the time they got him out that the doctor had to cut off a shoe and sock.

"Oh, Phillip's feet!" Jenny moaned. "He hasn't washed them since Saturday." In the excitement they forgot about Seranus Mast, who had gone down in the well to put the injured man in the bucket and had been left there.

Phillip was just able to be around and start getting in his crops when he lost his footing again. This time he fell from the hay mow to the barn floor. When they picked him up and carried him to the house, he told them calmly he was hurt inside and would never be able to work again.

"It's this pig business, Reverend," Jenny told the preacher bitterly. "Phillip never fell before in his life. It's as if he wanted to fall."

"I wouldn't say that to anyone, Jenny," he told her, but in the secret of his mind he kept wondering about it, for Phillip went from bad to worse. Dr. Gordiner called most every day from town and a pretty young nurse from Hancock came to stay at Jenny's house around the clock. It was pleasant enough to see her in white going about the yard followed by young single men from the valley who gave the excuse they had come to see Phillip or ask how he was.

But it was not pleasant for the preacher to visit Phillip, to see him who had been so ruddy and strong when they first came to the valley now a pale shadow of himself in bed or to hear him say terrible things about himself in that calm confident way of his, that he'd never get out of bed, that his bowels would never move again, and that he hoped the Reverend would look after Jenny and the boys when he was gone.

They had brought his bed down to the parlor to save steps for Jenny and the nurse. To see him lying with closed eyes beside the organ, with the stiff red plush parlor chairs around him, the sheaf of wheat on the wall and Jenny standing grief-stricken at the kitchen door, the preacher felt it almost as if he had come to conduct funeral services over his friend and neighbor.

"We're not doing enough," he told Jenny in the kitchen. "Phillip's still fighting that pig case. Don't say anything to him, but if I get the Piatts here to cut and shock his oats, I hope for his sake you'll be nice to them and feed them."

"I'll do what you say, Reverend," Jenny said. "If I must let them skunks on our place, I must."

But when the preacher came over an evening or two later, he had to confess it had not gone as he had hoped. The Piatts, he said, had been nice enough. They had listened gravely. They would like to have done what he asked. Unfortunately Oliver had to be home for notary work and a case coming up. Ray was delivering milk himself this week and had to go to bed early to get up at two in the morning. And Quincy had a felon on his hand. Then they all had oats of their own to cut. He added lamely that he had asked them to remember Phillip in their prayers.

"I didn't say nothing, Reverend, but I could have told you how them Christians would act," Jenny said bitterly.

All that week the preacher felt out of favor with both God and man. What was it, he thought, that made quarrels between real brothers and between church brethren more implacable and irreconcilable than between unrelated men? Whatever the cause, the phenomenon must have existed a long time, for far back before Christ, the Psalmist had pleaded, "Behold how good and pleasant it is for brethren to dwell together in unity." Could it be that love between brothers was an illusion? Or did love when turned to hate become deeper and more virulent than ordinary hate? St. Paul had said, "Love suffereth long and is kind." Could blood brothers and Christian brothers mistake pride in their relationship for love? And pride was one of the seven deadly sins. It never forgave or forgot.

"I ask, Lord, that I may never be proud," Harry Donner prayed in bed before getting up.

That prayer seemed to stir something around him. For the first time in days he felt a response when he reached upward. It gave him new hope. He went to see Phillip twice that day. Seldom had he interceded for anyone as he did by Phillip's bed that evening with Jenny and the nurse standing with bowed heads at the kitchen door and the little group of hangers-on, he knew, listening outside. He begged God to do something and not "stand afar off." He told Mamma afterward he believed his supplication heard because the strong scent of honeysuckle, like balm from Gilead, came into the room from the porch as he prayed.

But next day he confessed to Mamma he had not meant God to burn down the church. A hard electrical storm with heavy wind and little rain swept over Wetherill Valley before morning. The preacher thought the worst over and was going back to sleep when Mamma wakened him. He saw flickering light in the bedroom window and heard a long continuous ring of alarm on the telephone. He had no need to answer. He guessed what it meant. By the time he had pulled on his clothes and run out of the house, Jenny and the nurse and boys were helpless dancing puppets before the flames that licked the framework of the new sanctuary and Sunday-school room, from where they soon spread to the old adjoining church building, turning it into a huge box roaring with wind and fire in the black night. Pale and grim-faced men kept arriving, some on foot across the fields, some by road with horses. They tried to use buckets from Phillip's and the parsonage wells but, as Jenny said, they might as well had spoons. The heat, the roar of flames, the reek of ancient burning pine and hair plaster drove everyone back. In the end all that remained was the blackened ruin of foundations and brick bell tower standing stark in the dawn among the scorched and blistered trees of the church grove.

"We was like ants trying to stop a flood," Dave Ney said.

That day and the rest of the week the preacher found himself unfit for his duties. He could only stand around condoling with men and women who kept getting out of vehicles to gaze at the smoking ashes and blackened bell tower like a wrecked idol to Baal where for more than a hundred years a Christian house of God had stood on Manada Hill blessing the landscape and all who passed. But through the repeated worn phrases of commiseration to others he kept asking one question in his heart. If because of man's quarreling over his new temple, God had chosen to destroy it, why did he consume the faithful old church as well? Now his people were sheep scattered by the winds, with no fold in which to gather for protection against the night.

But when the next blow fell, he wondered if he himself had not unknowingly been the sinner. It came, of all people, from one of his own men, big, bluff, tactless Seranus Mast, who had once told the visiting Jess when he helped her out of the buggy that she was the lamest woman he ever saw.

"Well, the Piatts are taking it hard, Reverend," he said.

"We're all taking it hard, Seranus," the preacher answered.

"Yes, but not like them, Reverend. They've fetched their own preacher in it. They claim it was him done it."

Harry Donner heard incredulously.

"You mean me? They think I could control a bolt of lightning?"

The tow-haired giant in overalls and jumper stood there with lowered head.

"They claim it wasn't lightning, Reverend. They're saying somebody started it in the new church and it got to the old church by mistake."

Harry Donner didn't understand at first, and when the meaning broke over him, he couldn't believe it. After Seranus had gone, he went almost shaking across the road to Jenny in her summer kitchen to ask if she had heard anything. Her face grew cruel with feeling.

"Oh, I could have told you long ago, Reverend, but I didn't want to make you feel bad. All summer them Piatts have been saying you were so sick and tired of fighting over the new church, you didn't know what to do about it no more. They said every time a storm came and it cracked close, you went to the window hoping the new church was struck so you and everybody else could forget it."

Papa was white, Mamma told him, when he came back to the parsonage. He did not reveal what Seranus and Jenny had said. This was something between him and God, and this time he felt that God had gone too far. He was fifty-odd years old. Eleven of those years had been given to the Lord in seminary and service, and yet never before in his years as cleric or layman had anyone to his knowledge imputed what he would have denounced as a wicked slander against any Christian, let alone a minister of the Gospel.

"Now loose me, Lord, and let me go," he prayed during the night while Mamma slept. But nothing happened. No relief came, no light within or without. Nothing was seemingly going to happen to lessen his burden. This was his cross and he would have to bear it. A non-follower of Christ, he told himself, would have had it easier. He could have gone after his detractors and had it out with them tooth and nail. But a Christian was obliged to turn the other cheek, to walk the second mile, to let the veins of the flesh boil and yet be meekly satisfied with such thin comfort as Matthew, five eleven, "Blessed are ye when men shall revile you and say all manner of evil against you falsely for my sake. Rejoice and be exceeding glad, for great is your reward in heaven." Heaven, Harry Donner reflected, was a long way off, or so he hoped, whereas close at hand festered abomination and "all that maketh a lie," while justice was left to languish and wither on the vine.

His only comfort was that he would not have to preach to the Manada Hill congregation this Sunday while the anger worked in his blood. To be mild and submissive to the Piatts now would be an almost impossible task. Then Friday evening Jenny called that the council had asked for the barn floor for services since the farm stood nearest to the burned churches. Also, Phillip had a stack of oak and chestnut lumber that might be used for pews. Saturday morning Harry Donner helped a group of men fill sacks with grain from Phillip's granary. Upon these were laid the planking. Phillip's corn sheller was set up as lectern and pulpit.

No Piatt came then but Sunday morning they showed up for services. How they looked, the preacher didn't know, for he dared not turn his glance on them. In the end it turned out that all were there save George's girl, Esther, who had to stay home and keep the switchboard open. It must have been the fire, the preacher reflected, that had brought them out and most everyone else as well. The planks couldn't hold the congregation. Men sat on piles of hay thrown to the side of the barn floor, while boys and young girls climbed to the mows, where they looked pleased to attend church in a barn. The small door behind the preacher had been thrown open to give him light for the Bible he had fetched under his arm from his study since both pulpit Bibles had been burned up. The big doors behind the congregation stood wide open and through them the preacher could see Wetherill Valley rolling on to Fourth Gap, where Nippenose and Logan mountains joined.

It was a warm August morning but the air that drifted through the barn was cool and pleasant, bitten with the scent of dried grasses and wheat which Phillip's neighbors had harvested for him. Most of Phillip's cows were out in pasture but the preacher could hear the sounds of horses, calves and chickens in the stables below, and of Caesar, the old Holstein bull, rattling his chain in his stall. These were sounds and scents, he reflected, and this was a scene not unfamiliar to the Lord as a newborn babe, but never had the holy child had so lofty and fine a stable.

He kept thinking about it as the choir sang, their voices sounding curiously childlike and pure without benefit of an organ in this open place. He felt that at least for the moment he had his Old Adam under control. Still he didn't trust himself to look at Oliver Piatt, the chief slanderer, remembering that this wasn't the only mischief the man had done him. Here behind his corn-sheller pulpit, Harry Donner told himself again that of all human qualities, those of humility, meekness and forgiveness must be the most godlike and difficult for man to attain, for he had been trying for years to practice them, with very little success, he was afraid. Indeed here before his congregation in divine worship and the most humble and traditionally Christian of places, he himself, an ordained ambassador of Christ, sworn to walk in the footsteps of the Master, found it the hardest thing in the world to deny the hot blood of the flesh and affirm the spirit to forget and forgive.

After the service he made an effort to steel himself so that, despite the slander that everyone there must know, he might stand at the big barn doors and shake hands as usual with everyone that came out, especially the Piatts, with whom he must smile, chat and act as if nothing had happened. He noticed that Oliver did not leave with his family but waited to talk to other men on the barn floor. He was almost the last to go.

"Reverend," he said, shaking hands, "I think we done pretty good for a makeshift here today, but you know and I know it can't last. Winter is coming and we don't have much time. I think we should have a council meeting Monday and get started building as soon as we can."

"I think so, too, Oliver," the preacher agreed slowly. "But I don't know rightly where we can meet except at Phillip's since he can't go anywhere."

To his surprise, Oliver's face did not harden.

"Well, Reverend, I guess that's all we can do. In fact I said as much to the rest. I told them we got to get some kind of meetinghouse up in a hurry. We don't have time for wrangling now. I talked to all the council except Clint Miller. I'll call him up when I get home. I'll tell him like I did the rest to come to Phillip's tomorrow night at the usual time."

Harry Donner went home startled and a little mystified. He felt, as valley folks said, beat out. Here he had been trying in vain for weeks to get the Piatts, especially Oliver, to visit Phillip and break bread with him. And now the Lord had managed it in a little more than a day or two. Certainly Oliver wouldn't refuse Jenny's tasty rolls when she set out refreshments tomorrow night. Just the same, before he rejoiced too far, he better wait and see how the Lord managed it from here on. So far as he was concerned, he would keep out of it and let the Lord do it. Come to think of it, there was one thing he could do. That was keep a tight hobble on his "dutch" and act toward the Piatts as he had today. It was just possible he had helped the Lord a little without knowing it, holding his fire, treating the Piatts as decent honest men, returning good for evil. Once before in his life he had observed that when a man goes too far blackguarding another, he feels shame for himself in his heart and is ready next time to go a little more than halfway to make up for it.

CHAPTER THIRTEEN

The Rock Past Finding Out

Johnny tried to make out his father.

Once long ago he had tried and failed, but then he had been no more than a child sent to the store for a spool of darning cotton. Now he was almost grown, past his sixteenth birthday, and had been on a man's job in the city. He was experienced enough, he guessed, to see and understand what had been veiled to him before.

Just the same, all the way from the western part of the state he had dreaded the reunion. He was coming back jobless, defeated, a failure like the prodigal son. But if his father felt disappointment or disgrace, he gave no hint of it.

"Johnny!" his hearty voice called, and the black-garbed figure strode across the Wetherill station platform. The boy felt the well-known mustache-tasting kiss. "This is John, my oldest boy," he introduced him with pride to an older man on the platform. "He's been working for the Westinghouse Machine Company in East Pittsburgh."

As the host, he insisted on carrying the battered Donner-family suitcase, now back home again.

"No, no," he had protested vigorously when Johnny tried to hold on to it. "I'll have one of my members bring out your trunk. That's the new Wetherill school up there on Henderson Hill." On the way from the station he pointed out half a dozen landmarks. If he felt any less warmth for the son than in Mahanoy, the latter couldn't detect it.

"What do you think of our Pompy?" he demanded, pleased, stopping before an ordinary prick-eared bay hitched to a muddy-wheeled wagon. He stowed the suitcase under the seat and they started out grandly. "You're now going up Houston Hill," he announced, calling it "Howston" in the local manner, and later, "This end of Wetherill is called —— town, —— town," giving the boy a vigorous pinch on the leg before each word and laughing immoderately at his little joke on the name of Pinchtown.

At home Johnny thought he felt confusion in his mother's eye that he hadn't "stuck it out," made good in the city. But his father was in high spirits, especially at the table, relating jovial and even uproarious valley incidents. No one could carry things off like his father. After supper he took the boy across the road where the brick walls of the new church were rising from the ruins. For much of an hour he treated him as someone his own age, confiding all that had happened, pointing out future details of unfinished sanctuary and Sunday-school rooms, describing doors, windows and furnishings still to be.

"I have my text for the first sermon all picked out," he promised.

The boy heard with strange recurrent sensations. He had forgotten all this. Now he was back again among the old ecclesiastical influences, his ear assailed by the peculiarly dry and sterile vulgate of the church, his young life faced by the stern presence of rituals and sacraments, of vows and austerities, of obligations and constraints, all under the overhanging shadow of the cross. He remembered that his father used to speak of the church in his sermons as a river of life, and yet in this church as in many another the boy could feel only bare and empty walls and a strange mystic silence like that of the Sphinx in the desert. It was in the parsonage that to him the river of life flowed, the rooms and walls strong with refuge and peace, with freedom and the warm presence of his mother.

"I want you to see all the churches, Johnny," his father said with pleasure. "And meet the people. Wonderful people here. Maybe you'd like to ride along to male-quartet practice at the Frame Church tomorrow night."

What his father called the Frame Church turned out to be a rather narrow building standing lone and desolate on the top of a hill. Fields surrounded it but hardly a human habitation was to be seen, only the white stones of the adjoining cemetery. The other singers had not yet come. His father unlocked the door and took him in. The air tasted stale with the certain dry dusty smell of churches during the week. There was one large room, the pews straight and stiff, their color an archaic hand-grained yellow. Yet the boy noticed that his father's eyes had lighted as if he saw beauty here.

"I preached last Sunday on David and the eye of Mars," he said, giving a few points of the sermon, reciting in a dramatic voice, " 'When the eye of Mars looked down on the earth, it was red with exceeding fury, and the quality of mercy appeased it not.' " He added, pleased, in his natural voice, "Several people told me they liked my sermon."

The boy sat that evening on a back pew trying to fathom it out. The church lay in darkness save the square of choir lighted by an oil lamp or two flickering on the brown unpainted beams overhead and the faces of the four men. They went over their piece again and again. One verse haunted the watching and listening boy.

Ashamed of Thee, oh, sooner far
Let midnight blush to own its star.
He sends his beams of light divine
On this benighted, this benighted, soul of mine.

Exactly what it was he didn't know, but something troubled him in the melancholy words and minors, in the shabby furnishings of the church, in the remoteness of the scene, in the dim oil lamps against the ancient mystery, and in these four benighted men in the lonely reaches of this dark valley singing of the light of a mystical and incarnate star. But while it faintly chilled the boy, it warmed his father and the three other men. He could tell it by the way they sang. There was power of a kind here. The boy could not be certain of its nature or its source.

The power still lived in his father that night at the home of the tall farmer who sang second bass, and it had not burned out next morning when Papa, dressed and down long before his son, called vigorously up the narrow, twisting farmhouse stairs.

"Johnny! 'The sun is up and it is day.' 'This is the day the Lord hath made. I shall rejoice and be glad in it.' "

How his father had preserved such energy and well-being imprisoned as they both were in the spare bedroom without a single decoration on the white walls, Johnny didn't know. He had never seen him in better fettle. Last night at family worship before going to bed he had prayed, "When the fever of life is over and our labor done, then in thy great mercy grant us safe lodgings and a holy rest, and peace at the last, but if our toil remains and our life abides, call us up at the rising of the sun with morning faces and morning hearts," and here he was at the breakfast table giving joyful thanks "for the rest and care of the night, for having been permitted to look on the light of another day, for the air we breathe, the food we eat prepared by kind hands and for the raiment that we wear." He ate heartily and praised without stint the black coffee, the fried eggs, the sausage and especially the pancakes of dark home-grown buckwheat.

"This is wonderful, Mother, wonderful!" he said to the pleased old woman by the stove.

They left by midmorning.

"I want you to meet some more fine people, Johnny," he said on the yellow road, keeping tab on his watch and turning in to another farm in time to be invited to dinner where he prayed, "Bless us in things temporal and spiritual, in basket and store, in field and home. Grant to farmers and keepers of cattle good seasons and to travelers and harvesters fair weather." Later he gave a special prayer for the smaller children who didn't get to the first table and who kept coming to the door to show off in front of the preacher and then run before their parents could seize them.

They were on the road again by late afternoon. Pompy, full of oats, jogged along willingly. Johnny hoped they were headed for home but his father had other notions.

"I want to tell you a little something about the next place before we go in. They're fine people but they've had some hard luck and they've never got over it."

He turned into a long straight lane. Perhaps it had been his father's words, but there seemed to be something unhealthy about the low, heavy, flat land after the bright hill farms where the wind blew, and about the huge, gray, unpainted barn and darker weathered house standing silent and almost deserted-looking in the shadow of decaying maples.

"What sort of bad luck?" Johnny asked.

"Their son was hung," his father said. "Here's Mr. McPhail coming now. I'll tell you about it later. Just act like I didn't tell you anything."

A woodenlike figure was coming toward them across the field. At a little distance he looked red with the lowering sun but when he came close the boy told himself he had never before seen a face like dead meat. The hand given to Johnny was putty.

"I'll take care of him, Reverend," he said, meaning the horse. "You go on in. She'll be looking for you."

"What's the matter with him? Is he drunk?" the boy whispered on the way to the house.

His father gave him a nudge, and Johnny saw that a red-eyed woman had come out of the house and now stood waiting.

"How are you, Mrs. McPhail?" his father called, as if to visit such a place and people were the most agreeable thing in the world.

"Is it you, Reverend?" she asked. "I was hoping it was. I'm glad you remembered us. I was saying to him only yesterday, I believed you'd forgotten us."

"I was here only a month ago," Johnny's father reminded.

"But you wouldn't stay for a meal. And who's this with you? Not your boy. He don't look like you."

"This is our oldest, Johnny," his father said, pleased. "The one that worked out at Pittsburgh."

"Ah!" she said, taking the boy's hand and starting to cry. "I can remember when Marlin was just like him."

Papa didn't seem to mind her. He stood by, saying pleasant, matter-of-fact things till the woman remembered to take them into the house, where she opened the closed parlor and they sat around in the bleak room hung with the framed color enlargement of a youth. Papa tried to keep the talk on crops, weather and neighbors, but the woman kept bringing it around to the boy on the wall.

"We knew Effie was no good for him, Reverend!" she cried out once. "But we couldn't do nothing. They wasn't made for each other. She'd go home and he'd bring her back. This last time she said she was going for good, that she'd take his child along and he wasn't to come for it again. It was a day like today. Only it was Sunday. Hughie took me to church. Marlin said he didn't feel like going to church when he and Effie were fighting all the time, but we never dreamed anything like that. When we got home, it was too late."

She was weeping violently now. Getting up, she brought Johnny a tin object from the parlor table and put it in his lap.

"This is the last plate he ate from. They gave him his

breakfast on it the day they done that to him. He wanted ham and fried potatoes. He said that's what his mom always used to make for him. He said nobody could fry potatoes like his mom, and nobody could cure ham like his pop. This is the cup he drank his coffee from. He liked it strong. And this is the last knife and fork he ate with. The sheriff gave them to Hughie. He wanted to give the rope, too, but I said he could keep that. I didn't care what he done with it. I heard he took it home and now he shows it to everybody who comes to his house and says who was hung with it."

Johnny could tell from his father's resigned face that he had heard this several times before. He sat quietly, letting the bitter woman go on. When she was spent, he got down on his knees and offered a long prayer. After that she seemed better and got supper.

"Why was he hung?" Johnny asked when Mrs. McPhail was in the kitchen.

"For murder," his father told him briefly.

"But who did he murder?" the boy persisted.

"His young wife and child," his father said. "In the kitchen out there. He buried them under the manure pile. He told his parents he had taken them home to her mother."

The sense of ugliness and oppression that had been growing on Johnny turned into horror. He could scarcely eat supper in this place. He kept seeing the bloody bodies of a young mother and her child in the dark corners of the kitchen. On the other hand, his father remained as usual, sitting heartily up to the table, repaying the hospitality as always with prayer and compliments, ignoring the tragedy as though it had taken place in some past age and now all had been washed clean by time or at least diluted to a faint residue.

Throughout the meal the boy waited only to get away. Once it was over, he asked his father if it wasn't time to go.

"We can't run off the minute we eat, Johnny," Papa said firmly. "Besides, I want to visit with the McPhails a little."

As if his small word of sympathy had touched off her misery afresh, the woman started crying again. She had been doing the dishes and the boy could see drops falling into the dishpan.

"Now, now, Mrs. McPhail," Papa said. "Everything's going to be all right," which only seemed to make her worse.

"It's Effie's folks give her the most trouble," Mr. McPhail apologized. "They tell all the mean things they can about Marlin."

"Is it true, Reverend," Mrs. McPhail cried, "that a murderer can never enter the kingdom of heaven?"

"Well," Papa said thoughtfully, "we're told in the Bible that Moses killed an Egyptian. It's hard to think that Moses never reached heaven. We're also told that though our sins are scarlet, they shall be white as snow. You told me once that Marlin made full confession to his pastor and begged for forgiveness at the end. I think we can believe that his prayers were answered."

"But they claim he committed the unforgivable sin," Mrs. McPhail said brokenly. "They say that's what it is if you hate and destroy your own child."

"I'm not sure that Marlin hated his child," Papa said. "I rather think he meant to hurt his wife by hurting the child. There's a Greek myth along the same lines. I don't mean to minimize or defend his act, Mrs. McPhail, only to point out that God himself made us, understands us and is merciful to us, and we shouldn't impute to him our own human passions for vindictiveness and revenge."

Mrs. McPhail didn't seem to hear. She stood with hands helpless in the dishpan, her head bent over it. She seemed unable to see.

"They say Marlin's in the place of torment right now!" she cried out. "They say he's been there all this time since he done it. They say he begs day and night for a few drops of water but that nobody through all eternity can give it to him. They say when me and my man die we'll have to stand there watching Marlin in the sea of fire. We'll have to listen to him beg for water and never be able to give him none."

Johnny twisted unhappily over the tears and emotion, the baring of mind and soul, the sight of a grown man and woman standing in misery in their own house. He didn't know which room he hated more, the bloody kitchen or the second room with its revolting tin plate, cup and spoon together with the ghastly picture on the wall.

"I've got to 'go out,' " he blurted, and bolted.

Once in the darkness peopled with unknown shapes and shadows, he regretted it. He was still close to the kitchen door the murderer must have used. Under his feet lay the very path over which had likely been dragged or carried the butchered bodies. A few yards off his eyes could make out dimly the barnyard where they had been buried. Every mysterious stamp and bump in the barn gave him a start.

So this, he told himself bitterly, was beautiful Wetherill Valley that his father, mother and brothers liked better than Port Oxford! If he knew where the parsonage lay, he would get out of this horrible place. He believed his feet at first would little more than touch the ground. But he didn't know the way, and at night there would be no one to ask. It was getting late, and still his father didn't come out. He could hear the piteous voice of Mrs. McPhail running on and on in the house. At the end he climbed into the deserted buggy.

His father's hand on his shoulder wakened him. Sitting erect he saw Mr. McPhail with a lantern holding up the "shavvs" for the horse. The buggy dipped as Papa got in and picked up the lines. Pompy, anxious for home and stable, was already wheeling and breaking into a trot while his father called reassuring good nights to the McPhails.

"They're poor benighted souls," he said with feeling as they drove out the lane. "I guess I stayed too long. I phoned Mamma we'd be late. I had to wait till Mrs. McPhail settled down so I could talk to her. I wanted to give her what comfort I could that her boy would be all right."

"I don't see how you could tell her such a thing!" Johnny said, abhorrence for the place still upon him.

"There are three things I try to tell my people," Papa said. "First that God forgives sins, all sins including the blackest, if the sinner is truly sorry and tries to live aright. Secondly, that salvation, eternal life is open to all, even to the worst of us, through the grace of God. And thirdly, that these things are really and wonderfully true."

"How does anybody know they're really true?" the boy demanded.

"I know what I believe," his father answered him stoutly, and went on, quoting, " 'I know whom I have believed and am persuaded that he is able to keep that which I've committed unto him against that day.' "

"But belief doesn't make things so," Johnny said passionately. "Look at what the Hindus and Orientals believe. Lots of our own people, some of the most intelligent, say there's no God and no eternal life. They say when you're dead, you're dead, that preachers and missionaries and nuns and the saints who think the Lord or angels go with them and help them are only deluding themselves. They say that all those who give up everything for a religious life cheat themselves out of their real place in the world, out of pleasure and happiness, out of doing what they want to and making the most out of the only life they'll ever have."

His father was bitterly silent for a while.

"Do you believe that, Johnny?"

"If somebody proved it's true, I'd believe it. But would you?"

"Go slow, Johnny, on what you believe. The Bible says, as a man thinketh in his heart, so is he. You ask if it was proved that all I believe in and stand for isn't true but is a swindle, the greatest swindle on earth, would I believe it? I don't know how you or anybody else would ever prove it. But if some thought they did, I guess I still wouldn't believe it. I think I'm already doing what I want to do right now, getting a lot out of the only life you say I'll ever have. I think I'm already pretty well off, healthy, happy in my job, happier than most people I meet, especially those who don't believe in anything. I think my belief that God personally supports me, and that his presence and angels go with me, gives me grace to do what I'm called on to do and peace of mind while I'm doing it. Now let's take it your way. Let's say that what you and your wise men say is really true—that all I believe in isn't true, that the Bible and Lord Jesus, God forbid, aren't true; that going around preaching the Gospel and salvation and trying to do good like him aren't true. Well, in that case, when I'd die, I'd never find out it wasn't true and neither would you. So your belief doesn't give you any benefit there. Now let's take it while we live. Which way do you suppose I'd be the happiest and healthiest and get the most out of life for myself and those I try to do things for, going around practicing my belief and believing it true, even though it's false, or believing it false and going around believing it false, even though such a belief according to you would be true?"

The boy couldn't answer that one. It troubled him. He had always believed that truth was truth and best for you even if it killed you. Now he wondered if there was more than one truth about the same thing, one truth that hurt you and one that blessed. From time to time as the wheels rolled along, he kept watching his father. How could he sit there shaking the lines over Pompy's back so late at night after such an exhausting day, humming with feeling the air from the quartet last night?

He sends his beams of light divine
On this benighted, this benighted, soul of mine.

There was still light in the house downstairs when they reached home. His mother stood in the kitchen doorway. A wood fire burned in the cookstove and the smell of hot coffee hung in the air.

"Well, I'm glad you two got home before daylight," she chided them. "Is Mrs. McPhail feeling a little better now, Hal?"

CHAPTER FOURTEEN

Eve

Of all God's creation, the preacher thought, his finest work had been woman. She was, when you reflected on her, a most divine and marvelous invention, one that could feel tenderness for the weak, pity for the suffering, could delight man, make his bed and supper, not to mention her astounding gift to conceive and perpetuate her kind. Man couldn't begin to match her, but then God had made man first, more or less on the spur of the moment, and by the time he came to woman had had experience to surpass himself.

There were exceptions, of course, but all through life Harry Donner had noticed that women could endure more than their husbands. Already in infant baptism their superior character had begun to come out. They were less likely to protest water splashed from the font on their soft young pates, often laughed and gurgled to have their heads wetted. At two or three years they started to take hold of your coat or trouser leg. At five they were chubby sausages of delight to romp with. They wanted to be lifted up and hugged when you left. They always had a kiss for you. But it wasn't until they reached twelve or thirteen that the Lord's handiwork became clearly visible. They were gentler now, more reserved, susceptible and perceptive to the stirrings of young womanhood. Their eyes trusted you, gave you their unspoken confidences. Their faces were often a picture. When certain of them lowered their lashes to read aloud from their catechism, he thought their loveliness indescribable.

But it was at fifteen and sixteen that they reached the fateful hour of bloom, like the clover in early June, unfolded to completeness. They became shyer, graver, grateful for every word and glance, reverent to your face and merry behind your back. He thought of them as the young virgins the Lord had noticed in his day and spoken of in parables. Here on the remote reaches of back-country farms, with no models to follow or mirror, it seemed that the Creator's blueprint for them came to its purest fruition. There was something about tender young souls and bodies in rude calico and often bare legs that reminded him of the slightly coarse yet incredibly sweet call of the white-throated sparrow in the brambles, the one Mamma called the Canada bird because it seemed to say, "Swee-eet Canada, Canada, Canada." On the other hand, he fancied town girls and young Piatt females less unspoiled flowers of the race, more possessed, self-centered and appraising.

Wild or tame, he was devoted to daughters of all ages, having none himself. The pleasant honeyed thought of their presence ahead at this farmhouse or that lightened the lonely miles of pastoral travel. He had his name for each. "My girl" was his warmest endearment. "She's my girl," "Where's my girl?," "Here's my girl!" Only slightly less fond was "my sweetheart," "my Janie," "my pet." "Here is my nice little girl" was a diminished term although spoken with undiminished smile and heartiness. A host of lesser appellations poured out of him like nectar, "Topsy," "Sally wriggler," "my hanswascht" and "Nixnutz," which meant respectively clown and good-for-nothing. He loved to tease them but none, if he could help it, was slighted in his affection, none called pretty if a less attractive sister was around to hear or find out.

Of all the girl crop in his charge, the apple of the preacher's eye was Emma Severn. Emmaline, he called her, as he had his own sister of the same name. She came from an old unpainted house on the back road. It had chinked logs inside and out. To enter this rude cottage, black from time and weather, and find a beautiful girl like Emma was a delight like finding the yellow ladyslipper in the dark woods. She was devoted to church, seldom missed and invariably told back the text and sermon to her house-bound mother, who in turn would take pride in reciting his last sermon back to the preacher when he called while her daughter quietly listened, smiled and prompted when necessary. There was something about Emma's calm young womanhood and the silent way she went about the housework that made him think of young Mary in Galilee.

But he had to confess to Mamma that he couldn't understand what he heard was her choice of a man. Why, he wondered, was the tenderest flower so often picked by the heavy hand? What was the secret, almost devilish attraction between wildness and gentility? If he, Harry Donner, were young and unmarried, Emma Severn was one he'd think about going for, and yet her suitor, people said, was a worthless fellow from down below Allenburg. Jenny said he seldom had a dollar to his name, was crazy over horses and fed gunpowder to his bony nag to make him go faster. Every Wednesday and Saturday he put his red-wheeled runabout in the river to wash it.

"There's nothing wrong with that, Jenny," the preacher said. "I wish Johnny or Gene would wash our buggy and road wagon twice a week."

"It's about the only work he ever does around the place," Jenny told him. "You think he's good enough for her?"

"I wouldn't know that," the preacher said. "Emma's never brought him to service that I know of."

"She couldn't get him inside of a church," Jenny declared. "And if she could, he wouldn't have nothing to put in the collection."

"Now, Jenny," the preacher protested. "You and Phillip didn't have too much either when he started to go with you, did you?"

"No, but Phillip was no Jerry Wilkes," Jenny retorted hotly. "He never beat work or played fast and loose with a young girl like Emma Severn."

Now what did Jenny mean by that, the preacher wondered. He had not long to find out. One Saturday evening he sat in his upstairs study working on his sermon when he heard a rig stop outside. A long time passed before a knock sounded on the door. After a moment Vallie called him. He clogged downstairs and found a lean, bold-looking fellow with limestone blue eyes and a shock of yellow hair.

"Good evening!" the preacher said cordially, shaking hands, wondering if he should know him. "Can I do anything for you?"

"Reverend," the caller said in a kind of reckless unease, "my girl wants to get married and she wants you to do it."

"Why, I think that can be arranged," the preacher assured him heartily. "Bring her around sometime and we'll talk it over."

"She's out here now," he said. "Could you do it tonight?"

"Why, I guess I could." The preacher thought with a sigh of his unfinished notes on the desk upstairs. And yet a wedding was a more joyous occasion than preparing a sermon. But the fellow didn't go.

"She wanted me to ask what you'd charge."

"There's no fixed charge. Anything you want to give."

"Would you take a bag of snitz?"

"A bag of snitz?" The preacher was taken aback but he recovered quickly. "Why, yes, surely. Bring her in, and we'll see what we can do."

When the fellow had gone to the buggy, Harry Donner opened the door to the kitchen that Mamma had discreetly closed.

"The bridegroom cometh!" he told her in high spirits. "Can you use any snitz? I wonder if you'd call up Jenny and ask if she'd come over as a witness?"

He returned to the parlor smiling but he didn't smile when the bridegroom came with the bride-to-be and he saw that it was Emmaline. She had some early pansies from her garden pinned on her coat and carried a stuffed flour sack. She gave him a little smile, a brave pitiful smile, he thought. So this was Jenny's no-good Allenburg fellow? Well, all he could think of at the moment was St. Paul's assurance that the unbelieving husband is sanctified by the Christian wife.

Throughout the ceremony the preacher was conscious of the hard face of Jenny as she watched, and of the tender, almost holy face of Emma Severn soon to be Emma Wilkes. When it was over, he spoke to them jovially, bringing in his happy matrimonial phrases. Then he sobered and asked the bridegroom upstairs to his study while he wrote out the marriage certificate. He closed the study door behind them.

"Sit down, Mr. Wilkes," he said. "I hope you realize what a fortunate man you are. Emmaline is a wonderful girl and will make a worthy and excellent wife. However, I think she's worth a great deal more than your honorarium would indicate. I don't think you should let it get around the valley that you paid the preacher a bag of snitz for your wife."

"They're her snitz, not mine, Reverend," he retorted.

"I have no doubt," the preacher said. "I'm sure she picked the apples and cut and dried the snitz with her own hand. But that's no credit to you. I don't think you should offer the preacher less than five dollars in your case, especially in front of Mrs. Rodey. If you don't have the money, I'll lend it to you."

He opened his pocketbook and found only three worn dollar bills. Mamma kept little more than silver change in the kitchen, he knew, but she had a five-dollar bill in the upper bureau drawer, and this he took and passed to the skeptical-eyed bridegroom.

"Now I want you to hand it to me so Mrs. Rodey can see you when we get downstairs," he said. "But before we go, there's a verse from First Samuel that comes to me. 'The name of his wife was Abigail and she was a woman of good understanding and of beautiful countenance.' I strongly feel that this applies to your wife, Emma. Your responsibility, now that you've taken the step, is to honor and comfort her, sustain and support her."

"Reverend!" Jenny called up the stairs. "I wonder if you could let me sign the paper and get back to the house? The boys are alone over there."

Harry Donner turned to his desk, filled out the marriage certificate with a little less of his usual dash and flourish. Then they went together downstairs, where Jenny wrote her name as witness and left, followed by the bride and groom. Not until they were gone and the sound of the abruptly driven horse had died out did Harry Donner remember the five-dollar bill.

He said nothing to Mamma. She would discover the missing bill in time. It troubled him all that night, not so much about the money as for Emmaline and what lay ahead of her with this husband. He pondered the secret purpose of the Almighty that deserving men and women more often than not had spouses with opposite natures and dispositions. He knew the Lord's stern injunction not to judge. However, the Lord had not told him to shut his eyes, and it was one of the crosses a preacher bore that he had to join in holy wedlock from which let no man put asunder, couples who were unfitted for the trials ahead and some of whom might dearly regret the step they had taken.

All the next week he carried the cross. Saturday morning he spoke to Mamma.

"I feel I've failed," he told her. "I mean in making our young people understand the holy significance of marriage, that it's a symbol of the mystical and sacred marriage of Christ to the church, and should be approached with prayer and understanding and not with the blind passion of men on the one hand and the deceitful wiles and contriving of women on the other."

Mamma gave him a sharp glance.

"I don't know what you could have done."

"I might have preached some honest and informative sermons on marriage," he said. "I could have pointed out the terrible responsibility of any man who promises to be more to his young woman than her father and mother and all the friends she has combined. I could have warned him of his awful guilt in inducing a girl by fair words and promises to exchange her mother's house for some Dismal Swamp existence. I could have told him that I wouldn't so much blame a man for cheating another man out of a farm as I would for cheating a woman out of the happiness of a lifetime."

"It sounds very forthright," Mamma admitted. "Do you think that Cupid would hear it?"

"I don't know what you mean," Harry Donner said. "But I intend to preach such a sermon tomorrow."

He did, too. It helped to get some of his bitterness over Emmaline's probable fate out of his system. He had hoped it would do more than that. He gave it first at the Manada

Hill church. Almost no one commented on it, either then or at the Frame Church that evening. But at the Spring Garden church next Sunday afternoon, at least one hearer did, the widow of the late Harrison Todd.

"I liked your sermon, Reverend," she said. "I'd like to talk to you about what you said when you come to the house."

"I'm glad to hear it," Harry Donner said, pleased. "I'll be happy to talk to you about it."

The Todd farm lay in a great sloping meadow between Spring Garden Creek and Logan Mountain, excellent land, a square white house, a solid barn with stone ends and a number of outbuildings all white as the house. Harrison Todd had been a butcher and huckster. He had driven across Nippenose Mountain twice a week to market, where he kept a double stall the year around. His wife invariably accompanied him and her solid figure and rather pretty plump face were still a fixture at the market. She had kept up the stall after his death, driving over with her brother who farmed her land and lived in his own house across a small ridge. The lane between the two farms was well used as a road. The preacher took it today after calling on her brother's family first so as to follow St. Paul's advice of impartiality to all.

Mrs. Todd kept a hired girl but let the minister in herself. In the parlor with the inevitable organ and white walls they settled on stiff green chairs.

"Your sermon was a thinking sermon, Reverend," she said. "And it set me to thinking."

"I wish," the preacher said, "I might preach a sermon like that every Sunday."

"Yes, I thought about it in church. I thought about it at home. And I thought about it at market."

"I hope you approved."

"Oh, I'm in hearty favor of marriage," she assured. "In fact, I've been thinking of getting married myself again and I want you to tie the knot."

The preacher was taken aback. Why, it was no more than eight months since he had said the last rites over Harrison.

"Do you think enough time has passed?" he ventured soberly.

"A long enough time for me, Reverend, to be setting here alone."

"You're not exactly alone, Mrs. Todd. You have Nelly Sites to help you when you need her. George does your farming and goes with you to market. Don't you think you ought to wait at least a year? A longer time would be still more suitable."

"Not me, Reverend," she said. "When I want something, I want it."

He felt distaste rising in him.

"Marriage is a holy institution and shouldn't be rushed into. Also, the golden fruit of marriage is a house full of children. If you don't mind my speaking frankly as your pastor, Mrs. Todd, I believe you're of an age when you can no longer expect to serve God in this way." He thought that her heavy face looked a little thoughtful and he reminded her gravely that while she was acquainted with the drawbacks of her present state, she wasn't with those of the step she contemplated, especially if made in too much of a hurry.

The Widow Todd sat like a female Buddha.

"A man I want, Reverend, and a man I will have," she declared.

The preacher sat sobered.

"You have someone in mind?"

"Oh, I have him all picked out already."

"Well, I hope you're being led aright and that he is a Christian and God-fearing man."

Mrs. Todd looked stolid.

"He's a good enough Christian for me, Reverend."

"Do I know him?"

"Oh, you know him all right. He goes to our church. He sits in front of me every Sunday. I had my eye on him for a good while. I told myself this long time that he's the one for me. He owns his own place and got a good business besides. He has money in the bank and no wife in his house or bed now for ten years. You know who I mean?"

Harry Donner ran his mind over his Spring Garden congregation.

"You mean Jacob Reis?"

"No, he's my second choice. I want Arthur Scovel first."

So that was who it was! The preacher could see Arthur clearly in his mind as if he had suddenly stepped into the room, a tall spare man with dark eyes and red, almost purple, cheeks, his hat and clothes and spade beard dusted with the white from his mill.

"He knows about this?"

"Not yet but he's going to. I'd like if you'd talk to him and tell him what good you know about me."

The preacher grew stern.

"I'd prefer if you select someone else as your messenger, Mrs. Todd. I don't think it falls in the province of a minister."

The Widow Todd never budged.

"You're my pastor, Reverend," she said stubbornly. "You're the one who has to tie the knot and you're the one who has to help me get him. Unless you'd sooner see me get him foul than fair."

Harry Donner flushed but refused to be blackmailed.

"I had three years in the seminary, Mrs. Todd, but no instruction as a matchmaker or marriage broker. I was taught that marriage is a holy institution in which a man and woman are to be decently joined together in a civil contract for the prevention of uncleanness, for the propagation of mankind and so the contracting parties may be of mutual help and comfort to each other."

"That's exactly what I need a man for, Reverend," she

said. "I get cold at night. I need some red-blooded fellow to keep me warm. No matter how many quilts I put on, it don't help. My back gets like a sheet of ice. You can lay your hand on it right now, Reverend, and tell me if I don't tell the truth."

She began undoing her waist and the preacher's stern distaste turned into displeasure. He remembered gratefully the stern words of Vallie's father to the woman who wanted to show him the sore on her thigh. "Ich will's net sehna," he had declared. Thank God for the old preacher.

"As your pastor I have nothing to do with that, Mrs. Todd," Harry Donner said shortly. "You can ask Dr. Metzgar about it if you like. Now I must go. I've one more call to make on the Spring Garden road and get back to prayer meeting at Manada Hill tonight."

The Widow Todd looked alarmed.

"You're not going already, Reverend. I expected you'd stay for supper. You haven't taken a meal with me all year."

"I'll come and eat with you on my next pastoral visit," he promised. "I'll bring Mrs. Donner along."

The solitude of the buggy, the celibacy of Pompy and the austerity of the road had never seemed more solid and satisfying than today. Woman might be God's later and higher creation but some of them were a throwback to Eve. He gave Widow Todd a cool look when he greeted her in the Spring Garden church on Sunday, and no intimation to Arthur Scovel what had been revealed to him. He heard later that Mrs. Todd was taking her grain to Scovel's Mill personally, having it ground for what flour, chop, shorts and bran she needed. He heard other things, some that made him think of the verse from Proverbs, "Stolen waters are sweet and bread eaten in secret is pleasant. But he knoweth not that the dead are there." Mrs. Pumphrey, wife of the storekeeper at Spring Garden, told him she wouldn't be surprised if the widow didn't marry the miller.

Within six months Mrs. Todd herself asked him to perform the ceremony and all through the service she bore a secret and triumphant look on her fleshy face. Now that her marriage to the miller was to become an established fact, the preacher put into the rite and the prayer that followed every effort for an auspicious and heaven-blessed union, while in private talks with his Maker on the lonely roads of the valley, he requested that his own doubts and reservations in the matter be overlooked and forgotten.

Just the same, folks told him within the year that the miller had moved back to his own house by the creek, spending only Saturday night and Sunday with his bride, during which time, Nelly Sites said, they fought like cat and dog. Nelly also reported that the new Mrs. Scovel charged her husband for the oats and hay he fed his horse on the weekend, while he in turn deducted an eighth for the grain she sent to the mill to be ground. They still sat together during worship at the Spring Garden church but the preacher noted that they came to service in different rigs, sang from separate hymnbooks, took their respective offerings from their own pocketbooks and turned their backs on each other after the sociability at the door.

It made him a little sad to have the thing turn out this way, but not nearly so sad as to see the once lovely and promising Emma Severn now gaunt and almost slatternly, nursing her second child and giving her minister a reproachful look as if for not saving her but rather contributing to her misery. It troubled him. His prayer for couples joined together by him had always been joyful and expectant. He had prided himself that he "could tie a good knot," that his marriages had turned out well, that the participants remained true to each other and lived in seeming happiness. Now lately two products of his hand had foundered. Was his grace with God beginning to fail, his pronouncements in the name of the Father coming under divine disfavor?

He had been thinking these gloomy thoughts today when in the course of his pastoral rounds he called on Dan Singer and his common-law wife, Dolly. They lived on a little place near the river. Dan was a machinist with the chair works at Watsontown, a huge man with deep shoulders, a partly bald head and a tremendous face. He was a voracious reader, a longtime subscriber to the *Appeal to Reason*, and, it was said, liked to hold forth on politics and economics to Dolly, who confessed happily she could neither read nor write. She was a blond, blowsy woman always laughing so that her flesh shook like siterle.

Toward the end of his call, the preacher brought up again the old objective.

"I wonder, dear friends, if before I go you would do me a personal favor?"

"Sure. What is it?" Dan said.

"Let me say the common service over you and hear your responses?"

"He means civil and sacred marriage," Dan explained to Dolly.

Dolly laughed with embarrassment and looked at her man as if waiting for the pearls of wisdom to drop from his powerful lips.

"I don't think so, Reverend," Dan said judicially. "Now I hope you know I have nothing against you personally. If I believed in the dead dictums of the past, you'd be the one man of the cloth I'd want to do the job. But as you know, I'm a dissenter. No empty formalities for me. I take support from your own holy Bible. In one of his epistles your St. Paul tells you, 'Come out from among them and be ye separate.' Doesn't he now? At another place he gets down to cases. He says, 'He that giveth her in marriage doeth well but he that giveth her not in marriage doeth better.' Could anything be clearer? Even your great prophet, Jesus Christ himself, says very plainly in three different books, Matthew, Mark and Luke, that in the resurrection mortals neither marry nor are given in marriage but, he says, 'are like the angels in Heaven.' If you believe that, then what's the excuse and argument for civil marriage? As for me and Dolly, we're satisfied to remain on God's footstool like the angels in Heaven."

Harry Donner smiled ruefully. An ordinary person like himself could never hope to outreason Dan Singer. If he reminded him of the Lord's approval of marriage in attending the marriage at Cana, Dan would come back with a whole salvo of rebuttal. They had threshed this matter out before and the preacher had not come out a winner. Now if Dan and Dolly weren't childless, it would be a horse of another color. Then he would have irrefutable arguments. Indeed, if there were only one babe, already born or in store, he would throw himself into its cause and not give up until he had got the innocent a semblance of lawful parentage.

The preacher sighed. It was a pity for more than one reason. The marriage of Dan and Dolly Singer would be something to cheer him up at this time. He could pronounce them man and wife with a great deal of confidence in their happiness. It was a union to bank on, for already it enjoyed a true and tried basis to go on.

CHAPTER FIFTEEN

Water from the Well

Valeria Donner sat very still. She looked asleep but was thinking. Winter nights on Manada Hill the parsonage seemed like a shell. The wind from Nippenose Mountain shook it, rattled the windows, poured through the unseen cracks with icy fingers of draft. Up in Gene and Johnny's room, the snow often lay on their covers till morning. Those two read *Physical Culture Magazine* and insisted on opening their window on the coldest nights. Their bedroom lay over the second parlor, which had to be closed for the winter. The Reverend Cannons must have heated it, for there was a darkened pipe hole to the chimney but the Donners owned only one heater. Its isinglass panes glowed red in front of her in the parlor now.

They were all out tonight, Hal at the Frame Church, Johnny in town, Gene at a box social and Timmy studying with Bill Mast, whose big sister, Alice, could help with the homework since she was their Stone School teacher. The only family member left with her was Dixie, the yellow shepherd dog, good enough company except when he deserted for some female dog receptive to male callers, often miles away. He lay very faithful and domestic now, a furry lump on the carpet by the heater, his nose between his paws, never opening his eyes unless she moved or sighed, paying not the slightest attention to the occasional sleigh bells that passed. When first they lived in the valley she had expected the sound of every rig to be that of Hal. By now she had learned not to look for him till Dixie gave the signal. Long before she could even hear a sleigh bell or buggy wheel, he would be on his feet by the door whining to be let out.

Where would they be next year at this time? she wondered. Much of this summer she had observed that Hal was getting restless. She could detect the telltale signs, his preoccupation at meals, his deep sigh when he prayed, his zeal for preaching on Paul's missionary travels and on the text from Ruth, "Whither thou goest, I will go."

Oh, Hal had held out pretty well here, she thought, keeping away from the usual church and choir squabbles. He had endured the murmuring of certain members that he didn't take a meal often enough with them, that he was friendlier to others than themselves, that he had his parish pets. But these were minor complaints. He suffered more from occasional fault finding with his sermons, as when Ambrose McAndrew told him his preaching on the loneliness of Christ belittled the sublime sacrifice of the Lord of Lords and King of Kings. And for a week or two Hal had actually bled from a letter written by a valley sectarian and printed in the Wetherill paper, calling him a falsifier of truth and acolyte of the devil for declaring that God would forgive all who came to him with an humble and contrite heart.

But on the whole, Hal had ridden over these smaller waves. "This, too, will pass," he used to say. Oliver Piatt was the thorn in Hal's side that would not be withdrawn. It wasn't the pig business. That had been left behind. Neither was it Oliver's practice of inviting Reverend Cannon back to the valley to officiate at certain Piatt clan marriages and funerals, and not ask his present pastor to assist or even attend. When that happened Hal would be a little "down in the mouth" for a while and she would regret the loss of a five- or ten-dollar Piatt perquisite which the Donners could desperately use. But the cross always passed. Making Hal come like a beggar month after month for his own salary was the pernicious cancer in his blood. Jim Dietrich, treasurer of the Frame Church, paid his congregation's apportioned salary regularly in cash, and George Humphrey, being a businessman, sent his small check for the Spring Garden church by mail. Oliver might easily have done the same for Manada Hill, but he insisted on his pastor calling at the house to get it.

At first Hal had obliged gladly. Oliver had said simply, "Come and see us next week, Reverend, and your money will be ready." Hal thought he would make his pastoral call at the same time and kill two birds with one stone. But next month it had been the same. After a year of it, Hal had asked him to send the money, but Oliver always had a good excuse. He said he had "some things to talk over" or he had an old church record to show him or one of the family was ailing and would like to see him. It meant an extra two-mile drive in the buggy each way and, what was more, favoring Oliver Piatt with more pastoral calls than anybody save the very sick. After several years of it, Hal had rebelled. In the spring with the valley full of the bedfast and afflicted, he had stayed away and the second month after church service had asked Oliver for the money. But Oliver had been equal to the occasion. He had said piously that he didn't do business on the Sabbath. Besides, he never carried his checkbook or that much cash to church. Hal talked it over with Seranus Mast and Phillip, who had been trying for years to get Oliver out of the treasurership. They urged him to stand fast, but in the end when there wasn't a dime left, Hal had to eat crow and go to Oliver Piatt hat in hand.

Even so, Mamma thought Hal would have made the best of it if Oliver hadn't said what he had in front of the Manada Hill church council.

"You wouldn't run out of money, Reverend," he told him, "if you didn't let your three boys lay around the house all the time."

Criticism on himself Hal could take, but not on his boys. Why, Tim was still going to Wetherill High School and

Gene had graduated only a few months ago. Council meeting had been on Monday night and Mamma had heard about it from Jenny on Tuesday. Still she had no inkling of what was to come until she and the boys sat under Papa in church next Sunday and heard him preach what they afterwards called "his terrible sermon on failure."

"Failure, failure, bitter failure!" he had declared from the pulpit in a voice that shook them all. "What have we done with the time and talents that God gave us? He will say, 'Take therefore the talent from him . . . for from him that hath not shall be taken away even that which he hath. And cast ye the unprofitable servant into outer darkness; there shall be weeping and gnashing of teeth.' "

At the end in a voice strong with feeling he announced that he was leaving Wetherill Valley early in the new year. It startled Mamma and the boys. They knew he had no place as yet to go. Men from the three churches pleaded with him to reconsider and stay but Oliver was not among them, and Hal said he couldn't undo what he had spoken. Mamma thought she understood. He had held back his feelings too long. He could go on now only after a fresh start had wiped the slate clean.

Mamma looked down at the dog.

"You're going to miss it here, Dixie," she said.

They would all miss it. There was peace in this old country parsonage even on a wintry night. From time to time someone was generally passing, the telephone generally ringing to bring familiar faces from half the valley into the house. There were fourteen on the line, three shorts for the Manbecks, a long and two shorts for the Quincy Piatts, a short and two longs for the Ray Piatts, four longs for the Haverstraws, and four quick shorts for Dr. Metzgar at Spring Garden. Many a night waiting to see if it was their own ring, she had heard those alarming four shorts in the small hours, and said a prayer for the one who needed him and another for the good doctor who had to crawl out of bed and hitch up his horse. Their own ring of five shorts was never so sharp and demanding as Dr. Metzgar's.

"I'm going to miss the telephone," she told herself.

But in her heart she knew it was the people she would miss most, the valley's old-time American stock, individual, refreshing in what they did and said. How would Hal preach without old Bartholomew Maddox leaning forward on the pew ahead when he agreed with the sermon and sitting straight back as a post when he didn't.

"You pulled old Bartholomew front three times today, Papa," Johnny or Gene would tell him.

Valley people liked to be themselves, to put their own stamp on a word or saying. Some of their babies got "amonia" and were "so unrestless." Instead of "God is no respecter of persons," Dan Felty used to say, "God don't respect nobody." Martha Shellhammer said she didn't have time to go in her closet and pray. She had to do her praying and hymn singing when she could, mostly milking. She said the stock liked to listen, especially one old gray Jersey cow that had had lots of tribulation. Jake Loy would get up from a dinner for the preacher and say, "Well, Reverend, none of us shirked his duty." Jenny Rodey said "My land!" or "My stars!" at things you told her. Mamma had read those expressions in a book but she had never heard them spoken before. And Sammy Glass, the blacksmith, would yell when a horse or mule tried to kick him, "Dang your old liver pin!" Mamma had always meant to ask him what a liver pin was.

Whatever else you might say, valley folks were good company. They had funds of endless stories, like the one Jenny told about her sister, Naomi. Naomi had taken too much medicine and was out of her head for a day.

"Whose pants is them on the chair?" she wanted to know from her bed.

"Why, they's Will's," Jenny had told her.

"Who's Will?"

"Why, Will Greer, your man."

She lay a while digesting that.

"Can I get a look at him?"

"He's down for Elizabeth."

"Who's Elizabeth?"

"Why, your own daughter."

"Elizabeth, Elizabeth, well why don't he bring her? I want to see her if she's my daughter."

"She'll come. He's fetching her and the baby."

"What baby?"

"Why, Elizabeth's baby."

"Good God!" sitting up. "Does Elizabeth have a baby?"

"Why, of course. You ought to know that."

"Who was the man that done it to her?"

"Why, George, her husband."

"Oh, she got a husband," lying back again.

Jenny said her hair kept "raring up" as she talked and listened to her own sister. Oh, Jenny alone had told her dozens of stories. And Hal brought literally hundreds back to the parsonage. There was Tom Hildebrand, who told Hal when he offered to say grace at the table, "You can talk to the taters, Reverend, but it won't give you no more sausage," and his wife said, "Some folks choke their victuals down dry, I wash mine down with coffee." Then there was Hal's tale about Mr. Ott, whose favorite expression was "You bet," and favorite vice, tobacco. His wife died and she lay in the front room in her coffin.

"She looks very nice and natural," Hal had comforted him.

Mr. Ott shifted his quid to the other side of his mouth.

"You bet!" he said.

Oh, there were endless things to relate. She tried to pass on the best to Jess when she wrote. That reminded her. She owed Jess a letter now. She guessed she would have to drop Jess a hint or two about Hal leaving. One of the hints would be how Claude Mersey, the once dutchified country boy who had gone to school with Jess in Unionville, had written and asked Hal to come and preach in his big church in Brooklyn. But she would say nothing that Dr. Mersey wanted an assistant pastor and that Hal took the invitation as a trial sermon. You never knew. And she would say nothing about what Oliver Piatt had done to Hal. Jess still believed Hal head over heels in love with the valley and everybody in it, and so he was, Mamma thought. But a few here didn't love him so much as he did them. Just the same how could she and Hal trust themselves when it came time to say good-by to all their good friends in the valley, to Phillip and Jenny, to the Glasses, to the Billy Rosses and a hundred others? She hoped they both wouldn't break down.

CHAPTER SIXTEEN

Feed My Sheep

What Harry Donner liked best about his trip to Brooklyn were the train ride and the people. He enjoyed being among travelers in the day coach, sitting first with one and then another, getting to know them, handing them his card when they left, saying he hoped to see them again. On his return, Dr. Mersey—he didn't like to be called Claude any more—had offered to buy him a seat on the parlor car but the country preacher had declined. He told Dr. Mersey that when he went to Chicago to general synod, he had not taken a sleeper, preferring to sit up that night talking to fellow passengers in the smoker. He still exchanged letters with a man he had met on that train, a drummer from Ashtabula whose only son had been drowned.

Now as his train rounded the last sweeping curve of the river, he sighed and realized that his holiday was over. One of the boys would be on the platform to meet him. Pompy would be in the buggy up the street and the burdens of his charge waiting for him beyond Houston Hill. The boy turned out to be Gene, and once they were on the frozen valley road it was plain how in his fumbling boyish way he wanted to know how things had worked out in Brooklyn. His father turned most of the questions aside. He knew if he told Gene now, his thunder would be stolen. He would be talked out before he saw Mamma and the other boys. So he asked questions of his own about Mamma, about Fred Yorty, who had been kicked by a horse, about old George Washington Harmon and young Shelby Bashore, about Phillip's sick cow, about Mrs. DeLong's six-o'clock dinner and was it still on schedule for this evening, which was the main reason he hadn't stayed another day in the city as he should have liked to do, not wanting to disappoint Mamma, for Mrs. DeLong's dinners were a break in Mamma's stay-at-home existence and something to be talked about in the valley.

After Brooklyn and the warm friendly train, the parsonage looked cold in the December landscape streaked with snow under the bare valley trees. They all greeted him as if he had been away for a month. Dixie jumped up with sharp whining barks, trying to lick his face. Later the family sat around in the kitchen as it did after all his trips to hear a full account of his doings.

"Is it a big church, Papa?" Timmy wanted to know when he finished.

"One of the biggest I think I was ever in," Papa declared. "When I stood on the pulpit to preach it was like looking out over a city of faces. The stained-glass window behind the altar, they told me, cost I forget how many thousand and the organ five times as much. They don't have to have a boy to pump it like at Mahanoy. It's done electrically. The pews have green velvet cushions and carved crosses at the aisle like the Episcopalians. The Sunday school isn't just a big room with a smaller infants' department like ours. Classes have their own rooms like at college. There are I don't know how many bathrooms—and chairs, mind you, according to the size of the pupils. You never saw anything like it. The Bible class has hundreds of chairs and they were all filled the day I was there. I forget the amount of the collection but I could hardly believe it."

"Did everybody come to hear you preach, Papa?" Tim asked.

"Not everybody," Papa admitted. "They don't want everybody to come. Not at the same time anyway. If all three or four thousand members came, there wouldn't be room for some of them to sit down. In fact, they don't want any more members. They turn them away every week. You have to have mighty good references to get in there. Dr. Mersey told me they go over every applicant for membership with a fine-tooth comb. If they think he doesn't fit into St. Martin's, they don't take him. If they think he wants to join so he won't have to help build a new church somewhere else, they send him away."

"It must be a very rich church," Mamma murmured. "Did he tell you what the assistant pastor would get."

"He didn't say exactly," Papa hedged. "He did say they would be very generous, probably two or three times what we get here."

Timmy licked his lips.

"Tell us more, Papa!" he begged.

Papa obliged, warming to the memories of his visit. He told with enthusiasm of the trains, trolleys and ferries he rode in, of the street sights in New York and Brooklyn, of the size and importance of St. Martin's, of its rich yearly income, of his stay in Dr. Mersey's parsonage with two servants and twelve rooms, and what Dr. Mersey had told him of the prominent men in his congregation, the staggering figures of his budget and apportionment, his trips to Europe and the names of great people, churches and places of distinction he had visited.

"Twelve rooms!" Timmy said.

"Did he say anything about Unionville and the old days?" Mamma asked.

"Not too much," Papa said apologetically. "He doesn't seem to remember Unionville like we do. Of course he came from the country."

"He should remember his father and mother," Mamma said, and when Papa didn't reply, "I remember them both very well. His mother wore a sunbonnet and his father was a nice old man. He gave me an apple once. They both thought the world and all of Pap-pa. Pap-pa married them, I think, and baptized all their children."

"Of course we must realize," Papa said gravely, "that

such things may seem small to someone in Dr. Mersey's position. He's a very big man in the church now. It was nice of him to remember me and ask me over when I wrote him I was looking for another place."

Something in the way Papa said it made Mamma wonder.

"I hope he offered you the assistant-pastorship?" she said. You could see the three boys holding their breath.

"Oh, yes, he said I could have it," Papa answered. "If I wanted it."

"But you wanted it, didn't you, Hal?" Mamma persisted.

Papa said nothing. His lower lip stood out.

"Aren't we going to Brooklyn, Papa?" Timmy quavered.

His father looked unhappy. He faced Mamma doggedly.

"I tried my best to accept it, Vallie," he said. "I prayed hard over it but I just couldn't feel the call. The salary would have been wonderful, but the people in the church didn't seem to need me. I felt they could get along very well without me. I didn't talk their language. I saw plenty of people whose language I did speak and they looked as though they needed me. I would have liked to work among them. But they were in the street and I don't think St. Martin's would have liked me to spend my time with nonmembers any more than St. Peter's did. Besides, how could I go to these people with the Gospel when I knew my own church wouldn't take them in?"

The boys turned away bitterly. Mamma looked disappointed.

"Did you have your lunch?"

"I didn't want too much," Papa said, which probably meant that he hadn't any. "I knew there'd be plenty to eat at Mrs. DeLong's tonight. But I'd like to stop in at the Harmons' and Bashores' first. Do you mind if I call up Billy Ross and ask if he and his wife can take you? You'll have a fast ride behind his high steppers. Then I can get started right away and make a few calls on the way."

In a clean shirt he tied Pompy to the side of the old, closed, unpainted Harmon shop. He went to the back porch of the little house where young Mrs. Cal Harmon met him at the door.

"He's been saying your name ever since you went off, Reverend," she said.

The preacher took off his rubbers and went in. He felt suddenly refreshed, strong, filled with vitality.

"How are you, Mr. Harmon?" he greeted heartily.

For a little it seemed that the old, very old man lying on the homemade chair in the kitchen was unable to speak. He might have been a long abandoned corpse of skin, bone and hair except for his eyes, very dark and very alive in the deep caverns under his brow. They had fastened on the caller's face. When the voice spoke it was slow and abysmal as if coming out of the ground.

"So you're back, Reverend?" he said.

"Yes, and glad to be in the valley again. It's good to go away and good to get back."

"They tell me you were off in Brooklyn and you're going to move there."

"I don't know who told you that, but I guess there's nothing to it."

The strained look in the eyes relaxed. They warmed and moistened.

"So you're not going to leave us, Reverend?" he said.

The preacher took off his overcoat and seated himself on the chair the woman had pulled up.

"Let's not talk about leaving you, Mr. Harmon," he said. "Let's just say that I'm not leaving you for Brooklyn."

The old man lay silent a while.

"I've been thinking again, Reverend. All the time you were away I've been thinking how the Lord's forsook and forgot me."

"I don't think the Lord ever forgets anyone, Mr. Harmon. Our names are written in the Book of Life and all the hairs of our head are numbered."

"Not mine, Reverend. I know what it says, but it's had a slip-up somewheres. If a page ever had my name, it's been lost. The Lord's forgot I ever lived. For eleven years I been lying on this chair. For eleven years I been praying the Lord to take me. I'm no good here, I tell him. He can see I'm no good, only a burden to younger folks who ought to be doing something better than have to take care of an old wornout soldier like me. But the Lord don't hear me. I'm forgot. It's had a slip-up somewheres."

"It just seems that way to you, Mr. Harmon. No man knoweth the day or the hour when the Lord cometh."

"I know that, Reverend, and I always believed it. But he

wouldn't treat me this way if he remembered. You know I always tried to do what was right. I took my younger brother's draft. He had a wife and babe and I had none them days. I was at Chancellorsville and Antietam. I never dodged my duty so far as I could help it. I took over Pap's shop when I come home and took care of him and Mam while they was living. I never overcharged a man, even one I had no use for. Many's the wagon I made or fixed up and took corn or potatoes for it. The farmers them days didn't have the ready money. I've been a member of the Frame Church since I turned eighteen. For nigh onto seventy-six years my name's been on the church books, but it don't do me no good. I believe it was on too long, Reverend, and that's how I'm forgot."

"The Lord hasn't forgotten you, Mr. Harmon," the preacher countered warmly. "He promised you long life in Exodus. You know the commandment, 'Honor thy father and thy mother that thy days may be long upon the land which the Lord thy God giveth thee.' You took care of them. He's taking care of you now."

"It sounds good when you're young and strong, Reverend. But when you're old and helpless hand and foot, them days can be too long—especially when you can't get up to take care of yourself. Living to seventy might be all right or even eighty. But keeping you alive on a chair till ninety-four just because of a promise made in the Bible a long time ago isn't too much of a favor, Reverend. The Lord wouldn't do that if he come down and seen me as I am. A person can live too long, Reverend. Sooner die young when your name's still on the muster rolls and the Lord remembers to call you home."

"I'll always remember you, Mr. Harmon," Harry Donner said. "And if a poor sinner like me remembers, you can depend on it that the Lord does."

He stayed as long as he could, visiting, telling of people he met in the train, singing two hymns for the old man before he left. Never had he a more reverent or appreciative audience than young Mrs. Cal Harmon standing by the stove and the old man lying on his homemade chair, his dark eyes lighting up at the words of his favorite hymn, "Beulah Land, Sweet Beulah Land." After the prayer the gray cheeks had faint color in them and Harry Donner himself felt lifted that he could be of some service here.

But his spirit fell when he came in sight of the Bashore farm. There was something pitiful about the house, and a set look on Walter Bashore's face as he came out to put up the preacher's horse.

"Just give him a little hay, Walter. I can't stay long. I'm promised at Mrs. DeLong's for supper. She has something going on."

"Well, I'm glad you could stop, anyway," Walter Bashore said. He put off the inevitable subject. "Getting colder."

"Yes, it's about the time for it," the preacher told him.

They talked for a while in the barn, staying away from the small specter in their minds.

"How is he?" Harry Donner had to come to it at last.

Walter Bashore shook his head.

"Doc says it can't be long now. He says it's in the blood and nobody ever gets well from what he's got."

Both men braced themselves when they came out of the barn. Mrs. Bashore was standing without a wrap on the front porch waiting for them. The north wind over Nippenose Mountain blew her skirt and hair. Harry Donner's heartiness, so real and strong at the Harmons', felt slightly forced here. From Mrs. Bashore's face he knew the questions before they were asked. Why? Why must it be an only child like Shelby, a bright mind and a good boy? What had the Lord against a child who wasn't old enough to have done anything bad? She wrung his hand and they went in. The preacher spoke as warm and hearty with life as he could in these melancholy rooms. She motioned him to the stairs and he went up humming with a show of cheerfulness.

The boy in the iron bed in the back room tried to sit up when he saw him at the door.

"Am I going to die, Reverend?" he called out piteously and fell back. The words were to haunt Harry Donner as long as he lived.

It was warm up here, the room heated by a pipe from the kitchen stove. The preacher pulled a chair close to the bed and took the small blue-veined hand.

"No, Shelby," he said. "None of us ever die. On Calvary the Lord said to the man on the cross next to him, 'Today thou shalt be with me in paradise.' "

"But they'll put me in the ground!" the boy cried.

"No." The preacher felt a stubborn rush of something in him. "Life can never be kept in the ground. It always comes out. Every seed rises. It's God's law. All of us are praying for you. I'll pray for you before I go today and I'll pray for you tonight before I go to bed, and I'll pray for you tomorrow morning before I get up. All things are possible to God. The Bible says so. Now let's talk about life and living."

He told again about his trip to Brooklyn, about the trains and trolleys, the big buildings, the crowds of people, the church he preached in, the East River and the ferries and the lights at night. When the boy came piteously back to his fear of the ground, the preacher told how good the ground was, soft and rich to the plow, that it stayed warm in winter and cool in summer, how the whole world depended on it and its fruit.

It was time to go and yet the boy's eyes begged him not to leave him.

"But what if you're punished?" he cried.

The preacher sighed. Here again was the bitter fruit of some of those inexplicable things in the Bible. He sat thinking what he could say.

"When I was a boy," he began, "a little older than you, I lost my penny for Sunday school. All the way to the church

I prayed I'd find it. But I didn't. It shamed me that I'd have nothing for the collection. So I prayed harder. I promised the Lord that if he let me find a whole dollar I'd put it all in the collection. I'd no more than promised that when I saw something lying by a buggy wheel. When I rooted it out of the dirt, it was a silver dollar. Well, now that I had the dollar, I changed my tune. I told myself the dollar must have been there all the time and I'd have found it whether I'd prayed or not. Besides, who ever heard of anybody in my class putting a dollar in the collection? It would make the other boys feel cheap. So I ran down on Back Street where Pappy Haas kept his little store open on Sunday and had the dollar changed. I put a nickel in the collection and kept the rest in my pocket for candy and other things later on."

"Didn't God punish you?" the boy wanted to know.

"No," Harry Donner said quietly. "In fact he was very good to me and later on he called me to be a minister of the Gospel. I sometimes think that dollar had something to do with it. Of course, the rest of it was paid back long ago."

The boy lay back less troubled on his pillow. Harry Donner asked for a Bible and opened it at the Ninety-first Psalm. He had read it aloud when the yellow cat that had been in the kitchen when he arrived came into the bedroom, peered up at the bed appraisingly, then sprang on it and made itself comfortable.

"Did you ever notice, Reverend," Mrs. Bashore said,

"how that cat comes when you read out of the Bible? You'd almost think it could understand."

The phrase "the power of the Word" ran through the preacher's mind but he said nothing, only took a thoughtful and more sympathetic look at the cat before going on to the Twenty-third Psalm.

Mrs. Bashore had long since lighted a lamp. Now she asked that he sing a hymn for Shelby before he went, but he put her off. To an old man like George Washington Harmon it held comfort. To a young boy frightened of death it might be otherwise. He remembered how as a boy he had been depressed by certain hymns long after his sister Bessie's funeral.

It blinded him a little to come a half hour later into the big DeLong farmhouse bright with lights and gay smiling people.

"Where were you, Reverend?" they all reproached him. "You missed the dinner."

"I'm sorry but I couldn't get away," he said simply.

Mrs. DeLong, a big stout woman in lace, and much celebrated for her cooking, gave him a sad look.

"I won't soon forgive you, Reverend," she said. "Dr. Metzgar had to say grace. But I kept something back for you. I hope you haven't had your supper."

"No, Mrs. DeLong," he said. "I saved that for you."

It seemed, he thought, as he went around greeting everyone and later as he sat alone at the white cloth of the great table set with Mrs. DeLong's cherished English china used only on very special occasions, with the candles burning, with lively talk and laughter from parlor and kitchen, with the ladies in silk dresses, with a pair of white gloves lying on the table and a glimpse of Mrs. Metzgar with a gay lacy shawl around her shoulders, that here in this house death, sorrow and suffering had been shut out. But when he put his forehead down to his hand for silent prayer, it all came back to him. For a moment or two he had been able to keep dark things from his mind. Now already they were upon him and he must plead to his Maker against them.

Even after he raised his head and smilingly began to attack the plate piled high with chicken, mashed potatoes, gravy and two or three vegetables, and after he declared how good everything was to Mrs. DeLong, who had served him and now stood by to keep watch over him, he kept seeing the old man and young boy in his mind, one who wanted to die and must live and the other who wanted desperately to live and must die. It was hard to understand these things. He had heard some younger preachers speak as though once you were in the kingdom, an appointed servant of the Most High, all was made clear. It must be that he had only one foot in the kingdom, for despite what he fully believed and tried to perform, the mystery at times seemed only the greater and more inscrutable.

On the drive home Mamma kept talking about Mrs. DeLong's dinner. It had been, she said, one of the nicest parties she had ever attended in the valley. She especially loved the Christmas decorations and favors, but wasn't it a shame poor Dr. Metzgar had to be called out and missed most of the evening? Papa agreed. In reality he hardly heard her. He was thinking how the holidays had always meant to him a jubilant and triumphant season. He had loved the Christmas hymns and carols, abounding as they did in rich and splendid phrases such as "Oh, tidings of comfort and joy" and "Hark the herald angels, sing glory to the newborn king." He had liked nothing better than to take his three sons out on a snowy Christmas Eve and sing joyous words and tunes into the frosty air.

But this Advent the magnificent and exultant troubled him. There seemed to be too much misery in the world for glittering pageants and sumptuous celebration. Preaching about gifts of frankincense and myrrh meant little to poor farmers trying to raise a bit of Christmas money cutting a load of mine prop or lagging from their mountain timber, or to those who in good times drove a horse and buggy to and from woodworking jobs in Wetherill but were out of work today. For the time being God's magnificent heaven lay pretty far away. A mild and humble Saviour stood much closer, one born in a stable, who had been a carpenter and footpath wanderer, who had said, "I am meek and lowly" and "The foxes have holes and the birds of the air have nests but the son of man hath nowhere to lay his head." This Christmas he would devote his prayers and preaching to the lowly Jesus. For the season and an indeterminate time thereafter, the son of man rather than the prince of heaven would be his patron, the man of sorrows his intercessor.

Book · V

THE MOUNTAIN IN THE WEST

CHAPTER SEVENTEEN

Paint Creek

Valeria Donner came up the hill from Paint Creek to Blacksher, a slow, tall, heavy woman at sixty, she who as a young married girl had been so active and slender, climbing trees and running up stairs. But she could take it better now, both the hill and the soft-coal towns at either end. All three had been a struggle when first she came. Wetherill Valley had been so green. In Paint Creek hardly a blade of grass grew.

She had tried not to complain to Hal. Not a word that the two-thousand-foot elevation had shortened her breath, that the pains about her heart were sharper here or that she loathed the perpetual reek in the air.

"It smells like the infernal regions," she wrote Jess. "You can see brimstone burning on every rock dump and all the stones of the streams are painted with sulphur."

She felt most keenly the increased separation from Unionville, from Jess and even from Hal's folks, who almost never came to see them out here. The great mountains between them might have been oceans and she on the other side of the world. Most of those who passed on the street were foreign-born speaking alien tongues, Slavs, Poles, Italians, slight fierce Magyars with great handle-bar mustaches, and Greek Orthodox priests in their heavy fur coats and Russian Astrakhan hats, all breathing out vigorously in the frosty mountain air. The Johnstown trolley reeked of garlic. Somehow she had expected more Irish as in the hard-coal regions at home. The Irish she never considered foreign, having some of the blood herself.

But for Hal, Paint Creek might have been New Jerusalem. He preached with enthusiasm, giving his drab congregation the best of his Wetherill Valley sermons. The open welcome in his face was turned on one and all. His hearty greetings missed no one on the street whether or not English was spoken. His smile could not be misunderstood. He reported to her that Father Sukeena of St. George's and Father Yanulevitch of St. Nicholas's with the onion steeples were "fine fellows." His fervor for life returned. When she called him to dinner he would sing out from upstairs, "I'se a-comin'."

In their thirty years, Mamma thought she had heard such phrases repeated almost too often. But his pleased, almost idiotic grin when he used them was better than a long face, his favorite word "wonderful" better than complaint or gloom. The dinners he had had with parishioners were "wonderful." He magnified "the faithful" at Thirty-two, a Company mine patch where he had started preaching Sunday afternoons, and he did the same to the scenery on his two-mile walk each way. If ever he wished for Pompy and the buggy, he never mentioned it. "Whew!" he would pay tribute to below-zero readings and "My!" to Mr. Jonas's sugar maples standing tapped with kettles in the spring. Wasn't it wonderful to have sugar from your own sugar grove, he declared, although they had had a row of sugar maples untapped and unpraised at their late Manada Hill parsonage.

Yet, she told herself, she could never have lived here or in any other mining town without Hal. He was still mostly boy. "Did I put sugar in this?" he'd puzzle over his cup of coffee. "Dr. Evans doesn't want me to use a whole lump." He would break it in half, putting half in the cup, the other half in his mouth. More than once since here he had absent-mindedly addressed a letter to himself. "What in the world!" he had cried in dismay when it was delivered. He still half expected to find in his mail some notice of a bequest from the stranded old woman to whom as a young man he had given money for a railroad ticket. She had taken down his name to "remember in my will." He had always given his best to women, and yet he could never tell her how one of them was dressed. "Oh, something green or blue, I can't remember which," he'd say.

Mamma halted to rest her legs by the railroad, the border between the two counties. At first it had been something to write Jess about, the church in Cambria County and the parsonage in Somerset. It wasn't much of a parsonage, just half of a double house, scarcely larger than a miner's house, but if Hal could manage, she could. She mustn't forget their blessings. Johnny had found a job on one of the Johnstown papers, and Gene paid board at home out of his wages on a mine surveying crew. They still had friends back east. Their Christmas cards from Wetherill Valley and Mahanoy, many of them postcards with holiday tinsel, made a high heart-warming pile. Hal's congregation had given him a handsome purse and the minister's wife a real fur piece. Christmas Eve the Welsh choir from Blacksher had serenaded the parsonage. Hal had gone out to join in the carols and bring the singers in for a treat. Mr. Thomas, the leader, told her that Cambria was the ancient name of Wales, the land of the Cimbri or Cymry, and that if she visited Ebensburg, the county seat, she could hear Welsh spoken on the street. He invited her to come and see his wife when he would show her and the Reverend an open Welsh coal fire burning in the front room.

That was very nice. But, oh, there was still something lonely and foreboding here, something she had never felt at Mahanoy, something depressing as the narrow bituminous veins where the miners had to crawl on their hands and knees. Hal himself must have felt it at first. Weeks afterward Tim had told her what his father had said to him when they first came. It was in Rob Wagner's house, where they stayed until they could rent a house for the parsonage.

"Don't tell Mamma," Papa had groaned. "But I have the blues."

If he still had them at any time, Mamma thought, he concealed them well enough. She herself had grown resigned to the place, but never would it be home.

CHAPTER EIGHTEEN

I, the Sinner

The preacher felt confounded when he first heard it. He was up in Blacksher making a pastoral call on Swedish Lutherans. He hadn't been there long when Billy Potts, out of breath, was at the door.

"They want you in Paint," he said. "Jake Schneck's killing everybody."

"Who's everybody, Billy?" the preacher asked.

"Well, he shot Tom Staller. Maybe more till you get there."

"You must be mistaken, Billy," the preacher said.

"No, Reverend. Steve Kushko sent for the state police, and Lily Maddis told me to get you. Your missus told me where you were."

"Well, I'll come right away," the preacher said but he still couldn't believe it.

All the way down the hill he declared the presence of God against Billy's babbling. Oh, he knew that "in the midst of life we are in death" and that "as for man, his days are as grass." But Tom Staller was Jake's best friend, his crony. Furthermore Jake was a mild man especially fond of children and babies. Only last week the preacher had seen him, fresh from the mines, coming down Back Street, a short stocky, almost fat Dutchman waddling a little as he walked, his tin dinner bucket in his hand, stopping at every porch in his block that had young life on it. You might think a child would scare at a heavy face black with coal dirt, white of eyes and broadly pink of lip, but Paint Creek babies were used to black faces. Also, Jake had a way with the very young that no one who didn't understand that side of a Dutchman would suspect. They grinned back at his pantomimes and gurgled at his roughhousing. And now he was supposed to have done murder to his best friend. Harry Donner couldn't believe it.

But something must have happened to excite and terrify the boy. When they got to Paint Creek, people out on their front porches and talking in groups told him the worst. When he turned down Back Street he could see everyone in the street except in front of Jake's house, where it was conspicuously vacant.

"Watch out, Reverend!" the women called as he went by, and he felt suddenly and strangely exposed as he crossed the naked spot in front of Jake Schneck's house.

Steve Kushko, the constable, and half a dozen others were waiting just inside Jake's door. Jake's daughter, Lily Maddis, threw herself on him and poured out a wild stream, only half of which her pastor comprehended or gave credence to. He knew that ever since the Schneck girls had married, there had been trouble in this house. Jake had finally moved up on the garret where he had his bed, "like when I was a boy at the tipple," he told the preacher. Today the mines hadn't worked, at least not Thirty-four and Number Nine. The family was at home together, and that was its great misfortune.

"He fought with Lute and Wilmer all morning," Lily told him. "Then he said he was going up to his 'room' and none of us would ever see him again."

"Lil tried to go up and talk him out of it," Stella cried. "He told her he'd kill anybody who laid foot on the garret stairs."

"So we got Tom to come and talk to him," Lily went on. "If anybody could do anything with him we thought it would be Tom. He told Tom the same as he told me, what he'd do. But Tom never thought it meant him. They were always such buddies. He kept going up, pleading with Pop to put his gun away, and Pop killed him." She said it hysterically, covering her face with her hands.

"We heard another shot," Stella said. "We thought he'd killed himself. But when Steve started up, Pop called he wasn't dead yet and would kill the first person on the garret stairs."

Harry Donner groaned to himself. The Lord's words

came to him, "Oh, faithless and perverse generation, how long shall I suffer you?" He made a move for the stairs but they rushed in front and held him back.

"He'd kill you, too, Reverend!" they cried.

"Don't worry that I should ever tempt him or any other man, God willing. I just want to get his leave to look at Tom and see if he's still alive so we can get a doctor."

"Tom's laying on the garret landing, Reverend," Steve told him. "I couldn't see that he moved a finger after Jake blasted him. I wouldn't give him the chance to do that to you."

The preacher shook them off. It felt strangely quiet now in the house, almost peaceful upstairs. Here he was close to both murder and murderer, yet it seemed like a dream, an illusion, something that couldn't be. He had noticed this sense in him before, an inability to credit evil. The upstairs hall was like a box. An overwhelming sense of pity came over him for the three men and two women who had tried to live together in this tiny house. There was really no garret stair landing, only a spread where the steps turned. He could see Tom Staller's poor head and arms hanging down over the steps and the garret door open beyond.

"Who's that?" a terrible voice called.

"It's me, Reverend Donner, Jake," the preacher said.

"Did they tell you what I said I'd do to any man who tried to set foot on these stairs?"

"Yes, they told me what you said. And that's where you committed your great sin, Jake."

"Sin, Reverend!" he shouted. "It's them. They're the ones who done it. They drove me up here in my own house, holed me up like a rabbit in a stone pile. Then they made me get my gun in self-defense."

"Your greatest sin, Jake, was not with your gun but with your mouth."

The unseen man seemed startled, was still for a moment thinking that over.

"My mouth did no sin, Reverend. It only warned them what they'd make me do. If they'd had sense, they'd a listened."

"You know what Scripture tells us—that the tongue, not the hand, is the most dangerous member? James called the tongue 'a fire and a world of iniquity, that it defileth the whole body and setteth on fire the course of nature.' "

"I didn't defile anybody, Reverend. They defiled me. They've been defiling me ever since they moved in under my roof."

"You did worse, Jake," the preacher said relentlessly. "Don't you know your own flesh—how stubborn and willful it can be? Once you say something, the flesh says you must keep it. No matter the consequence. You knew this and yet you let your anger make the vow that you'd kill anyone who came up these garret steps. Once you said it, you were done for. That was your mortal sin."

"It was theirs for trying to come up, Reverend!" he shouted. "They know I never broke my word."

"There are plenty of times when it should be broken, Jake. Yours and mine, too. In heathen times the king Agamemnon vowed to sacrifice the most beautiful thing in his possession, which turned out to be his daughter Iphigenia. But Diana released him. She snatched Iphigenia away and put a stag in her place. And our own God sent an angel to release Abraham before he sacrificed Isaac. God would have released you, too, from your vow if you'd have got down on your knees and asked him before you took the life of your friend, Tom Staller."

An awful cry of reproach rose from the garret.

"Why didn't you tell me this before, Reverend?"

Yes, why hadn't he? the preacher groaned to himself. Oh, he could muster excuse and self-defense. Why hadn't Jake sent for him? Jake was like those parishioners who sent for the doctor but expected their preacher to come without word or call. But this was no time for self-justification. It hit too close to home. How could he forget his own willful tearing up of roots in Wetherill Valley, the sad resignation in Mamma's face, the hurt eyes of those he deserted? He had put on a great show of enthusiasm out here, had thrown himself with zeal into his work, but he would have given a great deal had he stayed and endured. After all, there had been only one thorn in his flesh in Wetherill Valley, not a whole crown of them as his Lord had borne.

"Yes, why didn't I, Jake?" he confessed. "Perhaps because I am guilty as you."

"You, Reverend?" in astonishment.

"It's true, Jake," he went on bitterly. "I lost my temper like you. This was in another charge. I vowed in my sermon I'd leave. I'd rather have stayed. I wanted to stay and there were many who needed me. But I'd given my word. God would have released me if I'd have asked. I shouldn't have cared what anybody thought. But I was vain and proud of my word in front of other people, like you were, Jake."

There was a long silence from the garret broken by sounds of hard breathing.

"Do you want to come up now, Reverend? I got to get to the outhouse. And if any son of a bitch tries to stop me—"

"Nobody will try to stop us, Jake," the preacher reproved him and started up the stairs.

He knelt first by Tom Staller, put his hand to his shirt searching for a heartbeat. With a little moaned prayer he lifted the heavy body down to the hall floor. Then sighing, he climbed through the garret door and sighed no more. He had seen hard sights before, miners crushed by a fall of rock, a child fallen into the thresher and the pitiful eyes of the dying begging for just a spoonful of life. But he was unprepared for this, a man he didn't know, just the carcass of a man sitting on the garret floor, his back against the iron bed, a gun in his thick hand, and blood and flesh all over him, soaking the bed behind him, blackening his shirt and pants, standing in pools on the floor. Part of his head had been shot away.

Now he struggled to get to his feet as the preacher appeared.

"Sit still, Jake. You can't go down this way," he told him.

"The hell I can't, Reverend."

"Wait, I'll get you a bucket."

"No," Jake insisted stubbornly. "I can take care of myself once I get there."

"There's a crowd down there, Jake."

"Are you helping me down, Reverend, or do I go myself?"

"I'll help you then, Jake," the preacher promised. "But you'll have to leave your gun up here. And you'll have to do something for the Lord."

"What's that?"

"Contain yourself to your girls and sons-in-law and everybody else. No matter what they say to you. Hold your tongue even if they crucify you. You failed to do that before. Now show the Lord you can do it."

Jake's blue eyes grew stormy and profane but he let Harry Donner take the gun and pull him to his feet. The man would never make it, the preacher told himself. It was a rank impossibility. Afterward he hardly remembered how he got him down the stairs, only the trail of blood behind them, the bloody smears on wallpaper and doorjambs, the horrified faces that watched them, first in the house, then from neighboring backyards as they went down the boardwalk. All the way the preacher could feel a terrible seething in the human wreck he half supported, half carried.

"Go way!" Harry Donner told them sternly in the backyard. "Leave this dying man in peace." But they hung about like flies on flypaper, closing in on the outhouse as they entered.

The rest he tried to forget. He almost wished these foolish people could have been crowded in there with him, to know the depths of degradation to which their unruly tongues could drag them, to taste to the fullest their own capacity for depravity and wickedness.

When the preacher came out alone, Al Weaver told him afterward, he looked like a bloody corpse himself.

"Is it safe to go in after him?" Steve Kushko asked, suddenly taken with his duty.

"It's safe," the preacher told him. "You won't need the state police. Tell the girls he said he wanted French's," naming one of the two undertakers in Blacksher.

CHAPTER NINETEEN

Harry Donner's Heathen

The preacher seldom gave a thought to his age. But last week he had had a birthday. Let's see, how old was he anyway? Sixty-four or -five. He had been born two years after Mamma. Why, that made him sixty-six! Well, it didn't matter. He might have a few more pounds to carry up in the pulpit but he could still get around. He remembered where as a middler in the seminary he had walked on his thirty-eighth birthday. He had to preach at a schoolhouse across the river. It meant tramping the mile-long railroad bridge, then more miles up a succession of hills. The schoolhouse stood on the very top, and when he climbed the last ridge with the sun setting in the golden river, he had sung half aloud, half to himself, the hymn ever afterward associated with the time and place.

The streets, I am told
Are paved with pure gold.
And the sun, it will never go down.

He hadn't taken much notice of birthdays after that, except those of his mother. They had been born almost on the same day. Of late years he liked to take the Sunday nearest her anniversary to preach on Motherhood. The sermons were all different, or so he thought, except, of course, some of the familiar phrases such as "Of all the names in the world, the sweetest name is Mother." When he brought in incidents about her, he often had to wipe his eyes. The boys used to criticize these sermons. They said he was too personal and sentimental. He couldn't agree and wouldn't change a line. He felt that what he wanted to say was a kind of public testimony to the small dark Welsh woman he could no longer say it to in person.

This year he had thought his "discourse" a little better than usual and had taken a pencil-written manuscript to the Blacksher *Era*. He didn't know if it would be reprinted or not, and a pleasant feeling ran over him as he opened the paper and saw the whole sermon in type. But he was startled to find that the paper called him "the elderly preacher."

The phrase shook him and kept coming back to his mind. It carried disturbing meanings. Why, his work had hardly begun, and now they hinted that it was nearing its end. What had he done with his life anyway? The Lord had said, "Go ye into all the world and preach the gospel to every living creature." So far he had gone into little more than four or five places to preach; Bairdsville, Mahanoy, Lost Run, Wetherill Valley and Paint Creek. The Lord had said,

"Work for the night is coming when no man worketh," and now the *Era* hinted that the dark cycle referred to was close at hand. He had always hoped to do something worth while for the Lord, something more than the small white church he had built at Lost Run or the brick one he had finished at Manada Hill, some holy shrine he could dedicate to St. John, a church of size and substance like Claude Mersey's in Brooklyn or the cathedral in Philadelphia he had once entered with awe. Had he started too late and was this now, so far as he was concerned, never to be?

Perhaps, he thought, he could still do it if the Lord gave him more time for bigger things. So many little daily duties came up, like the obligation put on him by Ralph Mace, a miner at Thirty-four and not even a member of his church. He said he wished the Reverend could go and see his mother. She was old and failing and had told her son she hadn't tasted the Lord's bread or wine in thirty years.

"I'll certainly visit her and give her communion if she wants," the preacher had promised. "Where can I find her?"

"Chadd's Cove. They ain't had a Lutheran preacher in there since she came over the mountain."

Harry Donner had heard only dimly of Chadd's Cove.

"I'll do what I can," he said and set down her name in his little black book so it wouldn't escape him as names of late were prone to do.

Next time he talked to Claude Barefoot, he told about the poor woman, hoping his councilman would offer to take him in his automobile, the only "machine" in his church. Indeed there were but three in Paint Creek and very few more in Blacksher. But the hardware dealer discouraged him. No fit road existed over the mountain to Chadd's Cove. The only decent road ran from the other end of the cove, and you had to go nearly to Bedford to get on it. Besides, the Cove had a bad name. Cove people, he said, were a poor lot who had come in early and killed off the Indians. When there were no more Indians to fight, they had fought among themselves. There had been three murders in his time and none of the men, so far as he knew, had ever been brought to justice.

"They marry cousins and stepsisters, so they're all related," Claude said. "If it had coal in there, they might have got civilized. As it is, they're still heathen. If you went in, Reverend, you might never get out."

The preacher's heart leaped at the words, exaggerated as he felt they must be. He thought how Peter and Paul had gone into dangerous places among the heathen.

"I'll have to walk it then," he said heartily.

"It's too far, Reverend," the hardware dealer protested. "I could take you to the top of the mountain and you could walk down if you wanted to, but it has no telephone in the Cove. How could you get back?"

"If the Lord takes me down, he'll bring me back, Claude," the preacher said cheerfully. "I'll be a thousandfold obliged to you for taking me part way."

It looked like rain when he left but nothing could stop him

on his missionary journey. He told Mamma not to worry if he didn't get back that night. He had cautioned Claude to say nothing adverse about Chadd's Cove to Mamma or to anyone who might tell her. Gloomily the hardware dealer drove him over the forested Allegheny plateau to a lesser road which he followed to the juncture of what looked like an abandoned logging road.

"You know the kind of place it is down there, Reverend, when they don't even have a road sign," he said. With his passenger out of the car, the driver seemed unwilling to go. "I hope I don't get in trouble for leaving you way out here, Reverend." He backed around slowly, stopped again, then drove regretfully away.

Once all sight and sound of his friend and car had vanished, the lonely remoteness of the place came over Harry Donner. He tramped on with energy but the only sign of life was what he thought at first an ax chopping in the deep woods but which presently grew far away, leaving the listener with a strange feeling of having heard a ghost or some giant woodpecker of the woods. Although midmorning, it had grown darker now, especially under the pines. He came to a fork in the narrow road and afterward felt unsure whether he had chosen the right branch. Reaching in his pocket to see if he had set down directions, his small red Testament gave his hand a feeling of protection, his Ministerial Acts a sense of anointment in the wilderness, feelings that had never come to him so strong in town or along the familiar roads of Broad Mountain. Had the Gospel, he wondered, grown richer and stronger also to Paul in dangerous places? The phrase "shield and buckler," so familiar in the Old Testament, suddenly grew clear. He went on feeling calmer. Soon afterward the road began to descend, at first moderately, then steeply over imbedded granite boulders that would have been impassable to Claude Barefoot's "machine" and difficult for a wagon. Almost at once he rounded a bald knob and saw far below him a narrow valley with green fields and unpainted buildings, some of them with blue smoke rising from clay chimneys.

He told himself he had never come upon any sight more welcome. The sounds of barking dogs and of a bawling cow rising from the depths sounded sweet to his ear. He could hear shouts of men calling to each other from a great distance, perhaps from mountain to mountain. There was something wild and primitive in the deep halloos, and he sobered a little at the sound, then brightened happily. These were truly the heathen the Lord had given him.

His reception at the first house confirmed his notion. At the sight of him boys dove into the nearest bushes refusing to come out. Dogs barked savagely while a man and woman watching from the door remained closemouthed to his greeting and questions. After all, he reminded himself happily, he hadn't been bitten, and he went on to a plank bridge sunken in the center where an old man listened to him with half-averted face, finally asking which Mace he wanted. It seemed that most of the people of Chadd's Cove had the family name of Mace, and when the visitor did find the right house, a plastered log cabin hanging to the side of the hill, it took patience and persistence to get in. All through his visit the old woman appeared suspicious of him and the bread and wine he had brought in his pocket. He told Mamma afterward that he had never given communion where it had "gone so uphill." Noon passed and she did not ask him to dinner or get anything for herself. Perhaps she had only a mite in the house, he concluded, and unfortunately he was not Elisha to multiply it. In the end, tired, his missionary enthusiasm thinned to a trickle, he said a fervent prayer for her and left for the long tramp home.

It had started to rain and before he came again to the sunken bridge he stopped for shelter at a two-story log house near the road. Two hounds grew absolutely frenzied as he opened the gate and knocked on the door. A preternaturally lean man whose bony face gave evidence of inbreeding came out and kicked the dogs into the road. Then he turned to the stranger in sharp silence.

"A fine rain!" the preacher said, beaming, and stepped into the house. He glimpsed a woman and three half-grown girls in the doorway to the kitchen, greeting them with warmth and pleasure.

Dark red streaked his host's face as if the caller had

broken some unwritten law, making advances toward his women.

"Where'd you come from?" he wanted to know.

"Paint Creek," the preacher answered benevolently. "I really live in Blacksher but my charge is in Paint Creek."

"You looking for coal?" Evidently the word "charge" meant nothing to him.

"Coal? No indeed. I came to give communion to one of your neighbors."

"Communion? What's that?" The Cove man looked suspicious.

"Communion?" A feeling of mixed pity and joy ran through Harry Donner, pity for ignorance of the sacred sacrament in this day and age, and joy that he had been led to this door. "It's administering the body and blood of our Lord, given for the remission of sins," he explained.

The man and four womenfolk stared back uncomprehendingly.

"What do you follow for a living?"

"I'm a preacher of the Gospel."

The man looked at his womenfolk and back to his visitor. "What do you do regular?"

"I do that regularly," Harry Donner assured him. "Sundays and weekdays, year in and year out."

His host digested this.

"Kin you preach any place or must you have a church to preach in?"

"Oh, anywhere," he said. "In a church. In a schoolhouse. In the open air. I've even preached in a barn."

"They was a preacher come in here six or eight years back, but he worked at farming and just did it on the side. Could you preach in my house?"

"I don't see why not," Harry Donner said. It came to him that he might base his discourse on Man's Hunger for God, first bringing in by way of illustration the hunger of man for material things like food. It might produce something for the inner man before setting back over the mountain.

"Wait a minute. My woman wants to say something." The man crossed the room and conferred with her at the kitchen door. "She says she'd like Al and Fay to hear your preaching. That's her folks. She says maybe we could give you a bed tonight and you could do your preaching this evening."

"I'd be glad to," Harry Donner said, pleased, also aware that his heathen had suddenly been watered down, that he was not now to be honored with persecution and hardship, let alone imprisoned like Peter and Paul. He needed time to think this over to decide whether he had been blessed or whether love and its chastening had passed him by.

But once the girls of the house had made up to him and smiled shyly as they went in and out, he was content. And when the fragrance of frying potatoes and ham began drifting through the house he felt the invisible wreaths of grace about him. They all sat up to the kitchen table with a huge round loaf of bread together with a coffeepot, almost as large, at the wife's hand. The host passed the platter of ham to the guest first.

Harry Donner set it down without taking any.

"Shall we pray?" he asked, smiling around the table his pre-supplication smile, full of good will and yet touched with a certain mysticism as if the inner part of him had already withdrawn and engaged in devotions with the Unseen. He put his elbow to the table, his forehead to his hand, sighed deeply and went into one of his most fervent and unstinted table prayers, giving thanks first for old Mrs. Mace, whose spiritual need had drawn him to the Cove, for the son who had invoked it, for himself that he had been led by God's hand to seek shelter at this "goodly" house, for his welcome by the host and his "good wife" and by "the sightly daughters growing up like Ruth among the corn" and finally for "all the manifold blessings" not the least of which were "these gifts prepared by kind hands." When he finished and came back to reality he was conscious of those around the table looking at each other and then at him in a kind of hush and bewilderment as if a bearer of gifts in the guise of a poor missionary had come to sit down and break bread with them in their house. That night when he lay on his straw tick, he gave thanks for a noteworthy day. This, he mused, was the pure and primitive reception the early Christian propagators of the faith must have found. It was among those living in ignorance of God's word, he reflected, that the most honest and childlike response came. This entire family, like the household of Stephanas, had become candidates for baptism in the Lord. Only the hounds remained heathen, unwon by his preaching, still growling a little when he stepped out of the house.

He was on his way up the mountain next morning rejoicing in sunshine after the rain when someone on horseback overtook him, a short burly man with an unshaven face.

"Good morning. A wonderful morning," Harry Donner greeted cheerfully and stood aside to let him by, but the rider had stopped threateningly.

"You the preacher that said things about me last night?"

"About you, my friend? Not that I recall."

"Don't you go lying to me! They say you blackened and tarnished me and my woman's good name. Didn't you say stuff about Dave and Sheba last night?"

"Why, yes, that's right. I think I did mention David and Bathsheba."

"You just said Bathsheba to cover over. Everybody knows you meant my woman, Sheba. You claimed we lived in sin. You told it in front of everybody. It's all over the Cove. Nobody can talk like that about my woman and not get beat up." He got down from the saddle.

The preacher kept a straight face.

"I think there's been a mistake, Mr.—"

"My name's Dave Mace."

"I'm afraid it's a case of mistaken identity, Mr. Mace.

The man and woman I referred to lived two thousand years ago on the other side of the world, in Palestine. They had nothing to do with you and your good wife."

"You said our names."

"It happens that you have the same names, at least in part. But I'm sure you and your good wife haven't been living in sin."

"No, we just ain't got down to Bedford to get married yet."

The preacher nodded gravely as though it was the most natural thing in the world.

"Well, that's easily remedied. Any time you decide on holy matrimony, I'll read the marriage service over you and pronounce you man and wife!"

"How much would it cost?" distrustfully.

"Whatever you choose to give. Nothing at all if you can't afford it."

"I don't want any cheap, piddling, second-rate marrying!" Dave Mace declared.

"No, of course not. It would be a complete, orthodox, religious ceremony."

"It would! When could you do it?"

"Whenever I get to Chadd's Cove again."

"And it won't cost nothing?"

"Not so far as I'm concerned. There's a state law that requires a marriage license. You'd have to go to the courthouse to get it. It will cost you a dollar."

The man's face fell.

"You mean I got to pay to get married to my own woman? That's agin my principles."

The preacher studied the heavy face for a moment.

"It's not against mine," he said. "Have you any children?"

"Three, and one on the way."

"Well, I'd like to see them and your wife have the status and rights of wedlock. You know what David, the man you were named after, said, 'Thy wife shall be as a fruitful vine by the sides of thy house; thy children like olive plants around thy table.' You owe them the dignity and protection of lawful marriage."

He took out a thin pocketbook and from it a thinner paper dollar. He went on.

"But you'll have to go down to Bedford and get the license yourselves. You and your wife. You might do that the first chance you get so I can tie the knot next time I come over."

The Cove man looked a bit dazed as he took the bill. He roused suddenly.

"Git up in the saddle, preacher. My nag'll pack ye up the mountain!"

All the way to Blacksher Harry Donner felt warmed by a certain overdue recompense. His failure long ago to persuade Dan and Dolly Singer to the authority of church and state had at last promised to be compensated for. He came home tired but glowing. For nearly an hour he sat at the kitchen table telling Mamma about Chadd's Cove. His face shone. He had new work, his life a new lease. It was a great privilege, he told her, to minister to those deprived of the Gospel. He could forget now that the *Era* had called him "the elderly preacher." His long tramp over the mountain had repudiated it. But Mamma said she wished the boys were still at home so one of them could go along with him when he walked so far.

He found himself talking now of Cove people more than his regular charge at Paint Creek. A sense of urgency seemed to possess him, as if he hadn't much time. He had four marriages the first several months and ran out of baptismal certificates so that he had to take the trolley to Johnstown for more. What helped him, he told Mamma, was the snake that had stuck its head out of the log wall in the schoolhouse. It was during his sermon on the text "And the seed of the woman shall bruise the serpent's brow." A long mountaineer had stood up and crushed it with the stove raker. It was a cool day and the preacher believed the fire and warmth had drawn the snake out, but Chadd's Cove people said, "Your sarment done it, Reverend." They never tired of reciting the text or of retelling the story. It gave him a reputation far and wide in the mountains.

Before the year was out he had formed a Cove church council. The men, he told Mamma, had already begun to fell timber for a church home. Fine men, wonderful men, he told her. She was never to see the church of Chadd's Cove, except through Hal's eyes, in which Cove, church and people shone with an aura of goodness and splendor. It was a little shock when two rough, seedy and almost degenerate-looking men who said they were from Chadd's Cove, stopped to ask for Hal and to have dinner with them at the parsonage, and a greater disappointment later to hold in her hand a snapshot of the rude log building, not quite plumb, something like a sprawling schoolhouse in the wilderness, with its rough belfry and the bell that Hal had begged from a Somerset County farmer's summer kitchen.

But you would have never known its limitations from Hal. He went about with fervor and enthusiasm. He persuaded Dr. Madenford of Trinity in Johnstown to preach the dedicatory sermon, and Claude Barefoot to drive them some sixty miles around by Bedford and Kerry Mills. Before Easter he dug into his own pocket for some of the Cove mothers to buy goods for their own and their girls' confirmation dresses. It was a day of the Lord's bounty, he told Mamma. Some folks he had never seen before came down out of the hills to Easter services on the Sunday after Easter. Old Wilmot Mace, who they said had murdered a cousin, was on a back bench. The young folks had brought in armfuls of shad branches from the mountain. The pulpit was a mass of starry white blossoms.

The church grew warm and a bumblebee came from somewhere out of the logs and crawled over the white cloth and plate of bread. Jim Mace carried it out in his hand. He said it was white-headed and couldn't sting. During communion, Tod Mace's little girl followed him up to the altar. Her father threatened her if she didn't go back.

"Let her stay, Tod," the preacher said. "The Lord expressly suffered such as her not to be turned away."

Tod didn't like it but let her squeeze between him and his wife at the peeled pine-pole altar. When the bread was passed, the preacher gave her a piece, which the child chewed gravely and with as much sense seemingly as her elders. Later he gave her the goblet of wine, taking care that she didn't more than touch it with her lips. It was a wonderful service, he told Mamma. Only the singing left something to be desired. They had no organ as yet and Cove people weren't familiar with Lutheran hymns and tunes. He himself sang as strong as he could but he kept wishing for a good woman's voice to lead them. Several had told him of Emily Mace, who both played the organ and sang—like a bird, they said. Her father, Mahlon Mace, kept store at the lower end of the valley.

"You could hear her clean across the Cove," they said. "But she ran off with a Raystown Branch man Mahlon had no use for and forbid her to see. So he cut her out of his will and he told her never to cross his doorsill again. She won't get nothing out of him when he dies."

The preacher tried to talk the matter over with Mahlon, but Emily's "disloyalty" was one thing the storekeeper wouldn't talk about. Outside of that, Harry Donner told Mamma, summer in the Cove had glorified God and gladdened the heart of man. Farmers plowed up "extry" land, including some new ground, to give its fruit to the church, and the Lord did his part, bringing heat and rain at just the right season to fill out the grain. Harry Donner did have what he called "a spell in his leg." It came on him climbing back over the mountain in August. Dr. Evans called it a slight stroke but told Mamma not to tell him. It left in time for Harvest Home services. This was the service Cove men took to more than any other church day of the year. They filled up everything behind the altar rail with corn shocks and pumpkins, red apples and rusty pears, sheaves of wheat, oats and buckwheat. They especially brought the longest ears of corn they could find in the field and fixed them hanging down with their husks shucked back. The preacher could hardly make his way up in the pulpit. He told Mamma he felt like St. Francis in the bush preaching to the birds. All that fall he brought home the fruit of Cove men's rifles, bloody furred rabbits, limp squirrels and a wild turkey hen with a copper sheen.

The day after Christmas, Mahlon Mace died in front of his store lifting a hogshead of molasses off the wagon. Cove folks said his death was a Christmas present to his boy, Sam, who would take over the store, and to his girl, Ruby, who with her husband would get the farm. His other girl, Emily, came on horseback, taking a short cut over Maunders Ridge to the funeral, for her father couldn't keep her out of the house now. She said she just had time, when she heard it, to make the burying.

"A fine-looking woman," Papa told Mamma later. All through the funeral service in the house she sat without a tear alongside her brother and sister inheritors, and everybody watching to see how she'd take it. She walked along with the family to the graveyard and came back to hear the will read although she must have known what the words would say. This was what Harry Donner hated most, for the preacher had to read it. Others told him afterward she never flickered an eye when he came to the part disinheriting her and pouring out old Mahlon's bitterness for what she had done.

When he finished, the preacher wanted to tell her how he had tried but failed to soften her father, but she gave him no chance. Rising, she startled them by going to the old parlor organ and seating herself on the stool. Her strong feet worked the pedals while her chapped hands lay on the keys she used to know. Then in a pure clear voice strong with feeling she started singing an old song, accompanying herself as she went.

Mid pleasures and palaces
Though we might roam,
Be it ever so humble
There's no place like home.

A charm from the skies
Seems to hallow it there
Which, seek through the world,
Is not met with elsewhere.
Home, Home. Home, sweet home.
There's no place like home.
There's no place like home.

She sang one verse and chorus. Then she got up and left. Harry Donner called after her but she got on her horse and rode off the way she had come, with snow flurries in the dark woods and with the darker mountain and sky overhead. He was never actually to see her again but often on the road to and from the Cove he kept hearing in his mind her rich untrained voice and seeing her still down there somewhere in the deep mountain gulf going back empty-handed to her house and children.

CHAPTER TWENTY

Woman of Kronos

Valeria Donner lay, a long, gaunt, gentle body in her bed. Through the open window she could see smoke rising from Thirty-four across the valley. Sometimes she thought she heard the loaded mine wagons rumbling out of the drift and the faint thunder of unloaded coal at the tipple. Hal was over there this afternoon marrying a Slovak couple in the patch.

The preacher's wife doubted she would ever see Thirty-four at close hand again. If she hadn't known it, the way Mrs. Petchullis acted would have told her. Every now and then she came to see if the sick woman was all right. The latter would hear her feet on the stairs like those of a belated husband tiptoeing up at night, then see her round foreign face at the doorjamb.

"I come in case you want anything," she would say defensively but it didn't explain the fearful expectancy in her eyes.

Oh, why did they go to so much trouble trying to conceal the truth from her? Hal did it better than Mrs. Petchullis and Dr. Evans better than Hal. He was such a nice, fastidious little Welshman who explained how the half dozen kinds of pills and bitter liquids he left with her would make her a new woman. He and she used to joke about how young and beautiful she would be then, although both knew very well in their hearts it could never be. Valeria Donner didn't so much mind dying. She had lived longer now than she had ever expected. Also, when you've been a lively girl mentally and physically, loving social life, able to dance and walk for miles and then gradually have your license in life and activity curtailed until a monotonous weariness takes over, the approaching end seems a welcome and even considerate eventuality. She marveled a little how something, so fearful and unthinkable to her as a girl and as a young mother with three small boys to raise, could finally to an old, weak and defenseless woman seem harmless and mild.

What troubled her most wasn't her passing but spending her last precious drops of life so far from home and family among alien folk in an alien land. There were always people in Hal's charges she loved. But as a whole, his chosen people were not hers, especially out here. She agreed that heaven was made for them as much and perhaps more than for those with the sin of discrimination, but she couldn't help that she had grown up familiar to a different order, not so much the rank and file of her father's congregation as some other families of town, Lutheran, Methodist and Reformed, that her people moved with or were related to by distant blood or marriage.

Nearly all were dead now but still alive in her mind—Colonel Nuttal, who used to play dominoes with her as a girl of twelve and tell how he had wanted to marry her mother—General Acgrigg, who built the railroad to bring down coal to the canal from the collieries—the Ammons, Major and Squire, who were Uncle Gus and Uncle Ed, and their wives Aunt Doty and Aunt Mary although the relationship was difficult to explain—and the Markles, who like the Ammons had "libraries" with red leather chairs and couch: Dan's, where you were warned not to go without a companion, Lib's, where you could safely go alone, and Max's, whose girls, Sade and Annie, had such gorgeous voices. She had tried to be one with Hal's church people, his "salt of the earth," the rough and kindly who loved his sayings and Christmas jingles. But she felt in her heart that she had really never been accepted or successful. She had found, if she hadn't known it before, that the humble orders have their own exclusions and discrimination.

Secretly at times she thought how comforting it would be to die in Johnny and Henrietta's house on their place back near the Susquehanna, or in Gene and Ellen's hospitable brick house in the suburbs of Reading, or in Timmy and Anne's white clapboard house in the large college town where Anne was active in her alumni. But she didn't want to be any trouble. Out here she could manage to depart just as surely. Death was no respecter of places. Thank goodness that Hal was used to people dying and their funerals.

She consoled herself that it would be harder on the boys. She had thanked the Lord all her life that she had good boys. None of them had given her trouble. Or if they had, they made up for it now. Gene and Tim had positions with great corporations whose company names she loved to pronounce to anyone who inquired. And perhaps Johnny would make a name for himself yet. She had saved in her upper bureau drawer most everything he had ever had printed and in her Bible worn newspaper clippings about him. She often said that she was proud of her three boys. Church people came to Hal with their troubles, but her three boys had always come to her. The last years it had been hard to live so far away. It would be harder still to leave them. She had once wished her third son had been a daughter. Wasn't it sad now when she had three daughters and as many grandchildren that she would have to go away?

Of course, it would be hard to leave Hal, too. But there was a difference. Aunt Teresa used to say that blood was thicker than water. She wished she might have been a better pastor's wife. As a young woman, children would sit endlessly listening to her made-up stories, but she hadn't the Christian charity of Hal. He would walk ten miles to please a child or old woman, slave for hours with no pay or recompense but a smile. Jess liked to tell of the time when Polly had seen a quarter moon for the first time.

"Oh, Mamma, the moon is broke!" she cried. "But Uncle Hal'll fix it."

Aunt Doty had another story. She claimed a miner's wife from Lost Run had bought a pocketbook in the store with her last dollar. Hal had made the sale and then given the dollar back to the woman.

"Now you'll have something to put in it," he told her.

During the strike he had been unable to say no to starving miners who left him with thousands in unpaid debts so that when he left the store business he could barely get out even. Without her father's inheritance he could never have gone to college and seminary.

Oh, Hal was a good man. But the wives of good men, she had found, had their trials. It seemed to her that goodness on occasion escaped from itself and became improvidence. She hoped that as a minister's wife she wasn't past praying for, but she hadn't the pious immolation to follow the Lord's injunction, "Give all thy goods to the poor and follow me." It was too hard a command especially when Hal more than once did just that to a needy and sometimes profligate soul at a time when they had little or nothing in the house. Her spirit was willing but the flesh weak. She still felt shock and rebellion that he, who should have been a beneficiary, would head a church drive for money with an enthusiastic subscription of twenty-five dollars, a staggering sum to her. Where would so much money come from? In the end she would manage to scrimp and save it, and they never starved, though she often sighed when Hal, as he was forever doing, brought people home for dinner and she had to use her last egg or slice of ham.

Then there was the time they both needed new clothes. All winter and spring she had desperately wished for a good dress. Her shabbiness in church shamed her. She didn't see how as the pastor's wife she could face Holy Week. Saturday before Palm Sunday Hal had come home with a new clerical suit. Sunday morning he showed her with pride how well it fit, while she got into her split and rusty old silk.

"My, but it feels good to know that you're well dressed!" he had told her as they crossed the road to church together.

Now in another charge and another year, Valeria Donner slept a little, dreaming she was a girl back in her father's parsonage in Unionville. Such a good sense of security held over when she awoke, her feeling as a child that she and Jess and Peter were more fortunate than other children, blessed through their father and Uncles Timothy and Howard with a birthright that made them poor but royal relations of the King of Kings. Certain declarations in the Bible confirmed it in her mind, "Now are we the sons of God" and "I would rather be a doorkeeper in the house of my God than to dwell in the tents of wickedness." Of course her father was more than a doorkeeper, rather an ambassador of the Lord. Power and position not available to all flowed from other verses, such as "Eye hath not seen nor ear heard, neither have entered into the heart of man, the things which God hath prepared for them that love him" and "Beholding as in a glass the glory of the Lord are changed in the same image from glory to glory, even as by the spirit of the Lord." She hadn't known exactly what it meant, but it had given her a sense of vested participation in majesty and mystery.

She had thought these things would support her all her earthly life, but they had faded, grown a little dusty and distant. Only at some unexpected moment as today did they light up the past as when on a late winter day the sun comes out and suddenly the countryside and mountains beyond are flooded with golden brightness.

That was one great difference between Hal and herself, she thought. His call to preaching and title to heaven had never flagged. It still stood out in his eyes fresh and green as ever. In his sermons he liked to quote in a kind of intoxication the verses from Amos, "I was no prophet; neither was I a prophet's son, but I was a herdsman and a gatherer of sycamore fruit. And the Lord took me as I followed the flock, and the Lord said unto me, Go prophesy to my people, Israel." His passion for people had only intensified the last years. Some clergy she knew seemed mostly interested in the matter of souls, saving them, divesting them of their sins and stringing them up like dried rattlesnake buttons as a passport to heaven. Mortal man himself they seemed to think beneath them, unworthy, sinful, an animal carcass which without ecclesiastical reclamation would go to Gehenna. Hal, on the other hand, was devoted to man for his own sake. He admired most of the human race, doted on people as they were. He used to pray, "Grant that I may look all men in the face with the eye of a brother."

She had thought it a pity that none of his boys had taken after him, had felt no call to the pulpit. She guessed they were too much like herself. All her life she had shrunk from following the mendicancy of the Lord and his apostles that Hal so delighted in. "Neither gold nor silver nor brass in your purses, nor scrip for your journey, neither two coats, neither shoes nor yet staves." It was a disturbing, impossible command to her. More than once in Wetherill Valley she had protested against staying at a farmhouse for dinner and making the tired wife prepare it.

"You would deprive her of her gift to the Lord," Hal had protested. "It's something she can do for him. It's not for us."

Just the same she noticed that he was the one who strove to pay for it with prayer, song and ministration. He seldom if ever refused a gift. Hadn't Christ sent his disciples among the five thousand to ask for loaves and fishes, to a man in the city for a room for the Last Supper, and ahead on Palm Sunday for the borrowed ass to carry him to

Jerusalem? It was true enough, but she and the boys were never comfortable in mendicancy. She remembered how he used to take them to Sharp's Drugstore at Mahanoy and order five sodas, vanilla for her, chocolate, strawberry and nectar for the boys, and lemon phosphate for himself. All of them were aware it was not to be paid for. Hal would ask heartily how much he owed, and Mr. Sharp, a member of his congregation, would say, "That's all right, Reverend," whereupon Hal would warmly thank him as for a great blessing. On a summer Sunday when the evening sermon was delivered and the week's work over, Hal used to send one of the boys for a quart of ice cream, but he almost never gave him the full price. "Ask for twenty cents' worth," he would say, and sure enough the quart box would come filled to the very brim.

There was a ring at the doorbell. It couldn't be the doctor, she thought. He always walked right in. She could hear talking. After a time Mrs. Petchullis appeared.

"Mrs. Weaver was here. She left a crumb pie, the kind the Reverend likes. She said she couldn't come up now but she asked about you."

The preacher's wife nodded. The Weavers were Hal's intimates and admirers.

"He always has so many cute things to say," Mrs. Weaver once told her. "You know he never says, 'You're welcome,' but 'You're welcome as the flowers in May.' "

The preacher's wife stirred in her bed and sighed. Yes,

Hal was a delight maker, particularly away from home. Hallelujahs came easy to him. He followed closely the admonition to come before God's presence with praise. She envied his ability to take things as God's special and personal dispensation. "It was for me he hung upon the tree," he would sing. "Ah, yes! It was for me." At that moment when he drew out, "Ah, yes," his holy joy was very real. And when he sang, "Between that fair city and me, I can see, I can see," she herself could for a moment glimpse through his eyes the city in the skies, four-square, cloud-encircled, amethyst and gold shimmering in the light of the Lamb.

Still she wondered at times if she had done right in marrying him. Another woman might have entered more wholeheartedly into his world. She remembered wryly how people in Unionville had said she would make an ideal minister's wife. Some even whispered she had written her father's sermons and now could write Hal's. As a matter of fact she had never really written a sermon for either, although she had made suggestions when asked, discreet suggestions, for a preacher's daughter and wife must be wise as a serpent and harmless as a dove.

And now she would likely never have the chance to ask some anthropologist the meaning of Hal's lips, especially his remarkable upper lip, a kind of princely cape of the flesh. Was it a sign or token and had it anything to do with the unusual essence of his being? In all her life she had known of only two whose lips were like his—an Asian general whose photograph had been in the newspapers, and a legendary doctor pictured on a bottle of medicine for women's troubles. Had these men also, she pondered, been unworldly to such a degree? Would they, for instance, do what Hal had done to her old violin in the attic? Grandfather Scarlett had taken it from some unknown traveler on the Tulpehocken Trail who hadn't paid his Mansion House board bill. It was bereft of strings but you could still see yourself in the back, so polished had it kept over the years. Hal, to please and provide work for an old country cabinetmaker, had given it to him to overhaul, scrape and ruin.

The only thing of hers she had never let out of her possession had been her mother's cupboard. It stood downstairs now, scarred and dented by four movings, still a rich old cherry piece glowing red in the lamplight. Hal had to cut it down to get it into the low-ceiling house on Fighting Hill in Mahanoy. It had broken her heart and she promised herself that when her ship came in and they had regained position in some house with lofty chambers, she would have it restored to its former height and dignity. She had always felt her mother's cupboard must have suffered as she had in these boxlike houses with low ceilings. Lately she realized that, Hal being as he was, what she had dreamed would never come to pass.

But if Hal was impractical and almost helpless in some things, he wasn't in prayer. That was where he suddenly came into his own, took on stature, was able to take care of himself, become eloquent, persuasive, earnest and entreating beyond belief. She had seen more than one man and woman rise flushed and refreshed under his simple "I pray God's richest blessing upon you." He suited prayer to the occasion. On the Jewish Sabbath, he seldom failed to pray, "Give us thy Saturday blessing," as if it were different than that of other days. On New Year's Day, his words "on this first day of the new year" were like squares of fresh bread kept sweet and holy for communion.

The prayer she had thought about lately was his petition at the funeral of John Roberts, his old friend in Unionville. They had been called back for the occasion. Hal had spoken to God as he might have to his own earthly father sitting in the next room on the Morris chair with a gold scepter between his fingers instead of a cigar. "I commend to thy fatherly love and care one dear to me whom thou hast called out of the body to a higher life. Vouchsafe him light and rest, peace and refreshment, joy and consolation in the companionship of the Saints and in the encircling folds of thy great love. And if it be possible, may we be kept in communion in death as in life until reunited by the river."

She hoped that Hal might pray that prayer also for her. After all, she was Vallie, his wife, and had been closer to him than a brother.

CHAPTER TWENTY-ONE

The House of the Old

The old preacher stood up under the blow valiantly. He gave himself what robust comfort he could. Mamma had been sick so long while he went everywhere on sound limb preaching, baptizing, marrying, visiting, ministering. Now the circumstances were to be reversed. He had to go about imprisoned in mortal clay while she was free to run up the hills of heaven. What was that verse from Isaiah? "They shall mount up with wings as eagles . . . They shall walk and not faint." At least while she lived she had had the best doctor in Blacksher, and Henrietta had brought her sister, Mary, a registered nurse, to take care of her at the end. Mamma had said how good she was to come, the first trained nurse she had ever had. She loved to see the starched white uniform and cap, to feel the cool skillful hands.

"Oh, thank you," she would say, grateful for every attention.

When it was all over, the old preacher tried to keep going

as before, staying away from the empty shell of parsonage as much as he could, devoting his time there to letters. His hand that had always circled so energetically above the paper before starting a new paragraph still did so, making vigorous and flourishing defense against "death and all-oblivious enmity." His letters were filled with a recital of his doings set down in his favorite words: "epistle" for letter; "the Lord's house" for church; "tiptop" or "dandy" for well; "a dear old saint" for some woman who had given him his dinner. He was unashamed to repeat phrases in letter after letter. Most all declared, "I hope this finds you well and happy as it leaves me." He kept writing, "I am truly grateful for my blessings"; "for a goodly congregation on Sunday despite the inclement weather"; "for the good send-off I received for my sermon, which set me up"; "for being called on to offer a prayer" at some other minister's service.

If members of his church thought him too old, his letters never mentioned it. His only hint to Johnny was "I received a few digs." Suddenly at seventy-five, writing about his church at Paint, he said, "I think some would like to see me out. I know a minister at eighty who holds on like dear life, and I suppose I could do the same, but I should not like such a sad thing to happen to yours truly. So before they try to pull me down off my horse, I'm putting my feet on the ground. After all, I've reached the allotted three score years and ten and am perhaps entitled to the golden rewards of retirement."

He never cared much for those "golden rewards." He went to see his boys, from each of whose homes he wrote copious letters of doings and descriptions, multigraphing and sending them to a hundred or more friends and former church members. Tiring of that, he went back to Paint Creek and adjoining Blacksher.

"This," he wrote Johnny, "is where I served the longest, where my friendships are greenest and the memories of your mother the freshest."

When Johnny paid back five hundred dollars he had desperately borrowed during the stock market crash, his father reported the purchase of an automobile, the first he had ever owned. Gene wrote that it was old and secondhand, painted a loud, ungodly green, and when his father visited him at Reading, the son was barely able to turn the wheel. But the old preacher could find no fault with it. He called it "the faithful chariot that carries me over hill and dale." He wrote, "I am in good hands, have a snug and cozy sleeping chamber in the commodious Eureka Hotel managed by my friend, Vince McCarren. I have the honored place at the head of the table for regular guests, and you can depend on it that the fair ladies who preside over the dining room see to it that I'm not slighted." He reported plenty of companionship in the hotel, which he called "a welcome haven for fine fellows in the sunset of life."

Johnny felt reassured by his father's letters. He couldn't remember the Eureka Hotel, and two or three years later when he stopped off to see his father, was stricken with remorse to have left him here so long. The place turned out to be a dingy red brick pile with the close smells of ancient carpets, cooking, stale bed clothing and mortality, Vince McCarren, a gaunt grim man with a huge chin. What his father saw in him the younger man didn't know, or in the "fine fellows in the sunset of life," with all of whom he seemed to have closer ties of friendship than with the son himself.

That evening in the "snug and cozy sleeping chamber" with his father, he peered with distress at the shabby furnishings.

"You can't stay here, Dad," he said.

His father looked up in affronted surprise.

"Why can't I?"

"It's not good enough for you."

"But I have my work here."

"What work?"

His father stiffened.

"My ministerial work. I may be retired but I'm not on the shelf. I supply Chadd's Cove twice a month. You know Hadley at Paint won't go all the way down there every week. That isn't the only place. I supply all over Somerset and Cambria counties. I help out once in a while for Nicely at Johnstown. Then there's certain sick people around here and the Cove that ask for me all the time. I have to go to see them no matter what Hadley thinks. They like me to pray and sing for them. Not every pastor can sing."

"They could do without you for a while," Johnny said.

His father's face fell.

"I suppose they could. But the men here at the hotel count on me. They put on a good front to you but they get pretty down in the mouth. One of them killed himself a few years ago, shot himself on the anniversary of his wife's death. That was before I came. But I know how he felt. They tell me they're no use to anybody any more. They have nothing to do, nobody to do anything for. They might as well be dead. They think their children send them money to keep them here just so they don't need to have them at home."

Johnny winced, remembering his own monthly check to his father the last year or two. The latter went on.

"I take a couple of them along in my car when I can. It does them good to get out. Some are Catholic and going to a Protestant church sticks in their craw, I suppose. But they'll do anything for a change. Sometimes we're asked to stay for dinner. That's what they miss the most, getting into a house and sitting up to the table with the family."

"You need a change yourself, Dad," Johnny said.

"Oh, I have plenty of change. Every day something happens. Only last week a girl got off the Johnstown bus and came in the hotel. She had a dear little baby. They gave her the room next to this. I was sitting here reading with my door open like I most always do when she came to the door and asked if I thought she could still get supper. I told her they only served at certain hours and the girls had gone home. But I said I had some prunes and oranges and a banana in my room, and I gave them to her. At first she told me the baby belonged to somebody else, but the next day she let me know different, which I knew all along. She said the man was married. She expected him to meet her at the bus but he hadn't showed up. She said her home was in Florence and her people didn't know anything about it and she was going to Ebensburg and put the baby in a home. I told her not to do that but go home and face the music and keep the baby but if she wanted to put it in a good place, I knew a God-fearing couple who were praying to adopt a child and it couldn't get a better home. She said she'd think about it but next day this man who'd disappointed her at the bus showed up and took her away. I didn't know the fellow's name and she didn't introduce me, but I helped her down with her things and gave him a look that told him he was doing this girl no good. I heard afterward she put the baby with a couple that some people I know didn't think too much of, but they paid her a good deal of money."

He talked all evening, mostly about local people. Whether they were important or obscure made little difference. He enlarged on one as much as the other. It was long after midnight when his last pipe burned out.

"How about getting away with me for a while, Dad?" Johnny urged him again.

"Well, if you want to. I can drive you down to Gene's and

Ellen's in my car. We can take some of my friends along. Two have never been to Gene's and I've promised to take them."

They left next morning in the old green sedan, his father rakish in a checkered cap, proud of his automobile, telling his two old friends where to sit and put their overnight bags. One was Mose Leopold, who had had a clothing store in Cairnbrook for many years; and the other, Charley Adams, whom Vince McCarren called "the Hawaiian," a massive, slow-moving, almost blind figure with a shock of iron-gray hair, who would suffer no man to help him. Yesterday he had kept bumping into chairs in the lobby and when he reached an empty one, had sunk in it defiantly, his face upturned, his eyes unseeing, as if to wait out another bitter day. What such a person might get out of an automobile trip, Johnny didn't know, but today as if somehow bettered by the prospect, he made his way to the car without help or bumping.

For dinner his father picked the best hotel in Bedford. Johnny paid for it as well as for several fat cigars which his father bought and distributed to his guests. From here on he let his son drive while the three smoked. When the cigars were thrown away, his father started to sing, a practice that had always made Johnny uncomfortable, especially through towns. What was worse, his father induced the others to join, and the sight and sound of these old codgers pealing out, "Singing Pollywolly doodle all the day," must have been something for the people who heard them coming and stopped to look and listen.

They reached Gene's in time for supper. To Johnny's relief, Ellen didn't seem surprised or upset. Dad ushered the two guests up to their room, then took them in to see Tilly, about whom they had heard much but never seen, Ellen's older sister paralyzed in childhood, long bedfast, twisted in face and body, able to speak only a kind of gibberish which Ellen, her children and Dad claimed to understand. He called her "my pal" in her hearing, which pleased her no end, and out of hearing, "that woman whom Satan hath bound lo these many years," saying the latter with low anger that boded no good for Satan.

It was late as usual when they went upstairs.

"I think, Johnny," he said as they got ready for bed, "you ought to go up to Unionville while you're here. Mose and Charley can come along, and that'll be one less meal for Ellen."

The son knew he meant the cemetery and Mamma's grave. They drove up in the morning. The countryside lay still in the cool late-October sunlight. Many of the trees were bare but here and there a maple still burned and everywhere on the mountain the oaks glowed a dark red in the sun. The cemetery looked sad and deserted but his father led the way up the path erect and energetic. At the thick stone lettered "Valeria Morgan Donner" he relapsed into utter stillness for a few moments as he used to do on reaching the altar of his church on Sunday morning. Presently rousing, he pointed out the twelve or fourteen other graves on the double lot, telling things about each from Grandfather Scarlett down. That done, he conducted a tour of the cemetery, not forgetting the Donner lot and the graves of men and women he used to know, expanding with a kind of zest on one or the other, telling stories and laughing as if those who lay there unseen were still subject to the give and take of life.

"Well," he said at last, "I guess we better go down to the DeWitt House and get something for the inner man."

As they started back to the car, they came on a flock of birds in the cemetery. They had been feeding on the fruits of fall and now at the approach of the men flew up and circled overhead. Some came down again, but the main body of the flock circled higher and winged off for the south, soon mere specks against the sky until they disappeared over Shade Mountain. Johnny saw that his father had stopped to look after them with a strange wry expression at his mouth. As the three old men and one younger one went on, they flushed other birds from the flock which rose to take the exact course of their fellows as if guided by invisible markers in the air. Now only a few of the flock remained behind, and these seemed unquiet with their lot, reluctant to join their fellows, flitting from ground to bushes as if aware that the flock to which they belonged had migrated and with winter coming on they must go too, yet unwilling to make the break, holding back in this temperate clime as long as possible before their long mysterious flight into the unknown.

"You'd wonder how they'd ever catch up to the rest," his father said, half aloud, half to himself, as he climbed into the car. He still, Johnny noticed, had the wry expression at the mouth, an expression the son was not to understand until years later he felt it on himself in the same cemetery at seventy.

CHAPTER TWENTY-TWO

Here Am I

After Johnny's visit, his father wrote him longer letters than ever, six, eight, ten and once seventeen tablet pages, all handwritten, some in pen, some in blurred pencil. They catalogued a recital of doings, visits, social and church affairs, most of them accounts of people and of his own simple pleasures. There were also tragic, even sordid, accounts from life as seen firsthand from a pastor's vantage. After some revealing incident and surprising personal observations on it, he nearly always concluded, "I confide this in the hope it may be grist for your mill." The son felt his father anxious to convince him that he was not "on the shelf" but still engaged in active, useful work among "the quick," not the dead.

Even when his letters, now much shorter and fewer, started coming from Gene's address in Reading, his only complaint and confession was that he was "under the weather." In answer to Johnny's queries, Gene wrote, "He had pneumonia. The doctor don't know what's the matter with him now." Johnny, three thousand miles away, wasn't too worried. Typhoid, the flu epidemic, heavy colds on the chest had never kept his father from something he wanted to do. A sudden wire from Gene that he better come if he wanted to see Dad alive shocked and sobered. Yet he remained strangely convinced that all was well.

Gene met him at the train.

"We still don't know what's the matter with him," he told his brother. "When his fever cleared up, he wanted to stay in bed. You know Dad. You could hardly keep him in bed sick or well. Doc Hanneman didn't take him to the hospital for the pneumonia but he did now for observation. He wanted to find out why he didn't snap back. Since he was an old preacher, he could get him in for almost nothing. That's the only way Dad would go—if it didn't cost us anything. He knew he didn't have the price and he didn't want us to have to foot the bill."

"He must have started feeling bad in Blacksher and that's why he came."

"Didn't come for that at all," Gene said. "Came to do a favor to some young preacher. Wouldn't talk much about it but I gathered enough. This fellow had been a boy in his church at Paint. Do you remember a Mimm boy? Had yellow hair and glasses? Dad confirmed him, encouraged him to go in the ministry. Went to bat for him in synod and got him help in college and seminary. Sent him money of his own when he could. Not much, I guess. But the boy got through, had a church in Juniata City. Some Johnstown church got vacant and Dad recommended him. They asked him out to preach a trial sermon. Of course, Dad went to hear him. He said he preached two wonderful sermons. But there was no train back till next day and this young preacher had a funeral, was anxious to get home. You know what happened?"

"I can guess," Johnny said. "Dad offered to drive him home."

"Drove him over a hundred miles at night in that old car," Gene nodded. "And Dad seventy-nine years old! They must have got to this young Mimm's place pretty late. It was raining. They'd come through snow in the mountains. Dad wouldn't tell much. I had to get it out of him piecemeal and put it together. But when he got young Mimm home, I gather that the young preacher said much obliged, good night, and went in. At least I hope he said much obliged. I know Dad didn't even get a cup of coffee. He probably left Dad standing there on the sidewalk by his car. You know how Dad was, always inviting people to stay with us. I'm sure he thought he would get invited in for the night and breakfast. After all he had driven the guy a hundred miles to help him out and would have to drive another hundred miles to get back. You know how crazy Dad was to get invited in a house anyhow and be entertained. Especially a parsonage. He always acted like a parsonage was a kind of holy place and him the holy guest. He also liked to see and talk to the woman of the house and the kids. I don't blame him after living in that dump of a hotel in Blacksher all this time. But all he said to me was he figured he was halfway to our place, he might as well come the rest of the way. I guess he knew he wouldn't have the door shut in his face here. So he took the turnpike."

"This was one or two in the morning?"

"I don't know what time it was. It was in the middle of the night sometime. When he got off the turnpike he found he was short on gas. He made it to a country gas station but it was closed, the house dark. He said the needle showed empty so he sat there till daylight. Evidently this young preacher hadn't bought him any gas either. I asked if it wasn't pretty cold but he said he didn't mind. He knew they'd open up sometime. When the station man got up, he told him how long he'd been there. You know how Dad gets along with people. This man never saw him before but he took him in the house and his wife made him some hot coffee and breakfast. 'Wonderful people,' Dad said. He told me he said a prayer and left a dollar under his plate for the wife. When he got here, he claimed everything was fine but Ellen said he already had a cold from the trip. Also he acted a little embarrassed. You know how he was at fancy places where he didn't feel congenial or welcome. But he never acted that way here before. I think he was embarrassed for this young preacher and his kind of religion. Anyhow his cold got worse, settled on his chest and turned into pneumonia. Such a thing never happened before and never would have stopped him if it had, but it did now. He didn't seem to have any fight. I can guess what took it out of him. You know how much Dad thought of the ministry, serving God, his fellow man and all that. Well the way that young preacher made use of him and then let him down I think killed something inside of him. Doc pulled him through the pneumonia all right but he said he couldn't do much now if Dad didn't care whether or not he got well."

Tim was at the hospital waiting for them when they arrived. He had come by car yesterday.

"When he heard you were coming, he asked me to shave him," he told Johnny in the hall. "He said he wanted to look right for you."

That troubled Johnny.

"How are you, Dad?" he asked, bending over to kiss him.

For a moment the old teasing shape came to his lips, as when about to say one of his fun-loving pleasantries to children.

"If I said I was tiptop, I guess I'd be telling you a lie, Johnny," he said. Today there was a rueful smile with it.

All through their visit another smile kept coming, a facial politeness typical of him with certain parishioners, those he didn't feel close to or who asked too much of him, an effort to be hearty, pleasant, perhaps a little too pleasant, a side of him never shown to the family. It disturbed Johnny. The old hymn his father used to sing so much came back to him, "I'm a pilgrim and I'm a stranger. I can tarry, I can tarry but a night." Were those words early discernment? Had his father returned to his unknown secret self? Was he now again a pilgrim from some unworldly land, treating his own sons with the cordial formality of strangers?

The only one his father spoke of in the old unchanged way was their mother.

"I was thinking about her last night. And our wedding trip. You know she and I went to Philadelphia on the train and took the night boat for Boston. Since we were just married, I supposed, a bride and groom, we were invited to sit at the captain's table. I can still see her. Your mother. She sat right next to the captain talking and laughing to him. She could do that. All the Morgans could. They said she took after her English grandmother. I guess it was true. She kept calm all through her life like the English. She could see when things weren't right but she would go right on and not give notice. Now I was different. I could get pretty stirred up. I remember one time I got so provoked at her over something she did, or didn't do, I wouldn't speak to her. I think it was for two or three days. I'm ashamed to think of it now. But she never abused me for it, just went on the same. She was a wonderful woman, your mother."

After the three boys had gone, the old preacher closed his eyes. He was grateful to have got through the ordeal. The boys would never know what a struggle it had been. He had felt like a stone in the field. Also, he had confessed, got rid of that old sin. He felt glad it was out. The boys had been good to come to see him. Two had come from pretty far. What had the Lord said, "I was sick and thou visited me." Just the same he thought he understood now why a few old men wandered off by themselves and were found perished in some lonely spot. He used to pity them for having to die in such Godforsaken places. They were called queer. Now he knew better. They only wanted a little relief before the end, to escape their dependent lot and the vanity of man, the demanding solicitude of their folks, the fatiguing company of the strong. They wanted to find a spot away from human grief, fear and despair, where death wasn't so much made of, some primitive solitude of the Creator where it was the most natural thing in the world for an old tree to fall over in the forest at night.

"Now come quickly, Lord Jesus," he thought.

He remembered with a faint bitter smile how he had once hoped that when his time came, it might reach him in church, while serving God, like Frank Walschek at Paint. The council had thought it an act of divine grace to have been called to the other world while taking up the collection, a sign of the Lord's favor. It was too late, he thought, for that now, and was perhaps for the best. He had no heart to dramatize any more, to pain and perhaps terrify those who saw him fall, especially the children.

He lay trying in vain to clear the heavy folds of thickness that held him. Heretofore a sense of immediacy, of great need to intercede for another, had never failed to bring him almost bodily into the Presence. Now in perhaps his greatest need, his will and awareness of the Presence both unaccountably forsook him. Thoughts still passed through the brain but of their own volition, some without form or substance. When he tried to control them, to join phrases together in his mind, even the words of familiar supplications that all his life had risen effortlessly to his lips, the attempt seemed beyond him. It shook him. Did prayer then require physical strength? He had always thought it the easy-flowing utterance of the soul, as natural to the spirit as breathing.

In his extremity, the face of Mrs. Livingstone came back to him on her pillow in Wetherill Valley. When he had to take his leave, she had begged him to keep praying for her.

"I will," he promised earnestly, "but you must pray, too."

"I don't know how any more," she had said.

"You know the Twenty-third Psalm?"

"I can't remember the words, Reverend."

"Well, you surely remember the Lord's Prayer."

"I remember it, Reverend, but I drift off. It's too long. There're too many words."

He had gazed down a long moment at the pitiful face.

"You can always say the name of God. Just say it over and over. It's a prayer. He will hear you. You know what Isaiah said, 'Before they call, I will answer.' "

Never did he think then that he himself, a preacher of the Gospel, would ever come to such extremity. He spoke the great name softly to himself. Thank God this much he could do. If people only knew, he thought, the power of the Logos, the omnipotence of the Word, the reality of the Bread of Life. The uninitiated supposed them just words, letters printed on a page together. There came back to him an incident as a boy in Unionville. He had been sent to a little house on Mifflin Street near the railroad for yeast. He had gone through the white paling gate and come to the open door. Here he had halted at the sight of an old man reading a large open Bible on his knees and the smell of fresh bread on the air.

It was the interfusion of the open Bible, the light on the old man's face and the symbolic presence of bread that had stopped him as on the threshold of some sacred place. He had never forgotten it or its glimpse into mystery. And he had never forgotten another mystery, the face of a young girl he had confirmed at Lost Run. The name eluded him now and what had become of her but her pure pale face was still a sacrament in his heart. She had no need to speak or do anything. He only had to look at her. Was that, he wondered, why flowers were such comfort and joy to the sick? The sick need only lie in their beds and look on the purity and mystery of their being. Too bad, he thought, that he and Mamma had never had any girls. Three times

Dr. Sypher had come from the bedroom and said in that deep voice of his, "It's a little boy."

When the three brothers came back from the hospital, Ellen was coming downstairs.

"How's Dad?" she asked.

"Better," Gene said.

"Well, Tilly had one of her notions again. She told me that Dad was just in to see her. He was going on a long journey, he said, and came to give his pal good-by."

"What's this?" Johnny wanted to know as he went up to see Tilly.

"Don't pay any attention," Gene said. "She gets these pipe dreams every once in a while. If Dad could come and give good-by to anybody it would be to us, not her. We're his own flesh and blood. She's not even related to him."

The three brothers didn't get together very often. They were talking now over ice cream and coffee when the telephone rang. Gene answered it.

"What?" he said sharply. "Are you sure? When? Is that so? Yes, I guess so. Yes, he had a pretty long life. Well, much obliged for calling." He came back to the table looking grave and a little gray for Gene. "It was the hospital. That nice night nurse on Dad's floor. He died, she said, about twenty minutes ago."

So long as his father lay under another roof in the same city, Johnny felt he was still somewhat here with them, and it was so during the brief services in Reading and in the home church with the sermon on the text "I will bless thee and thou shalt be a blessing." Once they stood on the cemetery by the open grave, the son felt his father slipping away, and when they had come down from the place of the dead to the living town, Johnny had the strange feeling that everything was over and only a vacuum remained. It was as if the ground had closed not only on the body but on the soul, voice, smile and all the rest, leaving them a kind of dream without substance, as if all that had never really been.

Going over Dad's things with Gene and Tim only increased the notion. His possessions were so pitifully few. Was this all he had to show for nearly eighty years of life, most of them devoted to others, one suit of clothes besides the one in which he was buried, an old overcoat, two flimsy pairs of summer trousers, a coat of another vintage, a coarse sweater that buttoned up in front, a few white shirts and pieces of underwear, his old black Ministerial Acts, badly worn, most of the leaves dog-eared or loose. There was a well-used hymnbook in the hotel room but no Bible except what belonged to the Gideons. He must have given to others the Bibles bound in morocco and levant presented to him by various churches and Sunday schools.

They found a pair of dark-red book covers ornamented with golden flowers and a little girl putting a wreath on another girl's head. The girls were what must have made him buy it in the first place. It was stamped in gold, VALUABLES, and the boys opened it eagerly. They found only legal papers and accounts from the estates of Howard Scarlett and Elijah Morgan with the name of Harry Donner as executor; some of his own poems marked "Jingles"; some hand-copied verse he had recited over the years; sermon notes on the back of scraps of Johnny's manuscripts when he was still at home; yellowed sheets of music manuscript covered with his own unmistakable penciled quarter and eighth notes; a printed program headed "Blahoslaveni, kteriz probyvaji v dome Tvem, Zalm 84–4," with two lines in English, one, "St. John's Slovak Lutheran Church of Cambria City," and another, "Sermon by Rev. Harry Donner." There was also a typewritten assignment of his only life insurance, a policy for $1000 with entries of borrowings against it, including the old loan of $500 to Johnny. Little or no cash value remained.

They paged through his checkbooks and bankbook. Few deposits, they found, were over thirty-three dollars, his monthly church pension. Most checks had been drawn to "cash" for five, three or two dollars. The balance at the time of his death was a dollar and thirty-eight cents.

"Well, it looks like he followed the Christian injunction

and left the world with no more worldly goods than when he came into it," said Tim, who was a manufacturer's buyer and credit man.

The brothers opened a packet of letters tied in white cord string. All thanked him for something or other, succor, help, comfort given, loans forgiven.

"What I don't understand," Tim said, "is why a man like him groaned so."

"Groaned? Who?" Johnny asked.

"Dad. In his sleep. You've been out West and haven't heard him the last few years."

"I stayed at the hotel with him in Blacksher and at Gene's," Johnny protested.

"Maybe he didn't that night. He certainly did up at our place. Anne had me go in his room to see if he was all right. I found him talking in his sleep. I couldn't make out what he said. It sounded like he was praying. You know how he used to break your heart sometimes when he prayed. When I was little, I never believed God could stand up to it."

"It was probably something he ate at your place," Johnny said.

"It wasn't just at our place," Tim declared. "Caroline Moody told me he stayed at her house in Hancock one night and next day her neighbor said, 'That man must have been awful sick last night.' Caroline asked why. The neighbor claimed he had groaned all night. Their bedroom was right across from his window and he kept them awake."

Johnny was shocked.

"But why should a good man like Dad groan?" He looked at Gene.

"Maybe indigestion. He was always taking pills for his stomach."

"He wouldn't have indigestion every night."

"It used to bother Ellen," Gene dismissed it. "But it never did me. I was out on the job all day and at night I slept."

But it bothered Johnny. He wished he had known so he could have asked his father. Now they would never know unless someone who knew him better these last years could tell them. It sent him in vague search of his father. There must be, he thought, other traces of him still around. Their Aunt Jess was gone and he went to see her friend Mrs. Eckroth in Unionville.

"I knew your father a long time and I never heard of him groaning here. Anything but. You know the Eckroths were somebody in Unionville. When I first married Tom, he said, 'Don't be so common and talk to everybody.' I didn't mind since that's what your father did. I guess you don't remember old Solly Grieff? He lived in a shanty out along the railroad. They said he lived off other people's chicken houses and smokehouses. Nobody had much to do with him, but your father talked to him like everybody else when he came to town. He even walked down the street with him. Solly thought the world of your father. All the poor scalawags did. He used to call him 'der schoener Harry.' When Tom wanted to get my goat, he'd call your father 'der schoener Harry.' It always bothered me. I was like Solly. I thought the world and all of your father. I'm going to miss him on Decoration Day. He always got here if he could. He'd visit around on the cemetery. Mrs. Kurtz once said she didn't believe in having a social reunion on the cemetery. She said Decoration Day was a time to honor and grieve for the dead. We told your father what she said. He visited with her like everybody else and got her talking and laughing over old times. Now how could a happy, sociable man like him groan?"

His father's two-story stone church in Mahanoy, the son found turned into a Gospel Holiness chapel, but the small white church his father had built at Lost Run was still Lutheran and flourishing. Charley Freeman was at work in the mines, but old Mr. Sharp, the druggist in Mahanoy, still haunted his store. He and his forty- or fifty-year-old daughters who waited on customers, shook hands.

"Yes, he stayed with us one night a couple years ago," Mr. Sharp said. "I didn't hear anything but the girls did. What they told me next morning made me think of what Wiley Drumm said. You remember Wiley? The same week your father died, he drove off the Primrose road in his car and got killed. I guess he'd been drinking again. He used to say he knew mighty few Christians except your father. He said your father was never meant for this world, that he had the wrong notion every person was a good person, which made him due for some bad disappointments in life. I told him how your father used to pray, 'May we all be gathered by the river without the loss of a single one.' I don't think I heard such a prayer before or since."

Jenny Rodey in Wetherill Valley welcomed Johnny.

"So you want to know about his carrying on at night. Well, you come to the right place. We heard him a couple years ago when he stayed with us on his way up to Tim's. He always liked to come here. After he went, Phillip and I were talking. I told Phillip it sounded to me like he was still doing in his sleep what he done all his life when he was awake, praying for them poor souls he'd seen ailing and suffering in this world. Mind you, he visited a lot of them. It sounded to me like he was eating his heart out that God didn't always answer his prayers over them. It sounded like he was begging God that this oughtn't to be and that oughtn't to be, and he had no right to let all them poor people under the harrow while folks like the Piatts rode rich and free."

Mrs. Claude Barefoot in Paint Creek said somewhat the same.

"Oh yes, we heard him. He stayed at our house more than once the last years. At first we had the idea he missed your mother. He never complained but something always came in his face when he spoke of her. Then we came to think he had other people's troubles on his mind. He did a good many things we don't know about. One I do know about was for a niece of mine in Johnstown. She was in pretty bad shape with t.b. One lung was gone. Her mother and sister had died of it and her father thought if her mother and sister had had to live out their lives along the Conemaugh River, she could too. She told your father she heard how warm and dry it was in New Mexico and how some t.b.'s got well out there without doing anything. She had no idea, she said, she could ever go there. But he started working on everybody including me and Claude and got her out. She's still alive, teaching in some college out there. She wrote your father up to the time he died. She wrote me if anybody was a saint, he was, and if he groaned, it ought to be expected since all the saints were martyrs and groaned over the sins and tribulation of this world."

That afternoon Johnny drove to the church his father had built in Chadd's Cove. The logs were covered with clapboards and fresh paint now. A power line led up to it and a pickup truck stood outside. The peculiar green of the paint gave Johnny a start. He felt himself close on the trail. It was the very shade of his father's old car.

When he stopped, he heard curious sounds from the church. The door stood open. He went in and found a man with curly white hair and dusty black sleeve covers tuning the secondhand electric organ. The old tuner would insert a wedge to keep a key sounding, then go back to the rear of the instrument, where he worked on the reed till the pitch suited his ear, after which he would get up from his knees and go through the long circuitous routine again.

"It goes slow," he apologized.

"Can I help?" Johnny asked. The thought of being of service in his father's old church pleased him.

"Well, maybe you could take over the keyboard," the old man said doubtfully. "If you want to."

The visitor didn't know what he had let himself in for. It was tedium sitting on the bench holding down a key, enduring the long endless drone. "B sharp," he'd say, then after that was fixed up, "B natural" followed by "B flat" and so on repetitiously. It seemed hours till the job was done and by that time the volunteer had learned the life history of the tuner, his youth in Austria, his work on organs over Europe including castles from which a coach and coachman had met him at the train. His great passion, he said, had been organs and swimming. Now, he said sadly, he was afraid to go in the water.

When the old man finished, he covered up the back of the organ, pushed it into place, took off his dusty black sleeve covers, seated himself on the bench and ran his fingers over the keys. At first he played only chords to try it out, triads that ran into other triads. Suddenly such joyous music burst from the instrument that his lone hearer took another and more respectful look at the player. Abruptly, as if the old man didn't know any more, the organ was silent. Something else was begun, at first slow, religious murmurings, snatches of contemplative chorales and preludes succeeded by waves of livelier happier dances and finally a burst of fanfare and counter fanfare that ended with a triumphant blare.

"What was that last you played?" Johnny asked.

"Bach. It was all Bach," he said. "When I get to an organ and it's in tune, I play Bach. Especially in a Lutheran church. Some people claim the old Lutheran was tiresome and monotonous. They say he was too much like trigonometry. Well, I don't agree. He's strong medicine, if that's what they mean. He never gets tired. He groans a little but he never stops praising God. He was a praiser, not a mourner most of his life. When I play him, I praise a little too. I think, Thank God I'm still here. Thank God I can breathe his air. Thank God I can make my water. Thank God I can still hear and do my work. Listen now. See if you can't feel a little of what I mean."

Johnny sat on a choir chair bathed in the stream of sound. He looked through the open door to the green truck and greener world outside. He thought, all this improvidence of praise for God and good will toward men, lavished, wasted, on an obscure log church in an obscure mountain valley, poured out through the open door on stony fields, worn rail fences and a poor yellow dirt road that led to the small weathered barns and smaller unpainted houses of obscure unremarkable men.

A NOTE ABOUT THE AUTHOR

Conrad Richter was born in Pennsylvania, the son, grandson, nephew, and great-nephew of clergymen. He was intended for the ministry, but at thirteen he declined a scholarship and left preparatory school for high school, from which he was graduated at fifteen. After graduation he went to work. His family on his mother's side was identified with the early American scene, and from boyhood on he was saturated with tales and the color of Eastern pioneer days. In 1928 he and his small family moved to New Mexico, where his heart and mind were soon captured by the Southwest. From this time on he devoted himself to fiction. *The Sea of Grass* and *The Trees* were awarded the gold medal of the Societies of Libraries of New York University in 1942. *The Town* received the Pulitzer Prize in 1951, and *The Waters of Kronos* won the 1960 National Book Award for fiction. His other novels include *The Fields* (1946), *The Light in the Forest* (1953), and *The Lady* (1957).

February 1962

A NOTE ON THE TYPE

This book is set in a type called Scotch. Even though there is a divergence of opinion regarding its exact origin, a cutting of such a face was undertaken and recorded by Messrs. Miller & Richard, of Edinburgh, in 1808. Their specimen sheet of 1812 shows the undeniable features of the face. It is the "Scotch" version of a general renewal of style, the change-over from the pen-derived "Old Style" to the tectonically conceived "Modern" caused by the Didot-Bodoni revolution of the late eighteenth century. Its essential characteristics are sturdy capitals, full rounded lower-case letters, the graceful fillet of the serifs, and a general effect of crispness through sharply contrasting thicks and thins. *Composed, printed, and bound by Kingsport Press, Inc., Kingsport, Tennessee. Typography and binding based on designs by George Salter.*